THE CONTRACT

William Palmer is the author of four novels, *The Good Republic*, *Leporello*, *The Contract*, and *Four Last Things*. He lives in the West Midlands with his wife and daughter.

RIDDLE OF BEAUTIFUL GIRL'S FATE.

REVELATIONS OF LIFE IN LONDON.

SECRET DIARY AND LINER VISITS.

ALTHOUGH more extraordinary revelations were made yesterday regarding the double life led by Miss Starr Faithfull, the American police were still baffled to explain the mystery of how this beautiful 25-years-old girl met her death.

Yesterday's disclosures showed that Miss Faithfull associated with gangsters as well as wealthy, cultured men, and one theory is that agents, in the pay of someone who wished her death, murdered her during a visit to Long Island.

SOBBING WOMAN IN A CAR.

From OUR OWN CORRESPONDENT.

NEW YORK, Friday.

THE grand jury at Mineola, Long Island, to-day began its investigation into the supposed murder of Starr Faithfull, the beautiful, wayward girl whose body was discovered on Monday morning in the shallow waters of Long Beach.

The first witnesses called were members of the family including Stanley Faithfull, the stepfather, the mother, and sister, Elizabeth Tucker Faithfull.

William Palmer

THE CONTRACT

VINTAGE

Published by Vintage 1996

2 4 6 8 10 9 7 5 3 1

Copyright © William Palmer 1995

The right of William Palmer to be identified as the author
of this work has been asserted by him in accordance with
the Copyright, Designs and Patents Act, 1988

This book is sold subject to the condition that it shall not
by way of trade or otherwise, be lent, resold, hired out,
or otherwise circulated without the publisher's prior
consent in any form of binding or cover other than that
in which it is published and without a similar condition
including this condition being imposed on the subsequent purchaser

First published in Great Britain
by Jonathan Cape Ltd, 1995

Vintage
Random House, 20 Vauxhall Bridge Road,
London SW1V 2SA

Random House Australia (Pty) Limited
20 Alfred Street, Milsons Point, Sydney
New South Wales 2061, Australia

Random House New Zealand Limited
18 Poland Road, Glenfield, Auckland 10,
New Zealand

Random House South Africa (Pty) Limited
PO Box 2263, Rosebank 2121, South Africa

Random House UK Limited Reg. No. 954009

A CIP catalogue record for this book
is available from the British Library

ISBN 0 09 959341 6

The Random House Group Limited supports The Forest Stewardship
Council (FSC®), the leading international forest certification organisation.
Our books carrying the FSC label are printed on FSC® certified paper.
FSC is the only forest certification scheme endorsed by the leading
environmental organisations, including Greenpeace. Our
paper procurement policy can be found at
www.randomhouse.co.uk/environment

Printed and bound in Great Britain by Clays Ltd, St Ives PLC

In argument and proof of which contract
Bear her this jewel, pledge of my affection.

Henry VI, Part One, Act V, scene i

AFTER THE NIGHT'S storm the air was still, the last rolls of cloud vanishing into the land. The sun had been up an hour out of the ocean, lighting the man-on-horseback weather-vane over Miller's Hotel, slanting cool light into the windows of the small wooden houses, staring down the long roads that ran east to west of the narrow island, to the city beyond.

A car passed slowly in front of him, heading west towards the bridge. When it had gone, he crossed the road into the dunes. The tide was almost fully out now. The weed at the edge of the dunes was already starting to rot, the fleshflies crawling and hanging above, a few hoppers beginning to get excited by decay. The beach below was grey where the sea had not long gone out, silver where it had dried. Just off the horizon a long ship moved so slowly as to make it seem that the turning of the world into day moved fluidly under it.

The long beach was divided between the combers. Their demarcations had come about after a series of hard knocks and sometimes almost friendly nods and shrugs and beers. Once there had been a whole barrel of fuel oil that must have rolled off the deck of a freighter that he couldn't move on his own. Another comber had helped him shift it — and had half the proceeds, because that is the economy of those who have nothing, or nothing much at all; that they share it or get out.

He tucked his chin into his coat collar. Though it was June, at this hour there was a fresh cold breeze blowing off the ocean. He turned side on to the wind and began to walk forward and back, going in a slow zig-zag from the foot of the dunes to the bubbling, retreating edge of the sea.

He watched the sand for the valuable, which was always sought but never there; the cheap, which was lucky, or the barterable — sometimes. This morning there was nothing but valueless things. A hammer, its thin iron head rusted brown, with a white shank that with one blow would have crumbled to soft, flaky mould. A bottle with a wrinkled label written in French that must have come from one of the liners. A door with a little hinged window square of cracked stained glass, as if the entry to a church confessional had floated out to sea.

One day, a couple of months ago, he had found a huge radio, half-buried at an angle in the high sand. It was made of dark varnished wood, only a little lined and cracked. The front was decorated with a pine tree in fretwork against the round of dark blue fabric covering the speaker. A big, heavy job, nearly three feet tall; when he had taken it up no water had drained out, but dried sand trickled through its back vents when he got it into the house and stood it upright. He said to his mother that he would see if he could get anything, found a wire and plug, fitted it up, plugged the set in — with all the time his mother saying, No, no, Daniel, it'll explode, and that, no, she wouldn't come in but stay in the kitchen when he turned the switch. All that happened was — the green dial glowed, and music swelled out, loud as life. 'La Rosita'. The radio was still with them, still working. He could have got ten, fifteen dollars for it, but it was a good radio and you couldn't have bought better than the sea had given up for nothing.

He came to the second breakwater. Looking over to the next groyne, where the beams tapered down to the sea, he saw a glimpse of blue and white patterned cloth. Perhaps some blouse or shirt left over from the weekend. You found such articles quite often; the debris of children, bathers, and lovers; stockings, used rubbers, shoes — for some odd reason he had never figured out why you only ever found one shoe at a time, never a pair.

His eye was caught by the gleam of a dime wedged between two pebbles. He had to prise it out, the milled edge a little cog, as if the stones were grinding out money. God knows they ground small; not like the city back over there, the early sun lighting its towers gold, whose whole fluid and blood was money and more money — and, like fluids and blood, rarely seen, but driving, building, casting down; its presence the cause of action, its lack the cause of action too. He rubbed the coin on his lapel and slipped it into his top pocket. Halfway across and he could see fully into the next section of beach.

The cloth he had seen was a blue and white Paisley patterned dress. The young woman who lay so still in it was too far down the beach to be a drunk or sleeper-out. The bums slept up in the dunes and wrapped themselves warm to keep out the night air. And there was always something humped and unsettled about the occasional drunks, as if they

3

were about to be born again to awkward, aching life. This one sprawled too much at ease.

He had never before seen a body brought in by the tide. The older men boasted that they were quite common. That they could drift here from way out in the Atlantic, or the currents even fetch them up from South America. For the bodies that were unclaimed or unidentified or unidentifiable there was a patch reserved in the shadowed sandy back of the churchyard at the head of the island, a row of plain pine crosses which had cut into them in shallow letters only the words *Washed Ashore*.

He clambered over the breakwater, his heart bumping in his chest.

The flesh of her legs was white and here and there mottled in blue patches like bruises. He felt the indecency of looking at her in this way. He reached out a hand, drew it back, then put it out again and twitched the hem of her dress over her knee. This made him feel a momentary but tremendous guilt and he stood back and looked round him as if he was somehow the cause of her death and that a hundred eyes must be observing him from the dunes, the houses beyond, even from the far shining towers in the city. He forced himself to look at her again. He had heard of all the terrible things the sea and time can do to bodies, the bloating, discolouration, decomposition, the eating out of parts by crabs. There was none of that here.

Her arms were stretched out each side like a sleeper's about to wake. But she had lain there too long and the sand had sunk away leaving a grosser shape of her body in a shallowed surround. Her head lay back; her thick auburn hair was filled with sand. Her eyes did not stare at the sky but were directed slightly downwards and towards the dunes

4

and their blue had taken on a milky, deliquescent cloudiness. The left eye had slipped a little to one side and there was a tiny triangular pocket of blood in the corner. The right eye stared at him. Her lips seemed to smile, as if she were meeting, hesitantly, with a stranger. She might have fallen asleep there, but the sea had passed well above this point in the night and if she had been here last night she had been out and back, or been washed in from God knows where.

The Contract

HELEN

THE MONSTROUS NONSENSE they write about my daughter! And to make the rest of us out so queer that you would think us a family of cannibals or murderers. I would admit we were, we are, no ordinary family. People think it strange in this modern age to keep yourself to yourself; not to want to wash your dirty linen — if any — in public; to keep at a distance whatever neighbours you are forced to share. Would you call that queer? All normality has gone now anyway, hasn't it?

For, whatever is said, I will maintain that my two daughters had the best start in life that could be provided for them. I say my daughters, although to read the newspapers you would think I only ever had the one. Which is grossly unfair to Tucker. It is always harder for the youngest child anyway, and Starr being born first, and five years before her sister, had the best of our attention. Fathers never like their second so much, do they? One could almost wish oneself without any sometimes, for truly children are a charge and heavy responsibility. It does seem a sad end for a family to come to this scandal when you consider our background and beginnings. All a part of this horrid, modern world, I must suppose, that it besmirches and mocks at what we stood for, and when the best of people are treated the same as the worst. This latest misfortune has spoilt everything. We cannot even go any more to the cottage on the Cape as we used to. That is to be sold, and that will be the end of the past.

I brought a few things away from there; pictures, vases, small ornaments and such like, but I don't know if that was wise. They only serve to remind me of happier times.

Despite our troubles, our family was to be found among the finest in the land. We go back to the very beginnings of the Republic. Pride is reckoned a sin, but I can see nothing wrong in being proud of your blood and stock. How many after all are mongrels today, who can hardly name their fathers or the countries they came from, let alone their grandparents, and their parents, and back and back. I know the dates and names and marriages of our family as far as the Revolution. Ask anyone in Connecticut or Massachusetts about the Pierces – and it is the Pierces, just as it is the Lowells, the Cabots, the Lodges. We did not always have their luck perhaps, but the castings up or down of fortune are nothing to do with breeding. A general on Washington's staff was great-great-uncle on my mother's side. Pierce, the fourteenth President of the whole United States, was in almost direct line on my father's. A small portrait of Pierce hung in the library of my uncle's house in Andover and I had a copy made which has travelled with me all the moves I have made since I first left home.

Just as well, because my father left little enough at his death. Worse, he died in debt, cheated by friends — who always make the finest cheats, I have found — in a business venture into which he had sunk all of his own inheritance. Our large Boston house had to be sold up. It went, cheap enough, to one of my father's sisters. One of the many aunts who ruled our lives. She leased the house back to us at a smallish rent, so that we might keep up some appearance. Such charitable arrangements do not last for ever. And although she never directly complained, my mother felt, and managed to communicate to me, resentment that the family had not done more to help my father and that consequently she had now to live on their charity.

She sickened, and died in '03. Perhaps her death caused me to act too hastily, to secure my own future in the form of a solid, well-founded husband.

I married beneath me perhaps, but in those days, in the good houses of Boston, it was impossible for anyone wholly unsuitable to enter our society. A Harvard man, even one from St Louis, was not to be sneezed at, said Aunt Julia, who had never married. She knew that I was poor and so should be kept from quite the best-connected men — Mr Wyman was a passable substitute in her eyes. Certainly it was in her drawing-room that we were introduced. He called on me while mother was still alive. With the breaking up of the estate it was comforting to have someone on whom I could rely.

He was a tall good-looking man in an ordinary sort of way. What distinguished him in any room was his crop of red hair. The mixture of the two of us — if that doesn't sound indelicate — my black hair, his red — resulted in Starr's beautiful Titian colour. Although how my other daughter Tucker's hair came like it is, is quite inexplicable. Tucker's hair has always been a source of worry to me. From when she was very young it was darker than Starr's; it had at the front a white streak which has never grown out.

I'm racing ahead. Here I am talking about children, and I am not even married yet. That happened early in '04. We honeymooned at the summer cottage on the Cape.

I had begged it from my brother in the settlement of the estate. I found out soon enough from the mortgage on the property why he had been so happy to let it go. But I had such fond memories of the place, from when we summered there every year, and I had spoken in such glowing terms of the cottage to my new husband. The spring weather was still locked in winter when we went up.

'Oh but you should see it in summer,' I said as we got down from the buggy that had brought us from the ferry station.

'Well, it's not summer now,' he said, looking round him.

It was late afternoon, getting dark and raining. The woods around were denuded and mouldy-looking. He covered up his obvious disappointment with some joke or other and insisted on carrying me across the threshold.

Inside was almost as cheerless as out. I hadn't seen the place for two years before Mother's death, and not since. There were pale blanks on the walls where my brother had removed the good pictures. Some of the larger, heavier, more valuable pieces of furniture had gone too. There was no fire in the wood-stove, though I'd written ahead to a local woman to provide one, enclosing money for her trouble.

But after a couple of days we got the place a deal cosier. In that first flush of romantic honeymoon, as we sat by the fire one evening, I said as a fancy that maybe, as we had nowhere else, we could live on here for the rest of our lives.

'We could fetch the pieces I had from Mama,' I said gaily. 'We could shut the whole world out.'

'And what should we live on?' he said.

That's when I found out that Mr Wyman had absolutely no money of his own. He had no capital and the prospect of none. I, in turn, was forced to disabuse him of any notion he might have had that he was marrying into a fortune.

We returned to Boston a rather more silent pair than we went away. It was not surprising I should feel further dismay when he told me that we should have to leave the hotel where we had put up temporarily. He had, he informed me, quit the investment house where he was employed. It had only been a one-year contract anyway. A dead, stuffy place. He could do better than that, he said. He couldn't. Not for a good while.

'We must live somewhere,' I said.

It was with a sense of humiliation that I applied to Great-aunt Editha. We were allotted two unused rooms high in her house. Now, it was fine enough to stay in a relative's house as a young, unmarried girl. There were enough of those, sitting like fitments in Boston households, waiting, patiently or otherwise, for a gentleman to carry them off. Indeed, one of the chief products of Boston at the turn of the century was young ladies. It was preferred that they should marry wealth superior to their own, or at least equal. But for a married woman to come begging back?

Great-aunt Editha said nothing until we had moved in; a couple of days later she summoned me and, in the cold, disinterested way she had of imparting information, told me that Mr Wyman's leaving of the brokerage house had not been a matter of his own volition, but because he had failed to live up to expectations and been dismissed.

Well, being a young bride, I was still inclined to be loyal to my husband. There was little enough choice. Age and wisdom water our loyalty. Now, I can see why his employers may have found him wanting. He was ambitious, but too eager and impatient. Ambition in Boston society went in a cloak of idleness, a sort of arrogant indolence that masked ruthlessness or even ferocity in money matters. The sharks fed with good manners. In fact, every emotion there went under some other, more cautious name. So, 'love' was uncommon, a vulgar word, a toy for women and novels; a source and cause of scandal. A happy, more or less, arrangement, a fortunate combination of natures and fortunes, were what made a marriage. I think now that this is right. I was too fond of Mr Wyman in the early days. That sort of thing doesn't last. It would be ridiculous if it did.

We were not to be welcome at Great-aunt Editha's house indefinitely. That was made plain from the start in my aunt's behaviour to my husband. She was far too well bred for there to be any overt unpleasantness in her behaviour; rather she laid an increasingly unappetizing selection of alternatives before him, and successively forced and narrowed his choices. He had not yet found another job in the city. Therefore a job must be found for him. But a man with any sort of stigma cast on him by one financial house was unlikely to find a welcome in another. 'After all,' as Editha pointed out, 'they all dine at the same club.' Office managers', clerks' jobs were offered to Mr Wyman. A fiery man, he felt insulted by these and refused them. 'Boston is a rat that eats its own tail,' he said. When he went away for a few days to Pittsburgh — an agency had written him of a job out there — Great-aunt Editha said, 'Well, I guess anyone can get a job in Pittsburgh.'

I must admit that while he was away I was happier than I'd been for some time. It was made more pleasant for me in that house when he was not there. I found I was carrying Starr. I was only in the first couple of months, I had told no-one, but as I sat with Editha one evening, she laid her book to one side, removed her reading glasses, and said, 'So when is the child due, Helen?' Her sharp eyes threaded me. I stammered something like, 'Oh, not for many months yet. Many months.' 'Well,' said my great-aunt, 'let us hope your circumstances have helped you to a better situation by then,' picked up her spectacles and commenced to read again.

Whatever the promise of Pittsburgh was — it fell through. Mr Wyman came back, went away again to New York, pausing only to fight with me. Over the next few months he made many similar trips, punctuated by our arguments. I'm ashamed to say that I grew to look forward to his absences. Despite the stirring of my own child inside me, my life was almost the same as if I had become an unmarried girl again, with no responsibilities or ties. I loved the large, airy house; the servants; the carriages; the huge lawn as perfectly flat and square as a green silk table-cloth. It was my green and white cave, with Editha as the guardian dragon.

Then Mr Wyman cabled that he had found a position as manager of a factory office in Chicago. Two days later he wired the money for a rail ticket. One way. The night before I left I went up to Great-aunt Editha's room to thank her for all her kindness.

She showed no sign of relief, or regret, at our going. 'It has been a duty and sometimes a pleasure, my dear,' she said. 'You must come and see me whenever you have the chance. And your child too of course.'

There was no invitation to Mr Wyman in her tone.

We took a motor cab, getting deeper and deeper into an endless succession of brownstones until we reached the house he had rented in a terrace like all the others we had come through. 'It isn't Boston,' he said, going up the stairs, looking at me quickly, then away again.

'That it certainly isn't,' I said, entering the apartment.

We didn't even have the whole run of the house, only the top floor, up three flights of narrow stairs, with the carpet starting off miserably thin at the first floor, and ending up threadbare outside our door. One big living room, the kitchen curtained off to one side, two small narrow bedrooms in the L of the rear wing. No bathroom. A tiny toilet; the view from its hooked-up window was of saw-tooth factory roofs.

The place was furnished with that somehow heavy and yet rickety stuff you find in all furnished apartments, chairs with mortice joints showing, the sofa creaking and churning its springs around as you sat down. The large pieces of furniture I had of my own were in store. In the next few days, I placed about the few small pictures and ornaments I had brought with me.

I did the best I could. I cannot say that our marriage was now of the easiest. I carried Starr through the winter when the snow fell brown even before it hit the dirty streets. The stairs and windows and floorboards creaked. A tin bath we put up in the loft to catch the rain leaking through went pink-pink-a-pink all night long to drive me nearly insane. In the spring, Starr was born. To be confined in such a place with a crying baby. To have no friendly face near; to be alone all day; to be staring at, rather than through, a rain-smeared window, with the child held in your arms hour after hour until they grow numb with the weight.

It was not what I had intended for myself. But if I couldn't be in Boston, I could still be of it. Martha Phillips was my lifeline. I wrote to her every week.

Martha had been my closest friend since we were at school together. We were those inseparable, closed-off girl friends, who twine around each other like twins, who are forever in and out of each other's houses, who giggle at jokes not understood by anyone else, who compare endless notes on unsuitable young men, and who prefer their own company to any other. Exiled, she was my only ally.

I wrote her how I had settled into Chicago as best as I was able. I described humorously, but with just a faint undertow of bitterness, as only she would understand, the awful apartment, the joys and tribulations of having a child to care for, how my marriage was happy enough . . . And, to myself, I thought, perhaps this was how it was, how it was meant to be. We were not starving — he was a good, if limited, provider — or unhappy — a strong, kind, slightly impatient lover.

Martha wrote back, full of the intrigues and gossip of Boston. About the young men — two of them now — who besieged her.

And I wrote her about Starr beginning to walk and talk, the cat I'd got as a pet, how Mr Wyman was doing tremendously well. How we hoped to move any day. Some day. Back East. East to Boston. Mostly I made it up.

Then we did move. East. But not to Boston. Mr Wyman had been made manager of a plant in Montclair, New Jersey. The new apartment was larger, a little better situated — and tantalisingly closer to Boston.

The correspondence with Martha continued. In a few months the two young men dropped away from her. They were succeeded by this one and that. Fluff. An older man — heavily underscored, that 'older' — had asked her father if he might call on her. Something in politics. Rather sweet, not at all overpowering or vulgar as such types often are, my dear. 'I'll let you know if it comes to anything.' She had been to the new Opera House with him. He was well known to everyone. She couldn't think why she hadn't noticed him before. Aunt Julia had been unwell, but seemed to be getting better.

I found it increasingly difficult to think up enough events of any sort of significance to say in my replies to her bubbly letters. A year passed. Half of another.

Martha wrote more about this new man, Andrew Peters, Andrew J. Peters. But, 'it seems we are destined to be just friends', she wrote rather resignedly. Then, all at once, months later, a letter came saying that she was engaged to be married to her Andrew. The details flowed. He was thirty-five to her twenty-four, but already the congressman for Forest Hills — not the best of districts, but one that showed his heart for the poor, she thought. He had been at Harvard — 'as I think your Frank was' — and had left with a good law degree. He liked riding, was a good dancer, was most witty and droll — she gave some examples which didn't really come alive on the page — and had a bald head, which she didn't mind in the slightest. 'It makes him look so mature and kind.'

It hardly sounded a *coup de foudre* to me, but I was jealous of her calm pleasure in telling me these things, so that, in reading her letter for a second or third time, I screamed across the room for Starr in her pen to be quiet, God damn her. I never seemed to have a minute for myself; life going on and me not there.

Mr Wyman went to his job, came home. Starr grew. Another year gone.

Starr was four. I reported the news to Martha. Our letters had become scarcer and shorter; hers because presumably she had so much to do; mine because I could think of nothing to say.

We lived on in Montclair. We went nowhere except the local movie theatre twice a week. Mr Wyman's salary did not appear to increase; to pay off the mortgage instalments on the Cape cottage I was forced to rent it out in the summer months to strangers. I had little enough; soon my friend was to have everything she desired.

Came the large cream envelope with the white card engraved and printed in silver script. An invitation to Mr and Mrs Frank Wyman and daughter, Starr, to attend the wedding of Miss Martha Phillips to Mr Andrew J. Peters at Trinity Church. Just about the grandest place you could have in the whole United States. I saw beautiful Copley Square lit up by the early morning sunshine in my mind's eye and I cried.

Mr Wyman could not go. Pressure of business, he said.

I was relieved, though I made the conventional noises of regret. Marriage is an academy for liars. I felt as if I were running away from home as Starr and I boarded the train to New York, to transfer to Boston. Or rather, running to home.

We spent the night at the house of Martha's parents. Martha and I talked long into the night. We became girls again, our tongues rattling, collapsing into giggles and then gales of laughter at our not very ancient pasts. Then, just as we had decided we must go to bed or look awful in church in the morning it was already, Martha said, her face flushing, her eyes bright, 'But what is it like — marriage? What is it really like?'

What could I say to her? 'It's fine,' I said gently. 'Just fine. You'll be fine.'

I could hardly tell her that my own marriage was not very fine. And I hurried off to bed before she could ask my opinion on more confidential matters.

The next morning the church was crowded with all the best of Boston society; or, if not quite all the best, such a show of lace and silk and tails and shining top hats and shimmering dresses and all the handsome gentlemen and beautiful women who wore them, such an aroma of opulence and money that rose with the scents and colognes high into the cupola of the huge, grave church, and descended again, faintly dusty, and I breathed it in and felt both exhilarated and at the same time vaguely shabby and ashamed for myself and my daughter that we no longer shared fully in all of this.

The front pews were crowded with the parents and aunts and uncles and the children and grandchildren of the two families. We were placed a little way back with the friends and more distant relations. I was on the end of the row and turned my head as Martha came down the aisle. She gave me a nervous smile as she passed, but I don't think she really saw me. The bridegroom awaited her at the altar, a tall bull of a man, his prematurely bald head giving him the virile appearance such men have. When the service ended and the couple came back up together, Martha clung to his arm and now saw everyone and gave a little triumphal flutter of her hand and a beaming smile to me as she drew level.

At the breakfast, after all the speeches and toasts, and as

things were beginning to break up informally, she came down and dragged Starr and me away to the top table.

'Andrew, this is my dearest friend, Helen, and her daughter, Starr,' she said to her new husband. He boomed, 'Hello. Hello,' and crushed my hand in his grip and then swung Starr off her feet and kissed her on both cheeks and everyone laughed and no doubt the women muttered that it wouldn't be long before he was doing that to his own little ones. Everyone asked how I was, and why on earth they hadn't seen me, and wasn't Starr pretty, and I must come and stay whenever I liked. The young women all told me how well their husbands were doing, and what was New Jersey like? Smiling, I lied. New Jersey was fine. My husband was in banking. 'Yes, yes, I'd love to come and visit,' I said. 'I'm often up in Boston . . .'

I stayed at my brother's for three days — we never really got on — then at Great-aunt Editha's. I cabled Mr Wyman we would be another few days. Editha was most taken with Starr. What was to be done about a school? she asked. I had not really thought about it. 'You must bring this child up in a proper manner,' she said severely. She would see what could be arranged.

It was another week before we went back to New Jersey. It was late fall. To the north was that beautiful New England from which I travelled, my heart growing heavier with each mile, each telegraph post wiping past, each little farm or break of country bearing away not slowly enough into the distance, each small town after town sliding and leaping nearer and uglier and larger, until they merged together into one everlasting mean wall and its yards along each side of the track.

I changed in New York. That was the last few years you

bussed to the Hudson Ferry. I felt queasy and depressed crossing the unfamiliar water. It seemed already to be winter on the other side. Another train. In the clanging station I was met by Mr Wyman. There was no smile on his face.

He had reverted to bachelorhood during our absence. The floors has not been brushed, the bed was unmade, the ashtrays full of cigar stubs. After gruff greetings and Starr put to bed, he sat over the fire, looking into it, silent. I tried to chat merrily, saying how well so and so was, how fat Aunt Julia was getting — until he cut me off. My place was here, he muttered. I was his family now, not some old women in Boston. Where the hell had I been?

We argued in fierce hard whispers, so as not to wake Starr. We rowed every night from then on. He began to come in late. Once or twice he did not come home at all. He was never drunk, nor violent. But neither would he ever explain his absences. In some way to pay him back, to insist on my rights, I moved into Starr's room, sleeping on a fold-up bed. Oddly, things began to improve a little between us then. I no longer reproached him for staying out. He stopped picking petty quarrels about the housework or food. He still provided for the two of us, but I was sure some of his money was going elsewhere. I didn't know who she was, but knew he had someone. Many people, more than you realise, live like this, the world outside not suspecting what goes on behind their quiet, closed doors.

Let us agree, I said to him, to live amicably together for the child's sake. Then we shall see.

But I longed to get away again. At the end of the winter, I had an excuse to go. The cottage on the Cape had to be got ready after the winter for the summer guests. I had no-one to put the place in order, I said, and we couldn't afford the local people this year. I would have to go up myself. He raised no objection. 'If you think it's necessary . . .' I guessed he was looking forward already to entertaining whoever she was in our marriage bed.

That time we travelled through the new tunnel under the Hudson into the city. Starr clasped my hand tightly as the train rattled and swayed and clattered under the river bed with only a weak lamp showing our faces; she squealed with delight when we suddenly shot again into day. We changed at the equally new Penn station. I was young, my daughter was young, the city seemed to change violently and dramatically and hopefully for us each time we came to it. Everywhere dies down when you get older; you get to resent any change. This is when you begin to die. But then we were young.

The train to Boston ran up the coast through Connecticut, with views of the waters between the islands, and the ocean further out. Starr stood on tiptoe in her blue coat, her face reflected with such joyous eagerness in the car window of the train, pointing out at the water, islands, two leaping dolphins out in the ocean which were wonderful to her eyes. And my own worries dissolved along those tracks. The dark rooms of Montclair were a set of boxes, small, full of darkness and ill odours; now packed away. Never to be opened again? That's what I wished. And before us the white, airy rooms in the white and red houses of Boston. That was how I always thought of it — as going from darkness to light.

We broke our journey in Boston, and stayed with Martha and Andrew.

They lived in a fine, last-century house in Chestnut Hill. The house was large, blessed with many rooms, a gravel drive between lawns at the front, at the rear a long, broad garden, planted with poplars at its end, already a good height. Martha seemed perfectly happy; she was, she informed me in a happy, gushing rush, already expecting a child. 'Come down,' she said, interrupting my unpacking, 'come down. Andrew is home.'

Andrew was most welcoming. He was just in from business; tall, imposing, beautifully dressed, without any sign of the dust or weariness of the day that you see on such men in New York. 'Helen.' He took my hand. His eyes had a strange, soft gaze which looked wistfully into you. If you were a woman. I saw later that with men he was bluff and hearty, and a little calculatingly so. I'd heard that he was attractive to women. But entirely faithful. Certainly he was never in the slightest manner untoward to me. I must say that he was always genuinely and warmly glad to see me and my daughter and told Martha on that first time that we might stay as often and as long as we liked. And though Starr was a little big for such games now, he would take her on his knee and bump her up and down and make her laugh, and then go galumphing on all fours like a horse or a bear across the floor with her on his back.

'He's looking forward to the baby,' Martha whispered to me. 'He'll make a wonderful father.'

We stayed for a week, then left for the cottage.

Oh, but those were happy days — I will not have their memory taken from me. On the Cape, at the cottage, with all the windows open to air the house, the birds singing in the trees around, the empty, still dust-road through the wood, with Starr sitting on the porch arranging stones and shells, or running in and out of the house in her drawers, or with her skirt tucked up into them, or her skirt flapping.

Some afternoons our neighbours would call, walking up through our small back garden, and ask if I would like them to take Starr for the afternoon, or if we would both join them for a picnic at the lake about a half a mile away. They had a young boy of their own and wanted for someone, in the off season, to play with him, I think.

Girls and boys of that age, five, six, seven, eight, will not play together if they believe they are observed. Left on their own they will. It was the boy who taught Starr to swim. She had such a love for water. I remember well sitting on the lake shore with his mother while the boy and his father swam out to an island in the middle of the lake and we two could hear them laughing and chattering on the little sandy bank and talk back to them, quite quietly and entirely clearly without raising our voices, over the water.

I go ahead again. That journey is one we made for a few years. After the first one we got back to Montclair at last.

The apartment was tidy and freshly cleaned. I should have known that Mr Wyman had found willing hands to help him. But he seemed to want to make a fresh start with us. Whether this was guilt, or he had broken with whoever she was, I don't know. He stayed home nights. He talked to Starr and read to her. Summer and fall went by almost contentedly. It must have been the winter coming on, our drawing together for warmth, because I weakened once or twice towards him, and found myself with child again. He took the news well enough. Perhaps it stirred some fresh sense of responsibility in him. He was doing fine at his job — at least the happenings in the office had become only brusque, occasional news, which meant that he was in no trouble there. But then even the accounts of small disagreements, of little victories won over this or that colleague, dried up. It's difficult for anyone to realise nowadays, before the radio, or much music on records, or anything of that sort, just how quiet our homes were. How, if no-one talked, there was utter silence, perhaps broken only by the sounds of the neighbours running a tap or tipping out garbage. Tied to the home by a child, pregnant with another, I could hardly go out when I wanted. But he began to go out again.

One evening he came in and said that he had enrolled Starr in the local public school. She was to begin there at the end of the spring vacation. I had seen the little guttersnipes streaming home from this school. 'Oh, no,' I said. 'That's all to be arranged. Great-aunt Editha is to arrange all that.'

He sat, his face slowly flushing, his hands gripping his knees. 'You'll never let it go, will you,' he said quietly. 'Well, damn Boston. God knows I've tried.'

He got up, walked to the door and took down his coat. 'I'll send for my things,' he said.

Next morning, I got a letter with fifty dollars in it. Also instructions as to the only things he wanted, his clothes and personal effects. If I would pack them in his trunk. Two days later he sent a coloured boy and a cart for the trunk. The boy had another list of a few smaller things to collect, and an envelope with a hundred dollars in it. And a note, saying something like he hoped I would be happy in Boston. He would wire money to Mrs Peters if we needed anything — though he didn't expect they'd let us starve. He gave no address. When he had settled he would be in touch. He signed himself simply 'Frank'.

Two days later, Starr and I were on the train to Boston.

We stayed with my brother, with one or other of the aunts,

then at Martha's. After Tucker was born in that August, the foremost women of the Pierce family met at the Peters' house to discuss my future. Martha had told me beforehand that the state of my marriage was not of any concern to them; they had only Starr's and my welfare at heart.

Starr and I were ushered into Martha's drawing-room. There the aunts and some of the younger collateral of married women sat in a semicircle, straight-backed on straight-backed chairs, facing the sofa on which we were invited to place ourselves. Does this make it sound as if I was intimidated? Not in the slightest. I was back with my own, and Boston has always looked after its own.

Great-aunt Editha was their chairwoman of course. She led straight in. It was high time that Starr went to school, she said. A place for her had been found at Miss Parks', an exclusive school in Brookline. The child — the child clutched my hand — would either board at the school, or might better stay here with her mother — I clutched Starr's hand back — at Mrs Peters' during term time, it being the nearest family residence to the school. Aunt Julia, plump in her white collared dress, leaned forward to say something. Great-aunt Editha, consigning her to silence with the merest flick of a hand, went on relentlessly, addressing me. This arrangement would enable me to be with or near Starr until such times as our circumstances might change, or if I and my husband were reconciled in our differences.

That 'if' was made of ice.

I looked down at the floor. 'That does not seem very likely at the moment,' I murmured.

'Quite so,' said Editha, 'but whatever change may occur in your circumstances, it is proper that your child should have some measure of security and continuity.'

Martha smiled at me. 'Of course, you're welcome to stay as long as you please.'

'I cannot see why then the child should not be perfectly settled — and Helen too,' said my great-aunt, as if neither Starr nor I was actually present, and, inclining her head stiffly, she looked in her tremendous way first one way, then the other, along the line of them. They all nodded assent.

'The expense will not be great spread across the family,' she said. 'Your husband no doubt will wish to make a suitable contribution.'

'I have my lawyer, Mr Armstrong, working on an allowance,' I said. 'And my brother has agreed to help with a portion of the school fees.'

Great-aunt Editha bowed her head. This was acceptable. Now the others smiled, their eyes widening in welcome.

All was settled then. Starr was to go to Miss Parks' school. There was some consultation or, rather, instruction by Great-aunt Editha about suitable clothes and the like. Starr, who was most closely concerned with all this, sat quietly, rather pale on the edge of the sofa. I could not tell if she was terrified or excited. Both probably. That is the usual state of childhood. The details were being talked over, Great-aunt Editha's voice cutting suddenly now and then through the chatter.

We have lost them — those generations of great ladies. It is a thing I have heard many people of my age say — that the War finished us. That our generation was the last to inherit true beliefs and morals; that ours indeed was a Golden Age. Our good educations, pleasant manners, correct speech, our trying always to keep some sense of decency afloat in these dreadful times, attest to that. Certainly, when I was young, we thought that our Time would last for ever, indeed we did not think of time as such, certainly not as this series of sheerly bewildering events we have lived through; the War, the Crash . . . We thought that when we had children of our own they would grow up with all the old values intact. In that light, my family, in that year of nineteen hundred and eleven, had done no more than what they considered their plain duty, what was right, with only the slightest hint of charity.

So, everything was decided. Great-aunt Editha got up from her chair and then all stood and she waited for Starr to be walked over to her to be kissed on the forehead. Then she was gone out of the house, being pulled slowly away in her horse-drawn carriage, for she still refused to have an automobile. When she had left we relaxed. The children of the younger women were let into the room. The doors were opened to the garden because it was such a fine, late summer night. Ah, what a happy afternoon; to sit there with one's family and friends, the children playing in and out of the long garden, their innocent babble under our conversation. As evening came on the windows were closed, the youngest children taken off to bed, the lamps lit.

And I take this afternoon as typical of all our afternoons in those days. No-one lives in history — we live in the present, our past is particular and coloured by our memory, it does not consist of dates or famous persons or great events but of Martha and I and our friends sitting, talking in the evening gloom, then under the soft lamps, Starr and three boys playing cards on the floor.

And that evening, Andrew arrived home from his work in the city; tall, black-suited, his eyes shining, in all the pomp and happiness of a successful man and husband and father, stooping to Starr, swinging her into the air with his great hands under her arms, booming, 'My gracious, is this little Starr? My, how she's grown. My gracious. And you're to go to school, Starr? Here in Boston?' he said, setting her down. 'In the greatest city in the whole United States?'

'With the finest Congressman he'll say next,' said Martha, laughing. And all the ladies laughed, at the same time admiring her large, vigorous husband.

'Close your eyes,' he said to Starr. Winking broadly at us, he took out two silver dollars, hid one in each fist, then held them out to Starr, who stood with her eyes tightly closed. 'You can open your eyes now,' he'd say — because he did this trick many times. 'Whichever fist you guess, you get to keep what's in it.' And she would, each time, hesitate most charmingly and reach out tentatively to touch one, withdraw her hand a little, then waver to the other — Andrew beaming down all the time — and suddenly dart her fingers forward and touch one of his fists. And of course always win; unknowingly, innocent of the kind deception, with pure delight she would display the silver dollar she'd picked out of his opened palm, and we would all applaud, and Andrew would say, 'Clever child like that — she'll go far, Helen, go far,' as he covertly pocketed the unwon dollar.

How could all this go wrong? Perhaps life is just a dream — one would like to think so — and we all awake back in the good times.

The young do not understand — although Starr did some-how; Tucker doesn't yet — the remorseless tick-tock of time. How you stay in an apartment and do nothing and the clock goes on. Then you are all at once fifty years old and all your life is summed up and presented to you in one horrible event. And you feel, as in a dream, that it is really nothing to do with you. That it has been thrust, enforced into your life.

Well, it goes on. It went on. I had my new baby, Martha had hers; we were a happy nest, and everywhere we were welcome and fussed over, and Starr as happy as pie.

STARR

WHAT DO I remember of Boston? Darkness. Stuffed, stuffy darkness. Like the inside of the scarlet plush sofa I lie on one afternoon. There is a tiny hole in the right arm. I work my finger round in it — not idly, which is the word you expected me to write there — but purposefully, with intent to ruin. The tip of my finger finds a coarse, stiff forest of horsehair . . .

The day bright and summery outside; but only a small blue and green segment visible, framed by the heavy drapes that meet at the top and swag back in thick folds, gathered and tied into thin waists with braided dark-blue cords. Sunlight is controlled and patrolled over the lower part of the house by these heavy-hipped chaperones; it only pours in, pure and strong, under the cream blinds on the upper floors, all drawn exactly halfway down. The sounds too, from outside, are muffled and dispersed and put at a distance by the closed windows and drapes. Those inside are made more intense or nervous-making, because about to happen and not quite. A black, locked piano. Clocks that tick too loud and chime too soft on the quarter, the half, the whole of each hour. The shout, deep inside the house, of someone, instantly cut off. The people of our sort, as Mother would say, sit and drink tea, talk endlessly and too quietly, move only furtively and occasionally as people do on theatre seats; every one of them old and grave in front of their children, so that the children feel old and grave, look odd and old inside these houses. And in the rough grass at the side of the long lawn of that particular house, a tall laurel hedge curving over, the soil below home to long black beetles and tiny spiders and the smeary tracks of snails, is a green, filthily wet hollow where early one frosty morning I stuff a white, stained dress, saying over and over under my breath, 'Take it back. Take it back . . .'

Let me tell you about my childhood.

About 1911 or so, Mother and I moved to Boston. We transferred from what I remember as a dim, sticky-windowed apartment in a dim, smoky town, to Mr and Mrs Peters' grand house in Chestnut Hill. It was a journey we'd made often before. When, this time, we stayed and stayed and did not go home, that seemed natural and the other place began to fade. When my father still didn't come, and we made no move to return to him, I must have asked Momma where he was. For I did miss him. I always missed him. You live past certain things and don't realise their value until too late. When he came back to live with us a brief while in Boston — a few years later — it was not the same. So, my mother told me that Father had had to go away to work in New York, and, yes, of course we would see him again. She couldn't be sure when. I must have got from overheard conversations and those scraps of coded tittle-tattle children pick up like dogs from adults at the dinner table, that my parents had become separated in some mysterious way. I didn't see how that was possible for a mother and father. When weeks, then months passed and he still did not come to us, I thought I had offended him in some way. But five-year-olds are pretty robust and heartless. And nothing dulls memory for a child quicker than newness and attention from strangers, and a little luxury after hard times.

For the Peters' house was fine. Last century. Three storeys high, with three banks of windows, one each side of the white-pillared entrance. Wide lawns in front, a gravel drive to a pair of high, wrought-iron gates painted fresh black and hung from white stone plinths each with a stone urn flowing with stone fruit on top. Four gables jutted from the green tiled roof. The black telephone wires went in a long lazy loop from the topmost left side of the house to the still pale pine post on the verge of the road. Always on the drive were one or two black automobiles as big as boats. Behind the white façade of the house, room after room stretched through panelled passageways, to the back windows looking out on the long, rich garden.

I was soon at home in all of this. Mother and I — and then Tucker — had a little suite of three rooms on the top floor — while, as Mother put it, we looked round for something of our own. The looking took an awful long time. Aunt Martha was always expecting or just having borne a child it seemed, six in eight years — you can't accuse Andrew of not doing his duty. The Peters' family grew quickly, and I became almost absorbed into it. Sometimes it seemed as if my real mother, taken up as she was by Tucker, was my aunt, and Martha and Andrew my true parents.

Sometime after we had moved in, I guess I was about seven, my uncle jovially suggested that I call him Andrew.

My mother protested. 'Oh, no — Uncle Andrew. Please.' Then, immediately, she backed up, as if she regretted her bold speaking, her transgression of some unspoken limit as a guest, and turned her words round, blushing and saying to Martha, 'After all, we don't wish to be over-familiar, my dear. It will spoil Starr so . . .'

'All right. All right,' he said. 'Uncle Andrew it will be, but,' — turning to me, winking out of sight of the women, his voice dropping to a stage whisper — 'but Andrew when we're alone, eh Starr? Away from all these women?'

The two women laughed.

One weekend in spring, my father — who they all, even my mother, called Mr Wyman — came up to see us. I was so excited. You are always excited by the glamorous stranger.

In the drawing-room, Uncle Andrew gripped the tall red-haired man by the hand, and looked into his face with that warm, searching gaze that being a politician gave him, and said, 'Frank — it's been a long time. Too long. How the heck are you?' Though I don't think they'd ever met before. Then, as always, Andrew had to hurry away for some business, full of charming excuses, and 'Now don't you leave till I come back. You hear. We've a lot to talk about.'

Father sat with Tucker on his lap and me at his side on the sofa, Mother facing us, her hands clasped in her lap, a tense expression on her face, and they made awkward, deliberately cheerful conversation. People don't think that children notice anything. They notice everything; it's only later that they interpret what they have seen. I wasn't sure if I liked him.

After half an hour or so, Martha brought in her own two small children; one in her arms, a toddler at her skirts, and asked if we wanted anything, if Mr Wyman would like coffee. Then she bustled out, and came back in, and out, and when, having served us coffee and lemonade, she made to go again, my mother said brightly, 'No, don't leave us, Martha . . .'

And I seem to remember, to see, the two of them, my mother and father, on this or another visit, because he came several times before the War, walking out into the Peters' garden in the summer evening, my mother lagging behind a little and halting as they got to the middle of the lawn, as if that was as far as she was prepared to go, and my father turning to face her, stiff-bodied, his hands in his trouser pockets. They talked there for a little while, as if they were in a lonely place — that peculiar old Roman amphitheatre in Hardy's *Mayor of Casterbridge* where the lovers meet at twilight — the light and strangeness borrowed from literature I read only later cast back upon these two. They were not making up the quarrel between them — I know that now — but going through a sad dance, partly for my benefit, mostly for theirs, arranging, out of a sense of duty, to meet again now and then. Their words were never many and soon they came back in, my father suddenly bright and cheerful, playing and joking for some statutory time, looking at his watch, bending to kiss me, his daughter, chuckling at Tucker's sudden squall of crying, gathering up his coat. Going. Going.

My childhood lasted as long as that of some other girls I've met; longer than some.

Every morning, I'd be walked by my mother or a maid to Miss Parks' school a few streets away.

The school was in a large, ungainly house that, when I

drove past it years later, appeared too big for a house and not big enough for a school. I looked across at it from Andrew's car — and felt sick at remembering that I'd been happy there.

Four large main rooms on the ground floor, answering I suppose to the old parlour, drawing-room, dining-room, and library. The kitchen, where we went to eat at midday, was long and narrow, with a black range at one end, and runnelled oak boards running along the blind whitewashed wall. In the largest room, I sat with twenty or so other girls, all of us in pretty, crisp, cotton dresses, our hair ribboned, our faces rubbed to shining, each at one of those little slanted-top desks with a tip-up seat attached to a whole cast-iron frame, its base like the runners of a sled bolted to the floor.

Miss Parks taught us junior girls only rarely; she was a distant creature, stern, terrifying. To me she seemed very old, but I doubt now she was much more than forty; her brushed-back hair and spectacles hid whatever looks she might have had. She was married, but we hardly ever saw her husband. He was reckoned odd, a would-be writer who was scorned because no-one had ever discovered anything that he had published. If we had found any of his work he would probably have been made an even bigger object of ridicule. He 'worked', or whatever he did, on the floor above ours, in the rooms which made up their apartment at the back of the house. You would catch him sometimes, looking down at us when we took lessons outside in the garden on summer days; he had a long white face with ginger sideburns like a fox. If one of us glanced up, he would draw back hurriedly. It was difficult entirely to believe in him as Miss Parks' husband. She was Miss Parks after all, if only professionally, like an actress or a ballerina. I remember so well my own first teacher. Miss Ducamp, an actually unmarried young woman who spoke real French, and had black intense eyes and the most extraordinary red mouth. I might have liked her now.

A blackboard on an easel. An upright piano whose low notes grunted flatly and whose high notes cheeped. A large globe of the earth, with the big green-blue eye of the Pacific staring up, out of the tall window. Smells of chalk and slate and the black ink that came sometimes clogged like a spider's catch in your steel pen-nib from the desk well. Miss Ducamp with a long tapering pointer, leading us along the words on the blackboard, her precise, lilting, fabulously envied accent enunciating them, as we plodded, chanting along behind her, like climbers roped together.

I was your average better-off Boston child put with others of my kind. I coloured my pictures, read my books, wrote my innocent, mad stories; walked back and forth each day from the Peters', growing. Two years in, Mother got some money from somewhere — one of those little legacies that fell irregularly enough into her life, an afterthought at the end of a will. What with that and the allowance from my father and some she had from her brother she was able to take a small, neat house further in towards the city. As I was doing well and was happy at Miss Parks' it was agreed that it would be unfair to move me to some other and probably inferior school nearer to her. She took Tucker to the new house; during term time I stayed at the Peters' house. Aunt Martha was happy for me to stay; what with all the boy-children she had it was nice, she said, to have another female about the place. And Andrew was so often away in Washington.

Long days, filled with the happiness of well-brought-up children; of a comfortable house; of being treated as a confidante almost by Martha, despite my age. Their dog, Bruno, nosing over the side of my nightly tub ... A man reading this must remember some of this too. But perhaps boys live differently. There is a sort of waiting quality always in the female life; even as a child — of waiting for something to happen, of waiting to be prepared for something to happen; a preparation if you like for stillness, passivity, receptiveness. I think that boys, however young, must feel something else; must be led to believe something else; must feel life pulling them forward. Perhaps it's just their little cocks pulling them forward into life, before they hardly know what they are for.

Too knowing? Of course I'm too knowing. I was brought up to know ...

Schools. Schools. Doctors. Doctors — it's a long way from Miss Parks' School to Bellevue Hospital.

I was in there last year. I see the doctor now, a woman, scribbling furiously on a big sheet of paper full of little boxes, and squares, and oblongs, for describing her patients' conditions. She wrote, as I say, very quickly and illegibly, snapping out questions.

No, I said, I didn't remember how long I was unconscious. No, I wasn't a prostitute.

But she was some place away from me. A visitor to this dirty world who went home somewhere at night. She was a doctor, I was patient number god knows how many thousand and one. Her pen flew, halted, flew again, stopping irritably, her eyes staring down at the paper, flicking up to scan me; the next question rattling drearily out; her eyes, her inquisitorial pen, her watch, as she snatched a glance at it, insisting, Get this over with — I have other, more important, healthier things to do than look after drunken little tarts. Then I saw that she'd written the wrong name at the top of the form. 'Collins, Mary' and I said that's not my name.

'What?'

'That's not my name.'

I said my right name and Stanley and Mother's address at St Luke's Place.

'For Christ's sake, I haven't time to play games,' said the doctor, pulling another form to her, screwing the old one up with a quick, devouring fist. Looking at me straight this time, her eyes saying, if you can afford to live in a place like that, what the hell are you doing here? Now I was worse than a whore, because a traitor to my class, my decent, middle-class address. At the end of rewriting the form, she said coldly, 'Do you want your people contacted?' I said yes. Then the big woman nurse who had brought me took me back through the wards. A negro man we passed — he could have been forty or sixty — sat on the end of his bed, manacled by the wrist to the end rail, intoning over and over, in that grave, regal, melancholy voice some old coloured people have, 'Shit. Oh shit. Oh shit. Shit.' Taking no notice of us as we passed. The big nurse took no notice of him.

I felt almost at home.

Let me tell you about Bellevue. Simply, its size. It covers several city blocks and is always growing. It is a disease of its own. It is free. I've had several doctors, but they were all bought and paid for. Bellevue is there to mop up all the rest. It's a city on its own.

Imagine a series of vast, grey warehouses, separated, and joined by pseudo-streets, where the traffic is ambulances and police cars and men pushing stretchers and dustbins on trolleys; inside divided this way and that by endless corridors and air-shafts and stairwells; with wards and rooms stacked up on one another like crates, all foul or sour or smelling of cheap strong disinfectant. You think the place is made for animals, until you realise the animals are human. The walls painted dark green or dull orange to shoulder height, above that a dingy cream — in some corridors the green has turned almost to black, the orange to a shitty muddy brown — or the paint has fallen off altogether leaving ragged islands and archipelagos of grey undercoat or plaster, and where that too has fallen off, blood-red brick. And all this on the edge of the East River, so perhaps it's more like an enormous foul ship, slowly, endlessly, breaking up, and re-forming.

Too fanciful. What ship takes out with a ward full of deformed babies; arms like little flippers; or no noses, no eyes? Or with a cage for the demented, who are soaked with a hose-pipe when they get too dirty or fractious? Wards full of men and women who do nothing but stand all day staring into space, or performing one small endlessly repeated physical gesture, a tentative wave of one hand in farewell every few seconds, a fearful chopping motion with the arm with a full minute between each chop, or scissoring the air with their fingers, making some endless seamless garment. Utterly silent, or gabbling nonsense at a ferocious speed, or repeating the same words over and over like the negro — and sometimes a word more mundane and so more sinister than any simple obscenity. One girl that I heard kept repeating, 'The key . . . The key . . . The key . . .' God knows what some locked or unlocked door, or drawer, or closet held for her. Or from her. Wards for tubercular coloureds. For whites. For old women dying of syphilis. Whole floors for the dopeheads and alcoholics, with metal grilles like you get on freight elevators instead of doors. The windows barred against 'flyers'. That's what they called dying there — 'he's gone flyin' . . .'

I was in the Reception tank. Drunks are brought in all day and night from bars or street accidents or fights. After whatever first-aid they need they — we — go either out the door, to court, or to a ward for treatment. The bad, violent cases are hauled off to the padded drying-out cells. Where they can't hurt themselves any more — the theory goes. Or up to the fourth floor, where nobody goes voluntarily, and from where you never see anyone come back. At least, not as the same person. They come down, said the girl I talked to, with something missing.

I'd been brought to this place from a hotel near the piers. There was a party before that. One of the before-sailing, farewell parties on board a ship. The first time I'd been drunk for years. They weren't supposed to break out the booze till you were out of the twelve-mile limit, but you always took your own flask and when that was empty you could find some in the cabins. I couldn't afford to sail, couldn't stay away from those about to.

That was last year. I went to a lot of those parties. I wanted a taste of the life before it sailed away. And if you were young and quick witted and well dressed and a good sport you could always get in with some crowd. I knew a lot of them. I guess I was known to a lot of them. And the food and drink kept coming. Who paid? Why, the actor, or Chicago meat packer, or newspaper owner, whoever's party it was. That was an actor's party. I got talking, bright and loud, to a man. He was big and good looking and wore a not very good suit and a two-day-old shirt with a new necktie. There are hundreds of him. He said he was an actor. Then that he wanted to be an actor. Then that he could do as well as any of those cream puffs out there in Hollywood. A few drinks later, he said he was in business. In a store. I was past caring by then. When the ship was about to sail and we were being cleared off, he said, 'We'll go to a place I know.'

The hotel was right for what was wanted. He bought a pint off the desk clerk and the desk clerk looked through me like glass. Oh well, I thought I could go through with it, even though I had no pills or anything. I was still quite merry with the drink, but even with all the booze I knew I didn't want to be there. We got in the room and he shut the door. He put his arms round me and kissed me, wet-mouthed but not repulsively so. His breath smelt just of gin. 'Take your clothes off,' he said. So then I must have started swaying about, drunk but with a little hopeless guile to it. I kept telling myself that I shouldn't put on airs with anyone, that I was only a slut after all. 'Pour me a drink, will you,' I said. We sat on the edge of the bed and drank the warm neat gin out of one toothglass. In a ridiculous striptease I began to take off my clothes very slow, piece by not quite quick enough piece. I was always a poor seductress. Too slow for him. When I wouldn't do what he wanted, he started to slap me, soft at first, then harder, and I must have started to scream or something. 'Christ almighty,' he shouted. 'What's the matter with you. I paid for the fucken room and I'm gonna use it.'

So he did.

After, I lay on the bed and sobbed and swore and shouted and he sat in the chair and drank out of the toothglass and shouted back. After a while I quietened down and he poured me a big drink. Then another. This went on until someone hammered on the door.

There was a policeman standing in the room then. What the hell is going on? and all that. He might have been speaking Japanese for all the sense it made to me. The man said his name was Collins. That I was his wife. That we'd had a fight — this much I gathered from the doctor at Bellevue when the wrong name was put on my sheet. Anyway, God — I must have looked a disgusting object, naked on the bed. Everything went haywire then. Two men appeared, dressed just the same as each other in short white coats. They gave me a shot . . .

I woke on another bed. It was daylight outside, but not the same daylight. I was in a grey, rough cotton nightgown. There were other women in the long, high room, sitting on beds, drifting between, talking, smoking. The one nearest called, 'Hi, honey,' when I lifted my head off the pillow.

I felt as if I'd been kicked all over, inside and out. 'I must go,' I said. The girl on the next bed said you had to call to be let out to the lavatory. 'They'll call you for the doctor pretty soon,' she said. 'You get to go then.'

I lay back. Soon enough, a big, fat woman in a blue apron loomed over me. 'Collins? Doctor,' she said.

I said, 'No,' — meaning, No, not Collins.

'Doctor,' she said.

'You'd better,' said the girl on the next bed.

'Shut your mouth,' said the nurse.

The whole thing was mad anyway. I got up. 'Can I use the bathroom?'

'You better be quick.'

The bathroom was tiled yellowy-white halfway up and some of the tiles had dropped away. The floor was covered with linoleum, a sort of brown and something like white check that curled, showing black edges in the corners. A line of water closets with no doors along one wall. Two baths, side by side, in the middle of the floor; long streaks of green water scale on the enamel beneath the taps. On the wall was a tin mirror — they didn't allow any glass in there. All I saw at first was a stranger in dim, rippled light. I looked like a geek: my right eye was swollen to a black ball with a slit to see through, my lips had blown up into red tyres, a line of dried blood ran from one nostril to my upper lip, a black plaster covered half my forehead. I started to laugh, because that is all you can do when you get that low. The nurse, who stood behind me, said, 'Wash up, Collins. You're a mess.'

I still didn't know why she called me that, but I was the only one there. I washed my face in cold water. The water and the feel of my hands hurt. I saw that the backs of them were grazed and I didn't know where or how that had happened.

So that's when I went to see the doctor, and got my name straightened out.

'You sure picked a rough one that time,' said the girl in the next bed when I got back. She thought that I was a prostitute. I guess she was. I felt flattered in some way.

'Where are my clothes?' I asked.

'They don't give you those till you get out. When you get out.'

She gave me a cigarette and told me all about the place. She wanted to be friendly, but I hadn't even the sense not to screw this up too. When she said, 'You speak kinda nice. Where d'you come from?' I stupidly told her that I'd just got back from a trip to Europe. 'This isn't normally the sort of place I'm in,' I said. As a joke.

She stared at me, then said, 'Who are you kidding — we saw you come in. There's no need to bullshit in here, dahling. We're all here for the same thing.'

She got up off the bed and walked away up the room to where some of the other women and girls were standing at a window, smoking and talking. She spoke to one of them and they all looked down toward me and started to snigger and turned away. Nobody came near me the rest of the day. It wasn't until evening that the big nurse came to the grille and shouted, 'Faithfull.'

'Lady Fucknose's daddy's come for her,' the girl called out and they all laughed as the grille rattled open.

The nurse took me along an endless corridor to a long room like a parody of a theatre cloakroom, with a long counter and dresses and coats hung anyways on wire hangers behind, and bags and sacks overflowing with small clothes and purses and stockings. There was a man behind the counter who looked as if he enjoyed his work. He took my form from the nurse and went to hunt up my clothes.

When he'd got them, I looked round for somewhere to change. The nurse said, 'You do that here, young lady. This ain't the Ritz.' The counter man disappeared into his warehouse of underwear. I still felt his eyes crawling on me. The nurse sat down on the only chair and lit a cigarette as I took off the nightgown and hurried back into my clothes. My stockings were torn; there was no bra; blood on my silk blouse. I put on my coat and did it up to hide myself as best I could. I felt in the pockets. My few bits of money and everything else had gone. 'Have you a comb?' I asked. She shook her head and smiled.

'You were lucky this time,' she said as we went down in the elevator. 'Next time one of those bozos'll kill you.'

More corridors, doors, and there, in the bleak admittance hall, stood Mother in her foxfur wrap and Stanley in his thick English tweed overcoat that made him look even more like a stick-insect with his thin neck and goggled head poking out.

'Oh, Starr! For God's sake. What have you done now?' Mother wailed.

Stanley signed a paper and I was legally theirs once more . . .

Not many old girls of Miss Parks' school got to get to Bellevue.

But, I cannot take it back, can I? Children, like animals, are not much cursed with a sense of the future. So, her school was fine. I can't remember every day. Again, almost every day as a child is the same, isn't it? Until the day that makes a difference. You could drown the world in the tears of the unhappy children. All those born to grinding poverty or cruelty. I was never one of those. Despite Mother and Father breaking up, I was happy.

What does the word mean after all?

You are eight, nine, ten years old; you are well dressed, well fed, well schooled. You eat and play with children like yourself. You sleep on downy pillows, between crisp sheets. The world is quiet and well ordered. What polite sound there is you hear clearly, and you see through crystal. The whole world is more various and brilliant than any grown-up can guess or ever remember. Space and time are dilated; rooms higher and longer than the ones they move in; your days as long as their weeks or months. Whatever happiness you have is instant and intoxicating; unhappiness is huge, but trivial and transitory. Money is provided; you would only notice it by its absence. You are not troubled by sex. You have a tiny past that is recalled only by the big, lumbering mammals around you. You are a small animal, becoming slowly civilised by attending school, learning table manners and how to speak correctly, how to go to church and sing flutingly and energetically enough to please your mother in the middle row — your little sister looking round, puzzled and bored . . .

It all came to an end in '17.

We had just gone into the War. Mother and I marched in a procession through Boston, helping to bear a banner, which was half a white bedsheet with the words SUPPORT OUR BRAVE BOYS — BUY BONDS painted in black, in front of a horse-drawn float which, confusingly enough, was full of college girls in soldiers' uniforms. We'd stopped buying our groceries from the Weiss store, because they were Germans, and cheered when they had their windows broken as our parade passed. Mother helped, and I helped Mother, to make up packs of chocolate and cigarettes and improving literature for the boys at the front. I gave up willingly, unread, the copy of Ruskin's *Letters To Young Girls* that I'd had for a Christmas present. I don't think now that it was much use to the poor bastards over there, crossing the Atlantic to end up in some lucky doughboy's pocket. Or in the mud. More probably it's still at the bottom of a tea-chest in some vast Army store for such useless things. All the girls at school took up knitting comforters and sweaters. Mother crammed peach stones into gas masks, complaining that their roughness was ruining her fingers. She found a gentler occupation, chairing some Red Cross Committee in charge of Rolling

Socks, or some such valuable war effort. The point of all this is that Mother had the house taken up with these people on the weekend that I started summer vacation. I stayed, quite willingly, at the Peters' house.

Andrew was back in the city that fall. They were adopting him as candidate for Mayor, Mother said, and he would be voted in if the people had any sense at all. That weekend the big house was virtually empty. Martha was in hospital with another of her babies expected; this time there was some complication so she couldn't stay home. The other children were at the coast with their nurse. Andrew was pleased to have me about. Over dinner on Saturday night he said he would take me riding the next day, after his morning call at the hospital.

It was a fine, fresh Sunday morning. It bored me through and through. I lay on the bed in my new riding kit and tried to read a book and rolled over and stared at the ceiling, and through the window, up at the gathering clouds, hoping it wouldn't rain. When I got tired of this I wandered down through the house, avoiding the kitchen, where I knew Mrs Fitzpatrick, the housekeeper, was. The remaining servants were nowhere to be seen, having no-one to attend to. As a child you do not realise that servants have an independent existence; they simply vanish when they have done their tasks. The only person I saw, looking out of the drawing-room window, was the gardener, a small elderly Irishman in a long black top coat despite the warmth of the morning, only the top button undone, raking the lawn with one of those thin springy rakes like a hollow iron fan.

I waited all morning for Andrew. I went back to my room, read a little longer. Then Mrs Fitzpatrick called from below and I went and had some lunch with her in the kitchen. 'I thought you'd be home, my dear,' she said. 'Haven't your holidays begun?'

'Oh,' I said insouciantly, 'I'm riding with Mr Peters this afternoon.'

'That'll be nice,' she said, pouring herself more coffee.

I went back to my room and waited some more.

You might say I had a childish crush on him. Was I innocent? The night before I'd dined alone with him. He'd given me a glass of wine, watered, he told me, but it made my head spin.

'You'll have many beaux, Starr,' he said, 'but you'll always be my favourite.' Then he said what a pity it was that all his children were boys. How he would like a daughter of his own — but only if he could guarantee she would turn out as beautiful as me. I blushed so deeply, and picked on doggedly at my food, keeping my eyes down. Then I looked up at him suddenly. He smiled.

'You'll have to forgive me, Starr. I didn't realise I was embarrassing you. My apologies — but I'm a fool for a pretty face.'

My blushing became even worse at that. But I didn't say a word. After all, this was how a girl grew up. Men flattered girls. Girls blushed and got confused. It was in all the romantic novels I'd read. True, the girls were a little older than me, but I still felt flattered.

He broke his bread and mopped his plate, his voice becoming brisk as he told me how he must go to the hospital in the morning to see Mrs Peters, then drop into his office, but he would be back for lunch and then we would go riding at the Country Club. Tomorrow was the last time we would see each other for a couple of weeks. 'I'll miss you,' he murmured in such a sweet, earnest, serious way.

It was almost two in the afternoon before I heard his heavy tread coming up the stairs. I rolled off the bed just as he knocked on the door.

'You decent, Starr?' he called.

I ran to the door. 'I've been ready for hours,' I said.

'Well, let's go then.' He stared past me into the room, as if looking for somebody. He had to get changed first, he said. Come along — I could keep him company.

I followed him down to the second floor, then along past his family's bedrooms. A corridor dark with shut doors — I felt excited that I was being admitted to this part of their, his, other adult world, but at the same time reluctant, almost guilty, as if I was trespassing. He opened the heavy oak door to their bedroom.

'Come in. Come on in,' he said.

Now even more I felt that I should not be here.

The big bed, the enormous bed, covered with a thick blue and gold embroidered counterpane. A wall that was a whole row, a short city street of tall, closed wardrobe doors. A dressing-table with a double line of different size bottles and jars of perfumes and lotions, of combs and brushes and a jewel box whose lid was not quite shut because of the loop of pearls that hung untidily out. The table's mirror showed, tilted, the bed. The window drapes were drawn only half back, the blind down, the whole room in a honey-coloured light, and smelling of that thick, sweet odour of marriage, cut by clean linen.

Andrew went into the small dressing room. 'There's a magazine on the table,' he called. On each side of the bed was a small table. The one on the far side had a low pile of magazines, the top one *Harper's*. I didn't feel bold enough to go round for it. The action would have committed me to

51

that room, and I knew that it was someone else's and intimate and I shouldn't feel too much at ease.

'No — I'm okay.' I tried to sound as mature as I could.

'I won't be a minute or more,' he called.

Where I stood, fiddling with my riding crop, turning a little this way then that on each boot, biting on my lower lip, I could see him every now and then through the door left ajar. In his shirt and trousers, shoes off. Then, out of view, the rustling of his clothes. For a moment, awfully, his backside, naked, not quite covered by his long shirt tail, and his thick hairy white legs stumbled into view and away again as he pulled on his riding breeches. It was funny and disturbing at the same time. I looked away, round the room, the window, the bed, the magazines, the carpet, anywhere but into the dressing room. I'd seen men half-naked before — at the sea, or in the open air pool at the Club — but never inside a house. Not once had I seen my own father in any state of undress more than his shirtsleeves in summer.

Andrew grunted as he jammed on a boot, swore very softly as he pulled on the other. Then he came from the dressing room, beautifully turned out as a gentleman for an afternoon's riding. Black boots, grey breeches, a long black coat, white shirt, black stock at his throat . . . 'My,' he said, 'don't we look a handsome couple.'

But as I followed his quick strong stride down through the house I couldn't get from my mind's eye that other sight — of the half-moons of his big, ridiculous, black-haired buttocks beneath his shirt tail . . .

Then off we went in the big car to the Club, the two of us in the back, the chauffeur driving.

A beautiful afternoon. The sun burned overhead. The trees were as if asleep, nodding at the edges of the wide, flat, white-fenced fields. We went sedately up and down on our mounts; a pony for me, a great grey mare for Andrew. People sat up on the benches by the Club House like figures in a painting. Two parasols, one red and white striped, one green and white striped, paraded in front of them, as if carried by characters in a toy theatre, drawn forward gently on sticks. And the city behind us, broad, long, shapely, with none of the height or overwhelming character of New York, still something of a big town rather than a great city. A companionable, rich town, with whatever poor it had tucked away from our sight — the charitable concern of Andrew and the Aunts. For a while more we trotted up and down. I was very fond of that little pony, and proud to be beside Andrew — rider and horse both big and handsome. Oh, but I was proud of Andrew then. Of my association with a great man. Of the new riding outfit he had bought me. I've never been able to wear anything but good, well-fitting clothes. When I see poor girls and women in cheap get-ups I feel sorry and angry for them. I guess this is the limit of my social conscience.

Every time I come near to this, I slide away from it. With some silly joke or crass statement. Well, that is what life is sometimes. A silly joke. Here I am, eleven years old, proud as Punch on my silly horse in the silly park under the silly sun. Beside me is the future Mayor of this city, Congressman — what an apt title — Peters . . . At his shout of 'Let's go, Starr' we broke into a canter, and headed towards the trees, going faster and faster, my heart in my mouth, but with such a mounting excitement. I had never been let go before, never gone so fast . . .

I don't suppose that we were going all that fast when I was thrown. I don't know what caused it. Someone said a dog ran at the heels of my pony. All at once trees and sky whirled about and I lay on my back in the grass, winded, with Andrew bending over me like a great, solicitous, obscuring cloud, gently squeezing my arms and legs in turn, saying, 'No bones broken, eh, Starr? No bones broken.' Then a couple of other riders came over and stared down at me from their terrible height.

I heard Andrew say, as he picked me up as if I weighed nothing at all, 'It's all right. I'm her uncle. I'll see her home if one of you can pick up her things.' My tam o'shanter, my crop. I felt so silly and shaken as he carried me clear across that enormous field to the gates at last and the waiting car. He put me across the back seat and sent the driver to return our horses to the stable.

He drove me home. Or, rather, to his home. He insisted on carrying me in though I said I could walk now. When we got into the hall, Mrs Fitzpatrick cried out, 'My gracious, whatever has happened to the poor child?'

'All right. It's quite all right,' said Andrew soothingly. 'Just a slight fall. Open that door, will you, so she can rest on the sofa. Fetch me the bottle from the dressing-table drawer in my bedroom. The small brown bottle.

'Now, you just rest there — I'll be back in a moment,' he said as he lay me on the sofa in his study.

'I'm fine,' I murmured. I had not been often in this room. Alone, in truth not feeling badly at all, but enjoying the feeling of being spoiled, I lay and looked round.

There was a large desk with a neat pile of papers on the nearest edge. A wood and ivory mounted stand with red and black ink bottles. Two long, glass-doored bookcases. In the far corner a green-painted safe with J. GOTTLIEB & SONS, CHICAGO. EXTRASECURE stamped on the brass oval surrounding the lock. Framed photographs of law-student Peters, of lawyer Peters, of Congressman Peters — his hair gradually, then more and more rapidly disappearing — lined the walls. There were other portraits and groups, some including Andrew, of men shaking hands, exchanging scrolls or charters, or ranked in loose pyramids of heavy important faces and heavily suited shoulders, all smiling forward at the world, which was their oyster and which they had just swallowed. Smaller, darker pictures, paintings this time, of his or Martha's more distant ancestors.

I heard him talking to Mrs Fitzpatrick in the hall. 'They have no telephone. I shall send Fred over with a note just as soon as he comes back. To tell Mrs Wyman she needn't worry.'

He came back in, closing the door. 'Well, Starr,' he said. 'This calls for a drink. At least for me. It's quite a turn you gave us. Have you ever drunk brandy?' He took a key from his waistcoat and unlocked the tantalus on the sideboard. 'Good for shock,' he said. 'Especially for falling off horses. Though I guess you are a little young for it. I have something else you'll like much better.'

He had poured himself a brandy while he was talking. Now he took a small bottle from his jacket and poured about an inch of thick, slow-flowing liquid into another glass. He came across the room, smiling that warm, slightly shy smile that looked so nice on him. 'Drink that. It'll relax you.' His voice was tender.

The drink was a dirty brown colour. It smelt like medicine. The taste was bitter. But only a second or so after it went down, I was filled with a warm, swooning feeling. 'Oh, that is lovely,' I said.

There was a soft knock on the door.

'I'll leave you for a while,' said Andrew. He made for the door, then came back, took the embroidered sofa cover off and settled it over me like a blanket. 'Sleep now,' he said, and went away.

I felt heavenly: spilled, spoiled, flattered, flattened, sinking deeper into the cushions — the little Princess of my books. Francis Hodgson Burnett, George Macdonald — what do they know? It's all lies.

I must have drifted off into the most perfect sleep.

When I woke I was in the same room, now cooler, and dark, with the touch, suspended for a moment, then returning, of fingers on my hair, of Andrew, Uncle Andy, sitting on the edge of the sofa, stroking my hair, his huge ruddy face bent over me, his mouth saying, 'Oh Starr, you are so very beautiful. My beautiful Starr!'

•

The Account

HELEN

I wish that everyone could behave with the control and intelligence of our class. When Andrew's chauffeur brought me the news of Starr's fall on that summer evening I thought, for a moment or two, listening to his rambling, stupid account, that she was dead or mortally injured. My finger jagged open the envelope he handed me, my heart falling. Then I read, with that odd mixture of relief and annoyance that all parents feel when they know their children are actually safe. Andrew's note said that Starr had fallen from her pony, but that she was only shaken and bruised — 'every rider has a fall on occasion'. He had given her a mild sedative and thought it best she should sleep over at their house. There was really no necessity for me to come. The driver would bring Starr back in the morning. He himself was leaving for Washington early the next day, but Mrs Fitzpatrick would look after Starr. She would have the best of care. In a postscript he reminded me of the big party he was giving next week and hoped that I and the children could be there.

I scribbled a note back to Andrew, thanking him for his kind attentions. My love to Starr.

It was the following afternoon before Starr came home from the Peters'. Yes, she said, she was perfectly all right from her fall. But the rolled-up bundle of riding clothes was held tightly to her chest when I tried to take them for the wash. 'It doesn't matter,' she said. She would not be going riding again. She had no intention of ever riding again. And she hurried away with them to her room. I never saw them again. They were nowhere to be found when I came to look. They were of the best quality and had cost Andrew a great deal.

She remained in her room the rest of that day and evening, and for the most part of the next day too. She refused to come down for her meals at first but when I insisted she ate little, pushing away her plate. When she answered me there was something churlish in her voice. She had always had the most refined and precise way of talking, which came, I suppose, from being brought up so much among older folk. But for all its formality her speech had always been animated by fun and warmth. Not now. Of course, I worried about her, thinking she might after all have suffered some after-effect from the fall. But in the succeeding days she was well enough, though still taciturn and irritable. I realised I should put it down to the girl beginning to grow up. I tried to broach the *subject*, but I must have been awkward, or too oblique, because she only answered me in these new short, bad-tempered asides.

Or she answered my questions with ones of her own. Where was her father? Why wasn't he here? Why must we be forever on the move from one house to another? Then, contradicting herself — Why must we stay in Boston for ever? It was a hateful place. We had all been so much happier in New Jersey when we were all together. Before . . .

'Before what?'

She was silent for a moment, staring at me. 'Oh — before all this. Before you and Daddy . . . Before my stupid sister. *Before.*'

And Tucker, sitting at the table, playing with something or other, stopped and said, 'What does she mean, Mama?' and began to cry.

'How dare you speak of your sister like that,' I shouted at Starr.

Things hardly improved when we went to Great-aunt Editha's house on the North Shore. All the young people were organised into a swimming party off the rocks. Starr, a good swimmer, who loved the water till now, flatly refused to join in. 'I simply don't care to,' was all she would say.

At Editha's table that evening she was well enough behaved, but spoke only when spoken to, keeping her eyes down, almost hunching over her place.

'What on earth is the matter with the child?' Editha asked sharply, turning her long, yellow face on me when they had all gone to bed.

'Oh, she is growing up, I suppose. You know . . .' I said as lightly as I could.

'But she is only — what, eleven, twelve at most, surely?' said Editha. 'A little early for *that*, don't you think?'

She spoke in such a forceful, accusing way, as if somehow I was indecently forcing poor Starr's growth.

The morning we came back from the Shore, Andrew's chauffeur came over early with a note from Andrew to me, and a large rectangular package addressed simply on a silver card to 'Starr'.

He apologised for the fact that he had had no chance to speak to me since the riding accident. Business — and Martha's latest confinement — had taken all of his time. He hoped Starr was well and would not be put off riding for good by this unfortunate happening. The present was in way of recompense for his own slackness when she was in his care, a little something to aid her recovery and brighten her vacation. Perhaps it would also cheer her to know that she had a bonny new cousin. Martha had given birth to another boy. A little premature, but both doing well. Martha would be very pleased to see us all now that she was back at home.

'Starr.' I called at the foot of the stairs. 'Starr.' After a long moment or two, her door opened and she came out and stared down over the banister.

'There's a present delivered for you.'

She tossed the hair back from her face. She did not smile.

'Come down,' I said. 'A present's come from Uncle Andrew. And a letter saying you have a new cousin — Mr and Mrs Peters have a lovely new little boy.'

'Well, bully for them.' She made no attempt to move.

'Don't say it like that.' I could have lost my temper, but controlled myself. 'Now, do come down and see what it is.'

She came off the last step slowly, holding on to the rail. She looked so thin and frail, with her dressing gown pulled in at the waist and her hair falling forward over her eyes, that I had not the heart to chide her further. I put myself out to be pleasant. Perhaps I should have embraced her there and then at the foot of the stairs. But I was never one for spoiling the children. Instead I said, but not unkindly, oh, I am sure not, 'I've a good mind not even to give you Uncle Andrew's present. Do you want it or no?'

She shrugged in the mulish way she had developed.

'Starr,' I said, 'is there anything you have to tell me?'

I knew how awful my first time as a girl had been. The shame and confusion at having to go to my own mother; the admission into a secret I didn't want to share, the sense of inescapable uncleanness that it seemed was to be your lot for evermore.

'No,' she murmured. She did not look up.

'You're sure?'

'No. Yes. I'm sure.'

'Well then, come and see your gift.'

'Mama. Can I get up now?' Tucker called from their room.

'Five minutes, dear,' I shouted back. I led the way into the front parlour, Starr padding barefoot across the board floor after me.

The box, wrapped in red and gold striped paper with a cream silk bow across one corner, lay on the table. I took it up and held it out to her. Her hands were thrust deep in her gown pockets. At first she regarded the box with a distaste that I couldn't understand, though she could not conceal some sort of sullen and growing interest in the contents. Her mouth grew a tiny smile in what was obviously an attempt to please me.

'You open it if you like,' she said at last.

'It is for you.'

But she made no effort to take it.

I pulled at the bow and carefully unwrapped the paper. A black cardboard box with the name of *Baumgartens* — one of the best stores in the city — printed in gold on the lid.

I lifted away the lid, the tissue paper guards. Under them lay a white dress. As soon as I saw it I knew how good it was. I lifted it reverently out, and it unfolded sheer, creaseless, with the merest soft whisper. Pure white, with that under-shine of silver which is in the finest silk, a creamy embroidery of flowers at the low neck, a bodice decorated again with raised lace flowers, a thin red velvet sash to tie in the waist, the skirt pleated, half-opening like a flower in the most delicate folds.

'Why, Starr — it's exquisite,' I cried. 'Come here — let me size it on you.'

She stepped one pace forward, with that same curious reluctance. I held the dress against her body. I drew back her gown, her hand twitched at it a little defensively. 'Don't be tiresome, Starr,' I said. The new dress reached to just below her knees.

'Why, it's perfectly in the fashion,' I said. 'Andrew *is* cunning. He must have got Mrs Fitzpatrick to measure your clothes at their house. My, you've nothing as fine as this. It's a summer dress — but far too fine for just playing about in the summer. Really — the difficulty will be finding some-where grand enough for you to wear it. Take hold of the shoulders — step back. Let's see how you look.'

Her fingers pinched the shoulders of the dress. I reached forward to drape it more to her body, smoothing her hair to the sides of her face. I stepped back.

'Oh Starr — it really is divine. You know why he's sent it over now.' I said, suddenly remembering. 'He wants you to wear it at the party. He wants you to be the belle of the ball. How thoughtful. Clever old Andrew.'

For the first time that morning she smiled, a little wanly, but better than nothing.

'Yes, clever Andrew,' she said.

I must tell you what the party was for. After his second term in Congress, and three years in Washington, Andrew had been adopted to run as candidate for Mayor of the city. The party was to celebrate his candidacy. His election was a foregone conclusion. If there was ever a man to clean up the city after the recent scandals — and there always were scandals of one sort or another — it was Andrew Peters. No one had a bad word to say about him. He was a gentleman of good, old blood, he had wealth, education, a family man . . . and that was what Boston needed.

Andrew had had a large marquee erected in the garden at the rear of the house — for his political cronies and helpers and their wives and children, for the party that started in the afternoon. The true party, for family and friends, was to come later that night, inside the house.

All the late afternoon cabs and automobiles and charabancs deposited those *other* guests, the not so rich and the ward workers from the city. Old Glory flew proud over the marquee. A silver band under the trees played marches, the sun glowing on the instruments. There were barrels of root-beer and great jugs of lemonade, whole hams and plates of clams and oysters, wheels of cheeses and baskets of loaves — and wandering, milling thicker and thicker over the lawn, the men in their summer suits or best and only black Sunday wear, the women in long dresses — variously good — and the children; the boys in sailor suits or corduroy jackets and knickerbockers, the girls in skirts to their ankles and black or white or lilac stockings, running about, growing more and more undisciplined as the sun dipped, cooling. And through them, as the evening drew on, like a collection of tug boats off the Charles, came the parties of important statesmen — the inside-the-house guests — in black and grey top-hats and black and grey suits, with their stateswomen plumped out with many petticoats, each holding on to her man's arm with one hand and, in the free hand, carrying a parasol with which they paced out the lawn, pocking it with small holes now and then as they bit down with the iron tips; all making their way gravely, talking among themselves, but nodding here and there to the commonalty, the Cohens and Ferraras and O'Briens, furrowing through the crowd towards the open French windows, where Andrew stood, black-suited, beaming, Martha beside him, still pale, her little ones, four of them now, clustered about her dress, a nurse beside her holding the latest baby . . .

And Andrew shook hands with the men, and the men all doffed their top-hats to Martha, ruffled one or other child's hair, stood aside to allow their good ladies in, then themselves mounted the steps into the darker interior of the house, clutching their hats by the brim.

The outside mêlée was a little loud and hot and vulgar, and in the half hour since we had arrived I had not managed to get near enough to Martha, she being so busy greeting her grand visitors, so that the children and I stood about among all the common folk. We waited as the afternoon wore on, until Martha and Andrew at last disappeared inside, the French windows were half-closed to, and at last I thought it decent to lead the children inside.

A few people sat about in chairs along the walls but I did not know any of them. Andrew and the political guests — those that Tucker called the Upside-Down Men because of their bald heads and beards when she saw them in the portraits in Andrew's study — had withdrawn further into the house.

As we got into the corridor the sound of the band dropped away. The chatter of women's voices came from the small drawing-room. Great-aunt Editha was holding court with the Aunts and the visitors' wives. She nodded to me as we entered and went on with her conversation.

At a pause, she beckoned us over and made room for Starr to sit on the sofa beside her. The Aunts who knew Starr smiled and greeted her by name, the other ladies smiled also and nodded to this pale, sombre-faced girl, who looked so beautiful in the new silk dress. And all the ladies complimented her on the dress and said how pretty it was and how it showed off her hair or complexion and made her quite the young lady. 'When I think of the heavy old things we used to have to wear,' said one old lady, and they all fell to, agreeing and disagreeing, in a kind of round, about the clothes of their own more or less faraway youths. And as always with the old and middle-aged and aspirant middle-aged the admiration of what was new on Starr quickly gave way to bemoaning every other terrible thing in the modern world. But Starr answered them quietly and demurely in one or two words only, enhancing her reputation as a splendid, if isolated example of how not all the younger generation were going to damnation double fast.

I suppose to Great-aunt Editha and indeed to the rest of us from the old world, this one *had* gone to hell. But especially to her older generation the sudden speeding up of the world must have been terrifying. No-one can resist improvement for long, after all — and America is the land of improvement. Not that the speeding world seemed to threaten our group on that day in that room. We should have taken the message from the mob outside — that with speed comes vulgarity, the rapid spreading of the common across quiet lawns.

Tucker and I stood by the window while the women talked, and Tucker pressed herself to the glass and said in a loud whisper how she wished she could be out there 'having fun' instead of in here, and I shushed her and pressed her hand and listened to the past talking behind us.

That evening — that long, golden, midsummer evening — was long in dying. It was August, and it was not until way past nine before it was dark. The tables were bared and all the barrels and jugs had run dry an hour or so before the light gave out, and most of the people had gone back to town for another rally. Only a few still wandered the lawns. At last it was over and looking out we saw the gardener lighting lanterns hung in the trees. Some woman called out for a lost child, 'Huey, Huey,' like a pigeon in a wood. The lawn was scattered with ice-cream papers that glowed pink under the lanterns, and the stub of a stubborn cigar smouldered under one of the wooden benches. Then our drapes were pulled to and they were all shut out.

The family, to which we clung so precariously, and their honoured guests sat down to feast.

My brother was on one side of me, Starr on the other. Tucker had been put to bed with the Peters' eldest. Starr was to sleep in one of the attic rooms, her old room being given over to one of Andrew's friends, a fellow politician from somewhere in New Jersey — an overripe gentleman who seemed to be bursting out of his dicky and evening clothes, his voice clanging down the table like a train bell; his wife — identified to me in a whisper by my brother —

looked across at her husband with aversion. But there were grand people too; representatives of families older than the Union, than the state even. And their host, Andrew J. Peters — a distinguished record in Government and Congress already behind him at the age of forty-five — soon to be Mayor of this great city.

Ah, but it was a grand party — at least by my shimmering impression of it, which is all that lasts in the memory. I felt privileged to be near the head of the table where Andrew sat, Martha presiding over the far end. Great-aunt Editha sat a little way below us, and I can't say that didn't provide me with some quiet satisfaction, though I shouldn't say so, seeing that she had been so good to us. In her own way. She had been sat next to the Chief of the City Police. Across the table his appalling wife, a thick-set taffeta column, speared food rapaciously into her red, oval mouth. Two judges sat opposite each other, as grave and as pale-faced as only they could be after our wonderful summer. Their wives, one of them surprisingly young; the other, a long, pink, kind face, a flash of gold-rimmed spectacles. The white and pink and mottled arms of the ladies rose and fell demurely at the elbows. The waiters gathered like flies in their black swallow-tailed coats over the dishes on the side tables. The butler, a fat, overseeing, stationary fly, hovered at Andrew's shoulder.

As I remember, Andrew introduced the dinner, gave names and compliments to all of his out-of-town guests, and went to sit down, on which they raised the call for 'Speech. Speech'. Andrew got back to his feet. 'I must decline, ladies and gentlemen.' He paused — a long pause. 'Before we eat. After is another matter.' At which we all laughed.

War or no, there was no stinting on food at that dinner. The War was hardly mentioned. And though there was no wine, Massachusetts being one of the 'Dry Twenty-four', some of the gentlemen seemed merry on more than lemonade.

It was nearly twelve before the last dishes were cleared away. Andrew stood and held up his hand for silence. Again the calls for a speech were raised, redoubled.

'Very well then — but I promise to keep it short,' he said.

Oh, I cannot remember all of it. It was a good, quietly thoughtful speech, full of reform, what business could do for Boston, what Boston could do for business, the danger of anarchy, of Bolshevism, the good old American Way, our Boys Overseas, better Government for Our Beautiful City, Reform. The toast — 'Our City'.

'Our City,' we all echoed.

Then Andrew sat down and the ladies rose to leave the gentlemen to their cigars and stories. And Andrew and the gentlemen rose to see the ladies out. Aunt Editha, of course, prepared to lead our retreat. 'Many congratulations, Andrew,' she said. 'We must all sincerely hope that the city is better governed by our kinsman than heretofore.' Like everything else she said, it sounded more of an admonition than a compliment.

'One must hope so, Mrs Pargeter,' he said jovially.

I nudged Starr to rise. The poor child was so tired she had remained seated. Andrew must have noticed it. The ladies were all turning away from their chairs when he cleared his throat loudly. 'And one last toast, my friends. To the future. To the one class I neglected to mention — perhaps the most important of all. The children.'

Everyone had stopped, and when he looked at Starr, they looked too.

'To the youngsters — and their exemplary representative

among us tonight. To the radiant, shining Starr, beautiful daughter of a beautiful mother.' The men raised their glasses, and murmured 'Starr' in fruity, growling voices — the ladies, having put down their glasses, stood around smiling. Someone tittered. I had gone bright red, I know.

Andrew drank to his own toast, gazing at Starr over the rim of his glass. Then everyone applauded. It was nearly very ridiculous, but he was a commanding man, so that the gesture carried itself off as kind and chivalric.

They all looked so beamingly at Starr. I put my hand on her shoulder. The gentlemen turned their attention in towards themselves at the table; the ladies started to go out in earnest, talking gaily, some of them bending to kiss Starr, or take her hand gravely. And she stood, confused perhaps, her head down, but not blushing or at all flustered it seemed.

Martha, sweeping up to us, said, smiling, 'Oh goodness, I do hope Andrew hasn't too severely embarrassed poor Starr.' Then in a loud whisper as she went out, she murmured to someone, 'I do believe Starr is a little stuck on Andrew.'

So the women went out merry. I ascended to the top landing to see Starr off to bed. I kissed her cheek and she went up to the attic room without a glance back, so exhausted was she.

STARR

THE SHEETS WERE cold when I got in. The gable window had no curtains, the night was starry and clear. The whole house went quiet. I waited for him. And he came.

For the next three years, while I was at that school and lodged with the Peters, he kept that room for us. He didn't take me to it often. Too many people. Pressure of business. Only for a short while. He was frightened in his own house, I suppose, of discovery. He rarely had time for the ether he had given me that first time. He got me allonal tablets. They helped me do those things to him. But it obviously wasn't satisfactory; the hurry and worry of it all. Something a little better had to be arranged.

'Let me take Starr off your hands, Helen,' he said, sitting in our small living-room, cradling a cup of tea in his hands. 'Let her see some of the country. I have to make these trips out of town — seems a pity to waste the opportunity. They're pretty miserable without a companion. Besides having her along as chaperone will keep me out of trouble.'

Mother looked flustered for a moment. 'Well, I don't

know, Andrew. All the way out to Maine? Vermont? To stay overnight? In hotels? What would people think?'

'What do you mean?' He laughed. 'What should they think?'

'Well, Starr is very young. Just growing. A girl. With an older man — forgive me, Andrew — not to say you are old, of course. I mean . . . would Martha be with you?'

'Well, sometimes, yes,' said Andrew. 'Sometimes no. Martha has the children, her charity work. It's not easy for her to get away, even if she wanted to. I just thought it might be an opportunity for Starr. I can't see the objection.'

'That's just it — you can't,' she said. 'Not everyone is like you.'

'I fail to see your worry,' said Andrew bluffly. 'Look at Starr moping about the house all the time — you've said so yourself, Helen — she ought to get out. See something of the world. What do you say, Starr?'

What could I say? I see myself, sitting on the edge of the sofa, my hands in my lap, gazing up at them as they turned to me.

How could my mother go against him? She had no cause to, except her natural unease at — what shall we say? — the unorthodoxy, the kindly eccentricity of his proposal. She could hardly voice any doubts. Even to herself, I guess. And she had so many reasons to agree with him. We owed him hospitality we could not return, money we could not repay, presents we could never match.

'Starr?' My mother insisted on my answer.

'I don't mind,' I answered listlessly.

Once he had put on his hat, wished my mother good-day, smiled his kind Uncle-smile at me, squeezed Tucker's cheeks with his soft big fingers, and gone out, and driven off, why didn't I speak out against him, break down and cry where I sat and tell my horrified mother everything?

Because a sort of bargain had already been struck between us.

It was a couple of months after the party — I'd been back to school and at the Peters' house, but seen hardly anything of Andrew, who'd been busy in Washington — I was at home for the weekend in Brookline, up in my room. Andrew had been expected that day; with Martha, to take all of us over to Aunt Julia's for the day. But Tucker was ill with a cold and Mother had sent a message to cancel the trip. I was surprised to suddenly hear his voice downstairs. I went to my window. His car was on the road. There was no chauffeur.

His voice rumbled on for a moment or so, then Mother called sweetly from the bottom of the stairs, 'Oh Starr, come down. Uncle Andrew is here to take you out.'

When she got no answer she called again, a little more sharply this time. 'Starr. Hurry up. He hasn't got all day to waste.'

God help me, I was trembling, but I even looked in the mirror to straighten my dress and pat my hair into place, like a little tart preparing her entrance in a bordello. My twelfth birthday still a few months ahead. The customer in his forty-sixth year.

'Martha only just gave him the message we couldn't go, but he came for you anyway. Isn't that kind? Take your winter coat, dear. It looks fine but it will be quite chilly up on the shore.'

'I thought we were going to Aunt Julia's,' I said.

'She won't want to see just us,' said Andrew. 'Let's get some roses in your cheeks, Starr. The summer's nearly out. We won't get many more chances.'

We left in the car, with Mother waving from the doorway, Tucker standing beside her, puzzled and forlorn as to why she wasn't going on the jaunt.

I wonder now how cunning Andrew really was? How long had he been watching me, waiting for me? Were there other girls? Boys? Women? But when I rode in the front of the car with him, then there were only the two of us; this bluff, hearty man and me, riding in an altered world. I don't know how much of this can have been in my mind back then. I wonder if there was anything in my mind then. I was numbed by an anxiety that pervaded everything I saw and did, and that changed all their meanings around. I wished I was anywhere but here, and whatever it was he had started, I hoped now it was over. Perhaps what he had done was a sort of madness, but he didn't look mad, only sane and important and the future Mayor and a man who pressed himself against me in the dark.

'Cat got your tongue, Starr?' We were cutting away from the city, heading north. We followed the coast till we came to a small town and drove through that to a large white clapboarded house facing the ocean. I didn't know it was a hotel until we got inside.

We walked from the lobby into the dining-room. It was almost empty, as the season was just about over. I can't remember the people in there. I reconstruct them as one or two lone men sitting at tables, eating stolidly. Perhaps they were salesmen. Perhaps they weren't there at all and I've simply imported them from a hundred other hotels like this one that stare at the sea. Perhaps too I make the linen too white, and the cutlery glint too brightly, as in the hotels I knew later in New York and Paris and London. And I exaggerate perhaps the size, the height and depth of the dining-room in this hotel, because I was small and hadn't been in many such places before.

The manager stood in front of us; a thick-set man, but very short, like a barrel, with a carnation in the buttonhole of his suit jacket. He greeted Uncle Andrew, knew him straight off, but called him not by his real name, but something made up, like 'Mister Jackson', or 'Johnson'. I remember that because Andrew didn't try and correct him, didn't bat an eyelid. The manager led us to a curtained-off booth where a small table was laid for two.

Andrew must have used this place before. Neither the name he used, nor the place we had come to, seemed that strange. They were just one or two more unaccountable facets of the world he had opened in front of me — a peculiar world where nothing at all was as it had been, as it should have been. To change a name in this terrifying adult world was as natural, it seemed, for large, important people like Andrew as it was for him to take off his clothes, or to slip my hand into his pants' pocket . . .

Oh, and yes, 'My daughter' — he introduced me as that to the hotel manager.

Sitting across the white-clothed table, in that booth with the curtain drawn almost to, there was the sound of a victrola playing somewhere higher in the building, a tenor voice, full, but sounding thin and tinny. When it had finished the aria there was only silence, as if the rest of the world outside this alcove had ceased to exist.

I was afraid to look at Andrew, then looked him boldly in the face.

'My, that's a stare,' he said, laughing. 'Like a frightened doe.'

He reached out. I was not quite quick enough to move

my left hand that had been twitching the fork and his great warm hand closed over mine.

'You like adventure, Starr. I know you do. You like something different. I know. I know you. This is different. Look on this as an adventure. Just you and me.' His grip slackened a little, but as I tried to withdraw my hand weakly, it tightened again. 'Just you and me. You haven't told anyone? I know you've not told your mother. About us. None of your little girlfriends? No, I can see you haven't.' His face relaxed into a warm broad smile; his grip relaxed too and he patted my hand. He sat back and folded his napkin into the top of his collar as the manager pulled back the curtain to take the order.

They talked about the food, the slowness of trade at the end of the season, the closing in of the weather. 'Mister Jackson' ordered for both of us, consulting his 'daughter' solicitously. She didn't want a thing. He laughed, ordering a little grilled fish for me. And all this time he was normal, affable, gladhanding Andy. When the manager had gone away, he carried on chatting, asking me how school was going, what were my favourite subjects. How was Tucker? The little dog we had?

'We don't have a dog,' I said.

'No? My mistake,' he said.

Then the food arrived; lobster or something like that for him; my fish. A bottle of white wine. 'A little naughty of me,' he said to me as the manager showed him the label. 'That's nice. You can't get much of this now. You won't tell, will you, Starr? Just a half a glass for the lady.'

When the manager had gone, and the curtain was fully closed, Andrew began, speaking between mouthfuls of food.

'There is nothing wrong, dear Starr, in an older man's

affection for a young woman. And you nearly are a woman, Starr, and should be treated as one. You're not a little child any more. You're growing up. Eat your food, it'll get cold.'

'I don't want any,' I said.

'Don't be foolish. Eat.' He sat with his fists on the table, his knife and fork pointing up to the ceiling. His face for a moment was stern. Then it broke into a smile, and he began to eat again.

'You and I — as I say — your whole family — can have good times, Starr. You can travel, have nice clothes, a good education. Your mother's not a wealthy woman, Starr, she can't afford these things for you. Your father . . . A sad business when families break up. I wouldn't like to see any of you unhappy, or not do my share in providing for you. Would you like to see your mother unhappy? Of course not.'

'I want to go home,' I said.

'I want to go home,' he mimicked a child's whining voice. 'Eat your food. It cost money. Oh Starr, Starr — can't we be pleasant to each other on our day out?'

So, in the end, I ate a little. I was growing. I was hungry.

He did nothing more than talk in that booth. Everyday gossip anecdotes about members of the family I did not know, gossip about people in the government I had never heard of. I yawned with the wine.

Leaving the place, the manager rolled over to us and said, 'Will you be wanting your usual room this evening, Mister Jackson?' 'Mister Jackson' said, 'No — we have to go back to town.' The two men smiled at each other.

When we came out into the clean salty air and afternoon light, I felt relieved, and at the same time guilty about what he had said. About some things he had said. It all seemed mixed together, the gossip and the other stuff, the stuff about me and my family where his voice had dropped and grown warmer. I wondered if I was mad, or dreaming, or imagining things he had said to me, giving me that bitter liquid. He was very good at putting me in the wrong.

'You want to go home, Starr?' he asked as we got into the car. 'All I want is your happiness. I'll take you home. I can see you're out of sorts. I have to make one call first. Won't take long. Official business. You know I'm an important man? You know better, eh? Let's go.'

We headed back to Boston.

'I have to visit a charity institution,' he explained as we drove. 'Do you know what charity is?'

Of course I did. Charity was doing good to poor people.

'It's a little more complicated than that,' he said. 'Charity begins at home. I'll show you.'

I thought charity meant bringing warmth, food, shelter to those without the benefit of those things; a dime in the hand of an unemployed panhandler — but the way Andrew explained it, you weren't doing them any good at all by such largesse. The beggar must regain his sense of initiative; by giving money while requiring no return you were making the beggar dependent on you, causing him to lose his spirit of get-up-and-go. What does he do, what can he do in return for your money?

'Only a dime,' I protested.

'Dimes add up,' he said.

We were coming back into the city. We had both fallen silent for the past quarter of an hour's driving. Not because we had argued; his face was quite serene and he kept humming some same stupid tune over and over again. At the big crossings, as we slowed or halted, policemen tipped their helmets — the English-style ones you see in the Keystone Cops — gentlemen saluted with the tips of their fingers to the brims of their hats, or with a more vulgar wave of a cap; women smiled; even the September sun smiled on Andy, showing his reflection in the flat glass windscreen — it was like carrying an admired portrait of himself through the streets, so broadly did his mouth smile, his head wag forward towards itself in the screen. Or like turning round at the movies and seeing all the faces, serious or laughing. You want to shout, 'This is not real — none of this is real.' But of course it is real, more real than life, the illusion. That's why we poor dumb bastards go to the movies.

Then we got into a part of the city I had never been to before, down towards the waterfront, slowly going up streets of high red-brick warehouses, no other cars to be seen, only a truck coming up from the harbour, pressing us over to the sidewalk, and no people on the sidewalks because they were all at work in the tall grim red blocks. Then we came to a street of dilapidated houses, and ragged coloured kids and whites playing ball down at the end, and behind their play the masts of a cargo boat and the river and sky. He drew to a halt here. Outside a Roman church. You can always tell them — they're either St Mary's, or Sacred Heart, or some determinedly non-Episcopalian name like that. The sort of place the Irish went. Not people like us.

'Not here,' said Andrew as I got out after him. 'You don't have to worry about your soul. Next door.'

Next door, attached, was a three-storeyed, stone-faced building, its lower windows guarded by iron grilles. Andrew led me up a short flight of steps under a Gothic pointed brick arch. At the top of the steps were massive double doors, shut; thick filmy dust lay in the lines of the carved panels, but the two brass knobs were polished brightly. Andrew knocked. We waited.

A slat of wood like a cigar box top high in one door slid open. A girl's face appeared, on a level with Andrew's.

'Who is it? Who shall I say?' she called out in a nervous voice.

'Mr Peters. To see Sister Zeidler.'

'Yes sir.' The girl's face vanished abruptly downwards. After a moment we heard the lock turn and the door opened an inch or so. As Andrew opened the door, it scraped backwards the stool on which the girl had stood. From what I learned of that place later, I guess she must have been about fifteen, or older. She looked younger than me: frail, pale face, pulled-back hair. She wore a navy blue dress of some coarse stuff which fell like a sack below her knees. Black stockings and shoes. A red armband on the left arm. Women remember each other.

'And what's your name, my dear?' asked Andrew.

'I'll run tell Sister you're here.'

'I asked your name.' It was a sort of kind command.

She looked wildly from him to me. I think that was the first time she'd noticed me, hanging back in the hallway. I don't think anyone had ever asked her name before.

'Mary, sir. Mary Murphy. I'm trusty for the day. On the door.' She pressed the armband with her fingers to reassure herself it was still there. I'm ashamed to say that I felt contempt for the little wan thing. Well, not contempt — that's not the right word. It was that sort of held-back, shunning pity we put on for those to whom we feel superior, and know we shouldn't. And I had never met anyone like her. She *was* contemptible in her poorness and thinness. Here was I, well dressed, in the company of an important man. I was something she couldn't understand. I felt pleasure in that. I'd really entered Andrew's world, hadn't I?

She hurried away. The glass panels in the inner pair of doors showed her going down a corridor lined alternately with portraits of old men and stout, closed doors. She stopped at the end door, knocking, waiting, entering, or rather, slithering her body between jamb and door into the room.

'Pleasant child,' said Andrew, tapping his cane against the outside of his boot.

I said nothing.

'Don't you want to know where you are?' he asked.

When I said nothing, he went on, 'This is a Home,' he said. 'Doesn't look very much like a home, I must admit. But it is. Like your home, but not so comfortable, eh? This is a "corrective" home. For girls they call delinquent. Though some are simply orphans or abandoned, I believe.'

Through the glass panels I saw the door at the end of the corridor open. A nun, tall, with a gravely beautiful oval ivory face came down towards us. Mary Murphy lagged behind.

The nun smiled through the panel, seeing Andrew; Mary scuttled in front of her and pulled open the door.

'Mr Peters — you should have told us you were coming.' Her voice was as cool and as beautiful as her severely beautiful face, the cut of her habit, the black dress and white hood against the rosy polished wood of the doors. Perfect.

'A surprise, Sister Zeidler. Now don't say you're unprepared — you're never unprepared.'

'You're too kind. Is there anything in particular we may do for you . . . ?'

'A short tour, that's all. We were in the neighbourhood

— my niece saw your sign — she takes a great interest in others — her mother works for Mrs Pargeter's charities — she wanted to see inside. Simple as that. We should have warned you I know, but she isn't a frivolous girl in these requests. Are you, Starr?'

I was silent, still, determined not to advance a word, or the slightest movement of my face to help him. She was something else, a person you would see and admire and remember from a fleeting glimpse the rest of your life. I warmed myself on the coldness of her smile.

'Of course, Mr Peters. Excuse me a moment please.' She turned away, took Mary Murphy's arm, drew her to one side, and spoke so quietly in her ear that I could not gather a word, all the while not looking in the girl's face, but with her eyes fixed on the lower right-hand corner of a heavy wood picture frame just behind Mary Murphy's head.

Everything, almost everything, peculiar seems natural to a child.

The girl hurried off to do whatever she had been told. When Sister Zeidler turned back to us I could see again how very fine looking she was; high brown eyebrows under a broad, clear brow, brown eyes in pure whites — she might have been made for her nun's dress, for those mute corridors, the dead, not quite plausible paintings of the faces on the walls.

I suppose I could say that the little crescent muscles at the side of her face stayed in position just a little bit too long after she smiled, and when she just the once permitted herself a half-frown you could see the lines accentuated that would deepen with age. I did see them, and I didn't — and I don't exactly invent them now so much as call them up to witness to what I saw without being able then to put into words. Does that make sense? That's what writers do all the time. It must be.

'What am I thinking of,' she said. 'Perhaps the comfort of my office? Coffee? I am sure we can offer you something . . .'

'No — thank you. We really must get on,' said Andrew decisively. 'But if there's anything you want me to raise with the Board of Governors — feel free. We do not visit you enough I fear.'

'You are our most considerate friend.'

'Shall we go in?'

After these pleasantries, we started our tour. Not before Bellevue did I ever see such a hole. What is worse I suppose is that Zeidler must have let us see the best of the place. Certainly she seemed proud of what she did show us.

An immense refectory, its ceiling going up two floors, electric lamps coming down on stiff stalks like elongated inverted iron flowers. Long wooden tables and benches. Shuttered serving bays, with trays of yellow-handled knives and forks and spoons in front. Our footsteps echoed on the boards. Through another door, which Sister Zeidler unlocked, and carefully re-locked again behind us. Along a corridor. We looked through the glass door-panel into a classroom with lines of single desks, each occupied by a girl in a navy blue dress. Andrew nodded. Zeidler opened the door a little. None of the girls looked up. The sound in the classroom was as silent as the corridor outside. The sister conducted us into the room. We stood, great man, governor of this building, and little princess in her fur-collared velvet coat and lilac high-buttoned boots.

Their tall, bony instructress greeted us. 'Sister Zeidler — and distinguished visitors, girls,' she said. Her arm swept round, untheatrically. A sort of smile leaked across her mouth. In one uniform motion, the girls laid down their pens and folded their hands on the copybooks in front of them.

'Good morning, Sister Zeidler,' they all chanted.

'And distinguished visitors.'

'And distinguished visitors.'

'Carry on, Miss Harvey,' said Sister Zeidler. The pens began to scratch again, the faces looking up and down at some improving text on the blackboard. Their lives looked as if they could do with some improvement. I heard not very much later that over half this school died in the flu epidemic the sailors brought back from the War. No doubt they filled it up soon after.

Andrew asked if we might see the dormitories now.

What else would they be? Straight rows of green-painted iron-framed cots, each stripped to show the two-inch-thick mattress, at the head one blue pillow, at the foot two blankets, dark grey, two sheets, light grey-white, folded army style. Not less than three feet between the beds, or perhaps a little more — enough at least to prevent two hands stretching and clasping for comfort. Those put in charge of those 'less fortunate than themselves' have this mathematical exactitude for inflicting misery. Not quite enough money for any tiniest luxury, not quite enough food to be altogether fed, not quite enough heat ever to feel warm: they are the geometries of the heart, the calculations of charity. And I wonder — as I've said before — how calculating Andrew was, what risks he foresaw, how he discounted them, how much he planned? I haven't seen him for five, six years now — I'm twenty-five years old — too old to still carry him with me, but I can't rid myself of him. He — what is the word — 'interfered?' with me.

Well, he did that thing from when I was eleven to nearly nineteen, if we are into numbers. And whenever I think of him now I am back to that age, either furtively in the attic bedroom, or, more at his leisure, swoonily, stickily, dreamily, smiling up at that great white body with its tufts of orangey hair like a great bald ape leaning over me in some anonymous hotel room ... Well, he was what he was. If he hurt me, and probably others too, then in some way, some way he didn't know about, he hurt himself too. I was always too kind to him. I've given him this satisfaction of remorse, of exculpation — certainly there was little enough of self doubt about him then, as he stood, his hands in his great-coat pockets, nodding his approval at the sleeping arrangements for the girls. And it's only now, writing this down, that I wonder if he had any of them — or rather, which of them he had.

'Most neat, Sister Zeidler,' he said. 'Most orderly.'

She smiled, showing her teeth like little white pearls.

'We try to instil in them the discipline they have lacked.'

Beside each bed was a wooden locker. On each locker top a white enamel dish with a square thin piece of yellow soap placed squarely in its centre. Behind each dish a rough face flannel, rolled up, and a dark blue cotton towel, folded in a square. There was nothing else on any of the beds or lockers. Along the walls at exact intervals were framed texts from the Bible; the frames were screwed to the wall, as if, for God's sake, anyone would try to steal them. The liveliest and lone human thing was a coloured Red Cross poster showing a wounded soldier with a nice lean brown face and a fetching white bandage round his head. It took on an extraordinary beauty and warmth in that place, where every-thing else had been calculated to a mean edge. There was overall a clinging odour of half-healthy, only half-cleaned, hopelessness in the air.

Sister Zeidler said that there were two other dormitories, if we cared to see them.

Andrew said jovially that if they were half as well kept as this one he did not think that necessary.

'Exactly the same,' she said proudly.

We turned and began to go back along the passageway. At one of the windows I looked down. There was a tree in a tiny square of earth in the middle of the small cobbled yard. The tree had had its growing head cut back so that it was an almost straight trunk, black bark peeling away, a few thin branches lopped to yellow-ended stumps at the top. They should have put a dress on it, to make it feel right at home.

A work room, where girls sewed. A row of three locked doors with iron peepholes. Above the lintel of the last one hung a board with *Requiescat In Pace* burned on in pokerwork letters.

'A small joke,' said Sister Zeidler, smiling up at Andrew. She turned to me. 'These are for wicked girls, my dear. Sometimes it is necessary for the body of the whole school to isolate them.'

There was no sound from behind the doors.

'Is there anyone in there now?'

'In two of the cells. The girls learn the value of silence.'

The corridor was cold. I shivered.

'Not all girls are as well behaved as my niece here.' Andrew placed his hand on my shoulder, caressing, twisting me firmly but gently away.

We stood outside. Black automobile. Dark red street. The boys had gone. The cargo boat still there, the River Charles; clear cold blue fall sky above. At that age we see clear and true and it is time that writes on all the rest, that invents and covers up and hides away in words like these. Last month, in Louise's apartment, drunk on gin, I wanted everyone to see me. Two men, first one, and then the other, had been whispering to me, amusing me, not amusing me, one of them propositioning me, the other trying to in that shy, frightened way that does not want to declare itself — that wants you to do all the work, and I got bored with this and said to the shy one, well, if that's what you want why don't you say it, and I got up on the piano. The phonograph was going and stopped as I stood up straight there and someone put on another record and the men began whistling and cheering as I started to strip off. While the coloured woman sang some dirty song I pulled my thin salmon-coloured dress over my head, then off, seeing them all looking at me, with their glasses raised and their mouths shouting things and Archie saying something to the man next to him and Isabel tilting her cocktail to her mouth. Then my chemise. Pulling the tapes of my brassière and holding them together behind my back just long enough for the whooping to start, then letting it fall, and I kicked at my dress and saw it slither off the piano and settle in a pool on the floor. Somebody shouted 'Starr!' and I was snaking my step-ins down over my hips, catching the garter clip on one of my stockings and standing there naked, with only one stocking up and the other peeling down and the record knocking in its grooves at its end and I choosing that moment to fall forward, dead straight, confident, gloriously, drunkenly sure in my deliberate dead straight naked fall that Archie would catch me — and ending up in a drunken giggling mess in his arms, and then being given to the girls to take me away and dress me . . .

We got into the car.

Andrew seemed in a good mood after his cheery goodbyes to Sister Zeidler.

'Well, what did you make of that place? Those girls, eh?' he asked.

When I said nothing, he said that what I had just seen, that was charity. Those girls had sinned, and must now be guided and disciplined. Taught a good plain trade so that they could pay back something to the city which had extended its hand to them. You cannot have something for nothing, he said again. What would America become if everyone took that attitude? A sea of outstretched hands picking fewer and fewer pockets. Bolshevism. The wealth creators bled dry to provide a living for the feckless and shiftless.

But they're all so young — I should have said, but didn't, of course. And, what chance have they had? What else do they know but that awful place? Those dreadful people supposed to be doing them good — in reality enjoying their power to stifle and regiment and make miserable. I said none of those things. Half the human race spends its time dreaming of answers it should have made to the other half in answer to questions posed an hour, a year, ten years ago. Old women and men go senile and talk to ghosts — giving them the smart answers they never did fifty years before. So I didn't say anything. I just sat still and listless, quivering a little with cold in my warm expensive coat, like that little piece of gold foil I saw once, at school in a science experiment, held in a clamp, quivering and shining between two electric poles — to demonstrate something that I and everyone have long since forgotten. Thin, cold, and golden on that still, cold day, quivering between Andrew and the world that fell away past us.

When he saw I wasn't minded to talk about it he shot me a quick, somehow sarcastic look and resumed his humming. Somewhere on Washington Street he drew up outside a big store.

'Won't be too long,' he said. 'I have something ordered.'

He got out and shut the door. I sat on in the great steel and glass box that he had earned and not had through charity. I tried to imagine that I was someone rich and beautiful and mysterious. And sometimes I succeeded. For some time. Across the broad street, a huge Stars and Stripes swagged down from the pole on the second storey of the newspaper office. There were cars and cabs parked black and glistening all the way up to the intersection and beyond. Four soldiers came down the street and looked in our car and one, putting his face right up to the glass, saluted me gravely. His friends pulled him away. Gentlemen. A hundred stout ladies stepped in and out of the store doorway, most in pairs, talking energetically to each other, their eyes searching the windows, the feathers in their hats nodding as they bent, indicated, walked on. Young women hurried by, their heads close together, giggling. Practising to get old. Here and there a solitary man or woman stalked by on some serious errand. A woman with a little Peke dog on a scarlet lead smiled in at me. A street car tolled past, two coloured boys, big caps on the backs of their heads, running behind, touching the end of the car every now and then with their fingers. Everything seemed slow and dreamy and stately, and all the faces that came past seemed filled with light, their eyes shining, all their movements full of grace and air, the air from over the ocean seeping through the white stonework and red brick, the glass in the windows reflecting them as if they moved through some marvellous crystal water.

Then it all vanished. Sitting quite alone, I felt his hand, warm and almost hideously real, between my legs, foraging like a soft rat, his thumb hurting me ... The crystal was shattered. The people who walked past were gross and ugly enough, but they looked into the car and saw something lower and dirtier and poorer than any of them.

The back passenger door opened sharply so that I flinched. A porter from the store was putting a large rosewood box on the back seat. Andrew stood behind him, a red leather case in his hands. He put this in carefully himself, smiling at me across the seats.

'Phonograph,' he said. 'And records. I've decided it's too quiet in Brookline. It's time you had some fun.'

'A phonograph? For us?' I said, looking back at the enormous box.

'For you,' he said. 'Though we'd better tell your mother it's for all of you. Eh?'

'Thank you. Thank you.' What else could I say? I was a well-brought-up girl after all.

The journey back seemed a lot shorter. Early evening was gathering in Brookline. He halted the car at the end of the street, a little way off from the house. He turned to me. His big face was solemn.

'You do see the point, don't you, Starr,' he said. 'You can either have a life of presents, good clothes, good times, see your mother and sister well placed and happy — and you too happy. Or you can be as those girls you have seen today — objects of pity; despised, fallen, diseased girls who can expect nothing from life but misery — at best, life as a drudge somewhere. For make no mistake, my dear Starr, if you should reveal our little secret, the first thing is that no-one would believe you. No-one. As a consequence you would be thought a most wicked, deceitful girl. Perhaps mad. And you would be put in such a place as we've been to today — or worse. Now you would not want that, would you? Nor would I. Now —' he took my hands in his and squeezed them gently — 'what do you want — to be happy? Or sad?'

He held on tighter, his brown eyes soft, like an eager dog's, his face large and ruddy and beginning to wrinkle in a smile. Or so I make him up now — dramatise him as I do with everything to try and invest it with interest in me. I know I looked away from him.

'To be happy.'

So we get used to, are broken into, our secret lives.

This room is utterly silent.

I must have drifted off with the stuff Stanley put out. I really can't describe the effect it has. If I could put it into words perhaps I wouldn't need to use it. It would be public then though. Anyone else could use the same words. Words aren't everything.

There are no visions of great beauty, or terrible night-mares. I've read pieces by so-called addicts and I don't believe them. They sound as if they're made up by priests or doctors or lousy poets. There is simply a profound peace and a sort of rocking into the softest, most velvety sleep. Only when you wake do you feel muffled, and distant, and anxious, and that's when the nightmares might come. Sometimes I've woken and beat on the door, and Mother and Tucker have come and led me to the bathroom and soaked me with cold water and slapped me about to get me around. Other times, like today, I'm locked in here to sober up after drinking. Bill said I should be a writer. This is all I can tell. I'm sorry it floats about so. I can't write those clever, witty, false letters to Bill any more.

If he wanted some light relief, I'd tell him about our life here. About breakfast a couple of days ago. It'll serve for the last couple of years. The night before I'd come back in a bit soused. To make sure I didn't roam, Mother locked me in.

At exactly five minutes to seven, Stanley eased back the lock of my door as quietly as he could, then knocked loudly to make it appear he was simply waking me. I know the exact time because I'd fallen asleep leaving the light on and saw the green face of the clock as his little mousy scratchings in the lock woke me.

'A fine day, Starr,' he called. 'Do you want breakfast?'

'I do hope, Starr,' Mother led off as I settled myself at the table, 'that we are not going to have any repetition . . .'

'Ah, now, Helen.' Stanley put a finger to his lips. 'We agreed to say no more about yesterday.' He smiled at me. 'No offence taken, none given.'

'None at all,' I said.

'That's my girl.' He rustles his newspaper open, holding it awkwardly with his right hand, while his left adjusts his spectacles on his nose. Then the same hand lifts his coffee cup to his mouth, holds it tilting while his lips sip delicately, places it down, lifts his napkin — blue-green, gold dragon motif — wipes his lips, places napkin down at the side of his plate, then with two hands shakes the paper out and turns a page. Same thing every day for two years, possibly more, probably many more — it's only the last two it drives me crazy watching him.

He reads silently for a moment, then lets out a little snort of pleasure, then says, 'It says here, Helen' — but glancing at me from behind the paper — 'says that Chemical Union have gone up sixteen points. I said that would happen. I said it. They have a new sort of Bakelite product. Charlie Wilshaw told me about it — and I told him that if that had been my company that would have been on the market five, ten years ago. The secret is to be there first. That's the American trick. Be there first . . .'

So he goes on. Where the hell did she get him?

HELEN

On TREMONT STREET, spring of '21, I think. The most absurd thing. I had been buying shoes for Tucker and a few other articles. It was a bit later than usual when I dropped into the restaurant and to my annoyance it was filled with noisy shop and office worker girls at their lunch. I was attracted to the place normally because of its quietness, its wood-panelled walls, its polite little waitresses in their black and white, and only a few ladies like myself out for the morning. Like most places since the War it had dropped a little in tone, but it was still possible to sit quietly and drink tea and look out of the window over the lace curtain to watch the passers-by; or to meet a friend or acquaintance and gently, or not so gently, gossip for an hour or so. Now I was forced to sit at the only available empty place.

The table was small, set for two, and jammed in an alcove next to the door to the kitchen. A man sat at one side of the table. I took him in before I sat down. Respectable enough, in a fairly good, tan-coloured summer suit a little light for the weather, steel spectacles, thin sandy hair brushed carefully sideways over his head in an attempt to hide baldness on the top. Thin face with a large nose. A senior clerk, or something of that order. Though dressed a little sportily for that. A businessman, or salesman perhaps. He was stirring his coffee with one hand and staring down at the tablecloth in a relaxed, thoughtful fashion.

It is almost a rule of nature that it is impossible for two women thrown together for the first time in such proximity not to strike up an immediate acquaintance. With a man it is quite different. The distance across a small tabletop can be as wide and arid as a desert. I sat down, busying myself placing my gloves on my shopping bags which I placed at the side of my chair. I sensed he was looking at me; blue eyes enlarged by his spectacles. But not once did I look at him. For we ladies are trained from an early age not to engage a man's eyes. We know what's there. It shocked me often when we were out together, and when she was still only a growing girl, to see how frankly Starr would stare straight at a man's face, as if daring him to look at her. I thought her terribly forward, even for her generation, and told her about it, and how they — the men — would get the wrong idea of her. At which she would smile at me, and say, in that smart, mock-innocent way, 'Why, Mother? What do you think they look at? Why do they stare so?'

They would get absolutely the wrong idea of her, I would say again. That there was little enough modesty in the world today.

'I like to see them put out a little,' she said. She spoke like a character out of a book. She was sixteen now, boarding at Rogers Hall, a finishing school upstate. I worried that she might have come under some bad influence there. That early change in Starr had not been welcome, but had persisted so that it became almost a normality. She was at times so shy, withdrawn and curt in her speech that I was terrified she would at any moment offend one of our benefactors. Her move to boarding school had come as a relief. And brought its own problems. I had had complaints about her, complaints that were made with reluctance it seems. Most of the time, the staff wrote me, she was an excellent, biddable girl, very bright, quiet, but polite and generally well behaved, it was just 'her little eccentricities' — that sometimes were harmless and understandable in a well-brought-up but shy girl — sometimes more worrying and bizarre. Such as? Her refusal to undress in front of the other girls. Her aversion to swimming. Her wishing to change roommates rather too often. An addiction — 'a positive addiction' — to poetry and to reading novels. Nothing wrong with that of course, but some of the books she read! They were not considered suitable for a teenage girl. I was shocked when they sent me some over they had confiscated from her. You know those novels that came out after the War, full of drinking and sex and profanity. Not to my taste, and certainly too old and sophisticated for a girl. She would not attend church on Sundays. Some of the words she came out with! It was a pity, they said — most times she was such a sweet and willing girl.

Well — this was my day. I shook her out of my mind. I sat in the restaurant, sipping at my tea, demure, a married woman, waiting for the stranger to be the first to leave. The gentleman — for by now I was reasonably sure he was one, by his not speaking to me — passed his napkin over his lips, folded it neatly — which I was glad to see, as I observed his every move minutely, while not being seen to be watching — placed it by his neatly emptied plate and cup, rose, stepped sideways out of the alcove, allowing himself the room to put his trilby hat on, settled it, then raised it slightly with one hand (white, delicate, long-nailed), said in a soft, rather kindly voice, 'Good morning, Ma'am,' bowed slightly and, my cup carrying on to my lips after the faintest of nods to him to signify somehow my agreeableness for his gentlemanly bearing, strolled off between the tables, out of the edge of my eye.

I did not expect to meet him again. But Boston, though an important city, was still small then — at least as far as the people who mattered were concerned. It was in the same tearoom, perhaps a couple of months later in the summer. This time at the quieter hour of about eleven. I had been unfortunate enough to get talking to Mrs O'Brien, whose husband had been ousted as an official when Andrew's administration came in. Andrew's four-year term was now up and she was loud in praise for his successor. She made vulgar comments about how the city would leap forward once more now that 'sloppy old Andy' was no longer in charge. I was casting round in my mind for one of Andrew's positive achievements as Mayor — when she interrupted her diatribe to say, 'Why, there's Vincent now. My husband. I must go.'

She gathered her bag, patting my shoulder, 'My dear,' as she hurried away. I glanced round. At the window, actually tapping at the window as if it was some cheap café down in the Port, and peering in, hands cupped round a big red face, was her husband.

I looked away. I composed my own face into an expression of amused distaste that was meant to be viewed by the other ladies, who might otherwise have thought this dreadful woman my friend, as true Boston reasserting itself against parvenus and vulgarians.

As I approached with extra delicacy the little silver fork to my cake, there came a polite cough, a shuffle of fawn trousers, and a man's voice saying, 'Permit me. Might I sit at this table? There seems no place else free.'

I smiled. Bleakly. Then recognised him.

'Forgive me,' he said, settling. 'I do believe I've had the honour of your acquaintance once before. At the corner table over there.' He pointed. My smile was somewhat less cold, but still neutral.

'You don't mind me speaking to you? If you have the slightest objection . . . My card.' He produced it with a quick flick of long white fingers, like a conjurer. 'Stanley Faithfull.' He echoed what I read. 'I couldn't help but notice you here again.'

'Mrs Wyman,' I said, so that he should have no doubt as to my married status. We shook hands. There was nothing else I could do, his hand appearing suddenly, crooked to that expectant position, across the table.

It was a surprisingly strong and warm hand for such a small, slender man.

That was how we met. I suppose I must have been lonely. I like to think now that it must have appeared to the other women there like an assignation, seemly enough, but I hope it gave them something to talk about.

They all knew my situation. But as I had no husband to speak of, there was no harm in it. I had long ceased to make excuses for Mr Wyman's absence, everyone now knew that we were separated for good. I would not divorce him yet — not and leave myself at a possible financial disadvantage. He still sent me a small allowance every month for the girls, but that had not changed for five years now. When I had written last year asking for an increase he had not answered and the bank would not tell me if he had changed his address. Still, the money, such as it was, kept coming. I had resisted all his offers of a divorce. I knew he wanted to marry his woman, but I did not see why I should give him satisfaction in his life at a possible cost to mine. His sense of responsibility to the children, Editha argued, would soon wither away when he had another family. Besides, my brother said, I might well find that any alimony awarded would be less than the amount he paid at the moment. At the same time, not being free and yet having no husband around, I knew I was sometimes the object of friendly pity — the worst sort — among the other women. All those I had known from my childhood were now happily ensconced with their own husbands in their own fine houses.

The only men I had seen for the past few years had been my brother and the husbands of my friends. They knew me too well, and a married woman who is separated but not divorced, with two children, known to live on partial charity, is not an attractive proposition. For that reason, and that I was lonely, the meeting of this stranger, this little man in his summer suit — the same one, I noticed, but now in season — was welcome.

'Would you like another — coffee, tea?' he asked me as he gave his order to the waitress. After the usual polite, necessary, meaningless protest, I accepted a cup of tea.

'There, that's better,' he said when the girl had gone away. 'I hope you don't mind if I say — but ever since our first meeting — you don't remember . . .?'

'I don't think . . .'

'Ever since then I've remembered you. Please don't leave.'

I'd made no move to do so.

'I mean,' he went on, 'you can at any time, but I'd rather
— much rather — that you didn't.'

The girl brought my tea.

He was so ridiculous. 'Well,' I said, looking at my watch.
'I must go in a very little while . . .'

So these things begin. I would hardly have expected him to
sweep me off my feet, would I? But I was intrigued; it all
seemed so pleasant and somehow adventurous. And I was
bored, and he was so accommodating to me.

When the *New Yorker* reporter wrote up those things
about us, years later, he said that he could not understand
how two such people as Stanley and I ever came to land up
with each other. At least, that was what was between the
lines of his piece. He only revealed how little he knew about
what makes women choose this man over another. It is often
no more than the simple question of being asked by this one
rather than another. And that depends on social closeness,
on the mutual attraction of those who have much in
common under the surface. For Stanley, then, was a quiet,
pleasing sort of man — if our life after became different from
that of others, well, that may be the fault of others.

Mr Stanley Faithfull was in his early forties; I was thirty-
nine. He was not a handsome man by any means, but he
seemed reasonably prosperous, his clothes were good, if his
wardrobe was limited — I came to know its few variations
very well over the following months.

What did we talk about that first, or rather second, meeting? The weather. Common acquaintances — we had few,
and those distant from both of us. The opera — to which
neither of us ever went. Books we had or had not read. The
tearoom in which we sat. A strike in the Harbour which

had led to a consignment bound for his company being delayed for two weeks and thereby losing an important order . . .

So he revealed himself to be a businessman. We agreed that there were no possible excuses for workers striking, that in the difficulties prevailing after the War the men were lucky to have any job. Why, he said fiercely, it had done him such harm he could have gladly gone down there himself with a carbine and shot the Red rascals. The thought of him with a gun amused me. I smiled and said ah, but that would be sinking to their level. I reminded him of the '19 Police Strike, and how that had been settled by Mayor Peters, making sure that he knew I was personally acquainted with Andrew. A good man, he nodded, but in the wrong party — meaning the Democrats. Well, I protested, Andrew had to have meetings with all sorts of people, including labour leaders, but he was still a gentleman. How daring I felt, to be sitting talking politics with a stranger. To change the subject I asked, or rather, asked if I might ask, what line of business his company was in?

'Chemicals. Infernally boring for a lady,' he said.

My eye caught the clock on the wall. Almost one o'clock. Time had fled away. Hadn't I said that I must go soon? I felt compromised by having remained so long.

He solved the problem by looking suddenly at his watch. 'That's my lunch-hour well over. I really must tear myself away from you. It has been most pleasant. Your name — it has another part?'

'Helen.'

'Helen — may I call you that? I know it's terribly presumptuous of me — but it has been so pleasant. Your husband . . .?'

'I'm separated from my husband.'

A funny, eager little man — he would not go back to his office, he said, until I agreed to another meeting.

'But your business,' I protested.

'The business can go hang.'

Over the next month or so I saw quite a lot of Stanley. All perfectly proper; drives into the country or to the sea, lunches, the theatre once or twice, even a hot, fetid movie house one afternoon. I knew hardly more about him after a month than I did when I first sat down opposite him in the restaurant.

One day, when we had motored out to the coast, lunched at an inn, and he had parked, bumping over the rough ground, on a headland overlooking the ocean, I decided to force matters along a little. I told him that my husband was seeking a divorce, but that I was undecided. I waited, but he volunteered none of the information about himself that I was waiting for. He simply stared on through the wind-shield. Then he said calmly, 'You know that I'm in love with you, Helen.'

'Oh,' I said, and we both stared straight in front at the sea and then, at the same moment turned to each other. He leaned over, catching his waistcoat on a lever on the wheel. Freeing himself, he kissed me. His mouth was dry and urgent, the moustache surprisingly silky. The sensation was not unpleasant.

'Forgive me,' he said, starting back. 'No, don't forgive me. I simply had to.'

'That's quite all right.'

'Then — again?'

This time our embrace lasted longer. His arm — touchingly thin and unmuscular, unlike Wyman's — lay lightly over my shoulders.

'Can we not go somewhere?' he breathed.

Indeed perhaps at that moment I wanted to. But I needed some greater imperative than a vague emotional desire. Does all this sound terribly cold? It is not meant to — it is no more than how we have to be. I was not sure of him. An air of mystery is always supposed to be romantic and perhaps it is, but there were things to be teased from him before I made any further sacrifice.

'Stanley, I must know, before this goes any farther — whether you are married?'

'All that was over a long time ago,' he said. His arm was round me still, but it now relaxed, and he drew it slowly away from me. He laid his hands on the steering wheel and looked down at them.

'Let me tell you about myself, Helen,' he said.

First, he had been married for the past sixteen years. No, he hadn't been deceiving me. His wife was an invalid, had been so for two years. She had a cancer. I would think him an utter cad to be consorting with another woman in such circumstances. Only — I was not another woman, I must realise that. His wife was slowly dying, but her condition came and went — that is why he could not see me sometimes, he had to be with her. At other times she was better. It was not an easy life. He had hoped to keep our friendship to a friendship. Only that. He'd hoped that the accord he had struck up with me had not been entirely unaffectionate on my part. If I wished it to end, I must say so now.

'No,' I murmured. 'No.'

His wife wasn't bedridden. How could he be here, if that

was the case? She needed frequent rest, but was able to go about quite normally in her good times. Perhaps he had been too dramatic in saying she was dying. He prayed not. Fervently. I must believe him. But the doctors had said her condition was inoperable. A matter of time. She was in no pain. A wasting complaint rather. She had no idea of the true seriousness of her condition. They had not been — I understood what he meant? — as a husband and wife should be for many years now. He had given her everything in a material way that he could. His business had not developed to its full potential because of the division of his concern. Could I blame him, not for seeking, but for accepting a little friendship outside the home?

'Friendship?' I said. 'Nothing more than that?'

'Ah, so much more than that,' he exclaimed, turning and seizing my hands. 'Oh, so much more than that, dear Helen.'

What a pair of noble lovers I felt we were at that moment. Quite like something out of a novel.

One result of our accession to nobility and love was that, once we had got our basic domestic situations out into the open, a thousand and one details spilled from each of us. I told him all about the terrible apartment we had had in New Jersey; the two children; my friends; my house; my family; my great-great uncle, the President; the cottage on the Cape; my girlhood; my mother; father's collapse and ruin . . . For which, in return, he gave me his English blood; his time in England as a boy; his interrupted education that prevented him from achieving the qualifications he most desired as a chemist; his years in Boston; the wonder that we had never come across each other before; his various business enterprises; the reasons for their failure — the partners who had cheated him, the tragedy of an associate murdered for a secret chemical formula that the two of them had discovered between them — 'in the War — the Germans had agents everywhere' — his only requiring a break to make some of his inventions really take off; America, land of opportunity . . .

In among this welter of mutual confession I still kept my head. Things had to be arranged on a practical basis.

We continued to meet; in out-of-the-way places, making our more public appearances in Boston so infrequent as to appear accidental. And I did think, I said, that we should not be too much alone with each other. To preserve the decencies. We were neither us free, I reminded him.

He looked unhappy. 'Legally no,' he said. 'But in our hearts?' Men have so much more of the romantic in them.

I sustained him with other assurances. He was — he was — more than a friend to me. Less than a lover, my mind said, but time might remedy that. I would allow him to write me at the Brookline house and he must give me an address where I could safely write him. I could not bear to think of one of my letters falling into his sick wife's hands. I surprised myself by how quickly I thought out the details of an intrigue, how much more exciting the surrounding circumstances were than the thought of an actual *affaire*.

He hesitated for a moment.

Not to his own business, he said. The letter might be intercepted by his secretary or bookkeeper. 'Write here,' he said, and scribbled an address down on the back of an old envelope. It was his name, care of a Mr Frishberg, Chemical Factors, a company in New York. 'Friend of mine,' he explained. 'Perfectly safe.' Frishberg would send on any letters unopened.

It seemed very roundabout. Why couldn't I just telephone him at his office?

'My secretary might listen in,' he said. Anyway, he was out much of the time. New York was the safest.

'We're not plotting a murder,' I said, laughing.

'No.' He took off his spectacles and began polishing them with his handkerchief. His face had a peeled, defenceless, unfocused look that was oddly touching. He put them back on, settling the spring ear pieces carefully back in place. 'No, we're not,' he said.

Confidences and confessions brought us closer together. I grew impatient to see him in our separations. I fell out of sorts with my teas and lunches with other ladies, my charity work with other ladies, the visits to and from other ladies — just, other ladies . . . I looked forward inordinately to his letters and chafed at their infrequency — though in fact he wrote at least twice a week when he was out of town on business. There even seemed something romantic in 'Chemical Factors' — whoever or whatever they were — the conduit for our feelings.

And yet. Stanley urged me to approach Mr Wyman for a divorce. I pointed out that he himself wasn't free to marry.

'What if I am some day soon?' He clasped my hand.

'Don't speak of such things, Stanley.'

'We must face them,' he said. 'My wife will not live for ever.'

But a little caution in these matters comes with maturity and experience of life. Feeling slightly ashamed of myself, I checked up through my brother on Stanley, telling him that I had the name of the owner of the business but did not know the name of the business, as I did not, and that someone had recommended them as a possible investment. Could he possibly find out about them?

My brother rang back a week later.

'Don't know where you got the name — took me a heck of a time to find them at all. Intercontinental Cosmetics and Foodstuffs is the name.'

'They sound awfully grand,' I said.

He laughed. 'A shack down in the Harbour district. I don't know where you got the tip. They don't issue any stock. Worthless if they did. It's in the name of three directors: Faithfull, Faithfull, and Frishberg.'

I remained silent a moment. 'Are they doing well?'

'Depends on what you mean by well. It's difficult to say. The bank says nothing is known against them.'

'Is that good?'

'Banks are very discreet. They rarely say anything positively against a business. "Nothing known" that can mean anything between imminent insolvency and just about keeping afloat — at the very least it is meant to be tactfully discouraging. Shouldn't touch 'em with a barge-pole, sis . . .'

I was mightily discouraged by this news. Hadn't Stanley presented himself as the head of a business, a man of substance? I was a poor prize, I thought, if he was an adventurer. Though, thinking back over our conversations, hadn't I rather over-presented myself, boasting of the family history, the fortunes made and lost, my hopes for my children through their connections with a powerful dynasty. But my house was a modest one; the summer cottage had much of its mortgage left to run — I admit that I had painted that in glowing terms, picturing myself and Stanley there, either side of a log-fire in the winter — and my sole income was made up of Mr Wyman's allowance, which would cease if I divorced and remarried, my brother's occasional gifts, Andrew's and the family's assistance towards Starr and Tucker's educations. Hardly a great catch.

The uncharacteristic absence of a letter from Stanley for over a week at that juncture allowed my doubts to multiply, until I put them, rather obliquely, into a letter to him. I said that, as neither of us was free to commit ourself in any other direction at the present moment, I thought it advisable not to meet for the present, to give us a term of grace of, say, three months, before we even considered meeting again. Nothing could be gained by any encouragement I gave him now, which could only be sustained by false hopes and result in even greater disappointment if it came to nothing in the end.

I must say I awaited his reply with great misgivings. Perhaps I had been too harsh. What if he tried . . .

His letter, when it came, was obviously written under great strain. What I was suggesting was hardly to be borne. But borne it must be, if I so wished. He agreed — with a heavy heart — that we must separate until we could be united with honour. Perhaps it was for the best. He could not anyway in all conscience now meet me. His wife was ailing. 'My heart is with you,' he wrote. 'My duty is to be with her.' He could wish for a miracle, that she would be restored to her previous health and vitality. But for her sake, not his. Alas, he feared it could not be — a merciful and swift release was the best that could be hoped for . . .

He must not think of that.

The nobility of this letter brought tears to my eyes.

STARR

To describe one's sexual conduct to another is to make it seem quite unbelievable — that Andrew could have done those things, that I could have acquiesced for so long. But all sex is a form of theatre. And as in the theatre, one of you is the actor, the other the audience. The ether, then, later, the pills helped with that — they distanced me so that I seemed to be looking from a great, amused distance at the fumblings and groans of my lover. My lovers. And it does amuse — you all want the thing so much. And Andrew? I was Andrew's audience, set down to watch his bits of this and that, his silly fleshy pipe sticking out — the thing he was so proud, so fond, of that literally his whole world revolved around it. Tell me, doctor, is it correct that the sex organs are actually in the mathematical dead centre of the body? And when that was filled, raised, his face flushed — well, then his world of politics and business, of signing documents, mounting platforms to speak, seconding this, passing that, shaking hands, the patriarch of the dinner party, playing with his children — those other games — all went, all shrank down to one afternoon hotel room with the drapes drawn, or the blind down — oh how carefully and worriedly he scrutinised the join of the drapes, the fall of the blind, to see that there was not the smallest, slightest, thinnest crack anyone could see through — even if we were ten floors up!

Then his ritual. First, in the earliest days, the ether bottle, the silk handkerchief, a few drops poured on. I must sit on his knee, breathe in the ether, both of us fully dressed, while he solemnly produces the book — of Havelock Ellis, *Studies in Sex*. Always the same book, the same passages that I must read in a hushed voice to him, my hand guided towards his unbuttoned pants, his hand groping up my skirt. I tell myself he must have been mad — but I was the one sent to see the doctors.

Did my mother not suspect? Or his wife, Martha? Did they think it was a precocious interest I had in politics, or an overwhelming fondness for the company of middle-aged men, that caused a very young girl to travel alone with Mr Peters. It didn't happen to other girls, waking into this nightmare, did it? It must be that if I was the only one, then it must be somehow my fault, my precocity, my wickedness, my temptation that caused Andrew to be weak. Because assuredly I must have some power over this huge, powerful man to make him whimper and moan. So then I felt a horror at myself. At school I could not bear to appear even half-naked in front of the other girls. The knowledge of what I did made me feel dirty and too old for my skin. I lost any taste for childish things long before I needed to. When I got to Rogers Hall, I read all the adult books I could get my hands on. Not old books, but modern books. I wanted to see what their adult world was — if it was anything like the one I saw with Andrew; if it was really as horrible and furtive as his version; if everyone else hid away from the world to perform these small, dirty, ritual acts. So I read Cabell and Hergesheimer and Booth Tarkington and Scott Fitzgerald and Sinclair Lewis and Somerset Maugham. I wanted to understand just how adults behaved — if they behaved in any way like the ones I knew. They didn't. Even in the most dreadful events in these novels, they came nowhere near to the sheer awfulness of dear kind Andrew, lowering his pants, or yellow Aunt Editha starting to smell of the cancer that was killing her. I found these books confusing; the whole notion of love that obsessed the characters, all the twists and turns they went through — I knew precisely what lay at the centre of the maze. I wanted to believe their high-mindedness, their kindness, their charity to each other — it simply was that I knew as I read that things were very different for me.

And, oh, but I used my knowledge too. It gave me some idea of the troubling excitement that a thief, or a poisoner, or spy, or poison-pen letter writer must feel. There is shame, but also a perverse pride in having a secret not known to anyone else; of which, you think, they could not even conceive. The thief stands in a room where he shouldn't be, where no single object has any connection with him, none of the photographs displayed is of anyone he knows, total strangers sit in those chairs, eat at this table, sleep in that bed; the thief can only subtract from his surroundings, the life he has chosen is solitary, a revenge upon the invisible others in these rooms; by taking from them, he adds briefly to himself. And the poison-pen letter writer poses as a kind neighbour or friend, gleeful in her heart — why do I think they are usually women? — as she sits in the company of the one, the special one, the one she has chosen to tease secrets from — and hears her own letter read out, and sympathises, consoles. The poisoner brings lovingly the medicine to his invalid wife's bed . . .

So it was at school with my friends — though I never allowed any of them to get too close, in case I might be tempted to tell. My knowledge of myself was the secret I must never, could never, tell; the theft, the letter, the murder. When they giggled over some hot pages in a new novel or looked down, hidden behind the curtains, at a new boy working in the garden below, I felt superior.

'Oh you're so pure, Starr. You're too good for this world. Wise up, kiddy,' said Sandy Cody — annoyed at my pale puritanism.

I could hardly inform her on Sunday, the day my kind uncle had come to take me out for a drive — that two hours later I was holding his plum-coloured dick in my hand watching it grow milky in its funny curved little mouth, while the ex-Mayor of Boston groaned and cried out, and his hands, holding onto my shoulders, dug the fingers in so tight that I had to ask to be excused gym the next week in case any of them should see the marks.

But these things didn't happen too often. Only on high days and holidays. I think that Andrew kept me as some sort of trophy, a prize for himself. Looking back, he visited me, wanted me most, when he had something to celebrate. Perhaps I was the reason for the success.

There was the night of the party of his candidature, of course. Then the day after he had been elected Mayor. Again, a wintry afternoon in the same attic bedroom. A whole six months after that on his yacht, moored off the North Shore, when some of his big political friends had come from Washington and he stole along to me in a tiny wood-panelled cabin after they had dined late into the night.

A summer later on a drive out to the country, when we were disturbed by an elderly couple out walking who happened to look into the back of the automobile parked in a gateway in the middle of nowhere. The sight must have made their lives. And in the Peters' own marriage bed when Martha was away in Europe; my mother in New York with Tucker — I forget which particular high spot in his life I was helping to celebrate that night. About once a year on out-of-town trips — those he had persuaded my mother would be good for broadening my mind.

Then I was seventeen, at Rogers Hall, a finishing school for the well-brought-up young ladies of New England, and at the age when every good American girl should get down to her patriotic duty of starting to 'date'. A euphemism for the first sexual experimentations of the young male and female. It is practically the whole point of the education of the American girl. That is, to lead on, repulse, strut before, give into, not give into, the American male of a year or two older. The whole complicated game starts up with the comparison of one physical specimen with another, the face, the hair, the nose, the teeth, the eyes, the social position, the availability, the latitudes of suitability. So the boy must not be overly handsome if the girl is on the plain side, but if she is pretty it will not do if he is in the slightest way physically deficient. The young of both sexes sort this out for them-selves, more or less without tears. The more complicated calculations involve parents or other guardians. Is the boy rich enough? Is his family good? Is his religion a correct match? What is his profession to be? You see how little the two sets of criteria have in common; those of the young are sexual, emotional, concerned with what they see as love; the mature people, the grown-ups, the overgrown-ups as my schoolfriend Dorothy — plain, sweet — called them, were worried only by the basics, to what it all boiled down to in the end — the money.

I don't think you can have any idea of what this intricate, silly, heart-breaking dance looks like from the outside. Which is where I well and truly was. The other girls at Rogers first made fun of me, then, in a gentle sort of way, they were puzzled. I became odd old Starr — to be tolerated, humoured, admired for my acid descriptions of all and sundry, my sophistication in other matters — books, music and sometimes gin.

'Oh, Starr's saving herself for something really special,' drawled Lindsey Pellew.

'A mayor at least,' said Sandy Cody and everyone fell about.

Their young bucks would call for them. For me? Here was Uncle Andrew, black-suited, bald-headed, advancing across the Rogers Hall lawn.

'Oh God, Starr, why don't you come with us, why do you have to go with him? It's not as if he's your father or anything,' said my friend Dorothy, seeing my face change as Andrew hove into view one Saturday afternoon.

The best was yet to come. A month's vacation at Andrew's summer place in North Haven. How the hell did he swing that? Why didn't Tucker come along with me? One of the times Andrew first broached the subject he told Mother that Martha was up to her earlobes in young children and would appreciate the help of us two girls. But, no, Tucker insisted she was spending part of that time with her own friend's family. I sometimes suspected from the way he looked at my little sister, all of twelve now, that he was somehow earmarking her for the future. Mother was for the idea. I would be bound to be among a lot of youngsters my own age — Andrew nodded sagely. Plenty of swimming — I grimaced. Open air — I scowled. Sailing . . . The true reason Mother let me go was her thing with this man Stanley.

Tucker and I had met this Important New Person in Mother's life only a couple of times when he had called on her in the evening — to discuss business, Mother said. It was obvious to me she was seeing a lot more of him than these formal visits — not that there was much to see. When I came home I had to act as big sister to Tucker when Mother went out; first waiting on the porch for a cab, dressed in her best, then saying she was off to visit friends, not to wait up for her . . . I could have recommended some swell hotels to her.

One Sunday morning, the first week I was home from Rogers Hall — she had been out the whole Saturday before — she called me into her bedroom. She was dressing. She had a reasonably good body for her age, though it was just starting to go that bit sallow under the armpits, and, with her top off showing her white plump shoulders, her neck and face looked a bit scrawny, the skin round her eyes showing tiny white creases and the top lip starting to furrow just a little.

'Shut the door, Starr,' she whispered. 'I don't want Tucker to hear.'

'Don't worry — she's out.'

'Oh. Where?'

'With one of her little playmates no doubt,' I said. Mother didn't seem to notice the acid tone in my voice.

'Well — as long as you know where she's at. Now, my dear, we don't seem to have had a chat for so long.' She had put on a white blouse and sat at her dressing table plucking the points of the collar how she wanted them. 'Sit down.'

She waved a hand at the bed, but I didn't care to loll there; instead I went and sat in the window, so that I wouldn't have to face her all the time, and could look out if she got too tiresome.

'I don't know if you've noticed,' she started off, 'but I have been seeing quite a bit lately of a certain gentleman.'

'Stanley.'

'Stanley? Yes, Mister Faithfull.'

'That's what he asked me to call him.'

'Did he? Well, yes — all right. We'll call him Stanley.' She hesitated for a moment then looked straight at me. 'Do you like him?'

'What's to like?' I said in a lazy Bronx drawl.

'Don't do that, Starr. It's horrible.'

'You're still married to Papa. This man, Mister Faithfull, he's married too, isn't he? Is there something between you?'

'Don't be impertinent,' she snapped. Then she softened her voice down again.

'You know I haven't lived with your father for so many years now. He has someone else — I may as well be frank with you. He wants to marry her. I didn't want to divorce him because of you children; there's still a certain stigma in divorce, even if you are the innocent party. But now . . . Well, I'm going to New York next week to put the matter in hand, as it were. Then I will be free. Mister Faithfull is a widower. Oh, Starr — you have no call to look like that at me. It hasn't been easy for me all these years. I know you've lacked a father's touch. And Mister Faithfull is a fine man. A good man.'

'Good, fine, and faithful.'

We both fell into a sullen silence. She smiled an uncertain smile, her right hand began to pluck nervously at the long points of her collar again.

'How long will you be away?'

'Two, three nights. Perhaps a week. Then there are other things to arrange. I'd rather do it now. You needn't bother. That's why I'm glad there's somewhere nice for you to go this summer. You won't be bothered at North Haven . . .'

So that's how it was done. It was convenient to everyone. And after all, had not Andrew shown us great charity and kindness through the past five years? Hadn't he time to concentrate on his fund-raising work for the Democrats now, having relinquished his duties as Mayor? According to Mother, I had seen only a small part of Andrew's greatness. The people hadn't deserved him. All those vicious articles in the papers, the cruel cartoons — they didn't know him as we did.

Andrew had come over to the house to discuss with my eager mother the last details of my trip. We would start, he said, with the two weeks at North Haven. Then, if I got bored with that, he had to go on a tour of the New England states, making a few speeches, pressing a few hands, calling in a few promises and favours . . .

'Why not let Starr come along with me on that trip too?' His jovial, frank question. 'Do her the world of good,' he said. 'We're not living in the old world before the War now, Helen. Young women have to learn to make their own way. She'll meet people who could be valuable to her in later life — see how the world wags. She is not stupid, she knows the good it will do her.' He spoke in his charming deep voice, tamped down from its booming public mode for this domestic setting.

He made this speech sitting in our best chair, in the one good, well-furnished room we kept for visitors. The rest of the house was a little under-nourished for furniture, for just us three to live in, and our rooms were getting neglected and dirty because Mother was out so much now and I could not be bothered — being the feckless, carefree girl of her imagination, on the edge of life — curled on the sofa, facing Andrew, her favourite, generous uncle.

My face, oval, slightly sunburned, was reflected in the mirror behind him. I often looked for myself in the mirror in my own room, but whatever the light in there, the electric lamp, sunshine through the open window, greyness of winter or warm amber evening, the tall rectangular wash-stand glass when I approached it cast up always only a cold white unflattering gleam across my face. And I would interrogate the mirror softly, like the wicked stepmother in the fairytale.

Who are you, Starr?

I am nobody.

You must be somebody.

I am nobody.

You must be somebody. Somebody else thinks you are wonderful and keeps telling you that and giving you things.

I am a dirty little nobody.

You can't be that. You have a man. A great, good man, who takes an interest in you.

Why does he?

It's love.

Is it the same for Mother and Stanley? Was it the same for my father and Mother? He went away.

You are a princess. He calls you that. My Princess Starlight.

And then he needs to frighten me.

How many girls have your chance? Your experience of life? They are nobodies compared to you, Starr.

Nobodies. No body — how I longed to be that. This absurd, stupid, unclean envelope that was so inexplicably desired by such an impossible stranger. The whole thing had never happened. It was a dream.

I would grin at the girl in the mirror, toothily, Huck Finnily, Saturday Evening Postily. The grin congealed into a rictus. Or smile, seductively, mysteriously, across a room at the beautiful young woman, myself, draped in one of Mother's evening gowns I'd borrowed. The smile faded into a sullen frown. I would sit and dress my hair in different ways, or contort my face into a hundred horrible masks, but every time the face resolved itself into the same prettiness, the same beauty admired by Andrew as he stroked my hair, my hand, my thigh, whispering, 'Ah, Starr, but you are so beautiful . . .'

The morning we left on our grand tour, my mother stood on the steps of the house and waved me goodbye with a radiant smile on her face that said, Free at last! In the trunk of the car I had a whole new outfit of summer clothes, swimming costumes, tennis clothes, evening dresses, daytime dresses — got on many trips to the best stores in town by Mother and I, charged to Uncle Andy's accounts. I was by now quite an accomplished whore.

Bowling merrily along, north out of Boston, the wind blowing in through the half open window, my hair streaming back, eyes sparkling — 'Happy, Starr?' he asked. 'That's the girl.' I kept a diary of the trip. Here, I've just got it out from behind some books in the case — for don't forget in all the fun that I'm still here — the car purring on under a blue sky — in this gloomy room.

Here's the diary. And a couple of photographs.

Myself, taken at North Haven. Not that year — must have been 1919, when all three of us had gone up there at Martha's invitation, Andrew being busy playing Mayor. Because in it I can't be much more than thirteen. I am standing in front of a white door with its window panel showing the ocean hazy in reflection. My hair is all windblown, I am tanned, but I look quite plain because my mouth is a little pursed, my eyes screwed up against the sun. I am wearing a loose white blouse with a sailor-boy knotted scarf, my arms are thin and sunburned, there is a silver bangle on my left wrist, my right hand is resting on the door knob, my left hand on the opposite jamb. I have baggy white shorts down to my knees, sunburned legs, white socks, and lace-up baseball boots which rest on a Greek key-patterned mat which identifies it as the backdoor to the Peters' summer home. A New England tomboy.

In the '23 picture it is quite different. I am in smart clothes, a little overdone and citified for the jetty on which I now stand; a tight skirt, a blazer, a silk scarf fixed with a silver and diamond pin — Andrew always liked me to dress a little older when I was away with him. He had had too many rather suspicious looks at this 'niece' of his.

I'll come to the diary in a moment. I want to talk about that fortnight in North Haven. It gave me the first insight into what I was and what I couldn't be any more. It's strange that I could still be so happy; that I can look back on part of that time as a sort of lost Paradise. Though of course, Paradise wasn't lost, was it? It was just fucked up.

The place itself was paradisal. A small island off the coast of Maine, a few holiday cottages, of which Andrew's was by far the largest and grandest, the whitest and most windowed, in a tiny village that looked like all those blue and red and white places along the ocean coast. The harbour had some fishing boats, and moored out, Andrew's yacht. He needed the size of house for Martha and the six sons she had produced for him since they married in 1910. She produced them quick, almost one a year until 1919, when either she or Andrew gave up on it. Of course by then, he had me. So, there were six boys aged between twelve and four, Martha, Andrew, a couple of maids, a cook, a handyman. And a young man, Paul Hamlin, summer tutor to the boys.

It was all very free and easy. Breakfast was an ongoing meal from about eight to nine, taken in the big, bare floor-boarded room facing the sea. When we were all together, Andrew sat, in white ducks, white open-necked shirt with a cravat and navy blue blazer; the boys dressed as boys; Paul in white flannels, white shirt; Martha summery, blooming; myself too, all in white. Lunch was taken on the run, in picnics, sandwiches, on the yacht. We all dined together at night in the house, and dressed slightly more formally; the boys looking like newly civilised savages with their hair neatly combed.

The first couple of mornings I got up late, hearing the sound of children going past the house down to the shore. Each morning Paul took the boys to bathe off the rocks. He was a good-looking young man, tall, with dark brown hair. I would watch them for a time from the house; then try to find something to do. It had not been a very good idea to come to where the major pastimes were swimming and sailing. I love the sea, but I was too self-conscious to swim. Especially when Andrew was around. On the third day the boys implored me to come down with them; when I made some feeble, female excuse they didn't ask again. I spent most of the time with Martha, talking to her for hours on end, in the kitchen of the house, or when we went into the village to the store — and I would talk to her and yet be observing her all the time, forever wondering at her evident normality and happiness, speculating on the amazement and revulsion she would feel if I told her about Andrew. But he was right — she would have thought I was mad. So we talked, endlessly, about nothing in particular. Or I would be in charge of the youngest boy, and spend all morning super-vising his play in among the rocks, examining pools with him; making ever more elaborate sandcastles, conjuring games of handsome princes and princesses and dragons and ogres out of a handful of pebbles and shells.

At the end of the first week, coming alone down the steps of the house, I went for a walk along the low sandy beach with two young married women staying on the island with their children in the other cottages; waiting for their hus-bands to come up from New York. The slightly older one twitted me about the young man who was with our party. Was he my brother? No? Then why didn't I start an affair with him? She said she would if I didn't. The other was quite shocked. How could her friend say such a thing?

'What do you think our dear husbands are doing in the city right now?' said her friend. She it was who asked inquisitively about Andrew.

The big fellow — Mr Peters? Was he my father?

No.

Oh — she thought I might have been his from a previous marriage. And me being so apparently close to them all, and all the much younger boys . . .

'He's my uncle.'

'Oh, that explains it'

The next day I let the two women go past, trailing their toddlers, before I emerged from the house.

It was always like this; I did not want to put myself in a position where I had to answer questions, or seemed too obviously to be avoiding them. So I would appear stuck-up, stand-offish, arrogant, conceited — choose for yourself.

Of course, Andrew had no opportunity, being surrounded by his family, nor, it seemed, from his bouncy, almost off-handed cheerful way with me in front of Martha, much interest in any of his usual activities. It really was as if I were a charming, but poor relation, taken on holiday by a rich family, considerate to me, but of course engrossed in their own affairs, and in the rituals of holiday which had grown up over the years among themselves. The same went for Paul, in a different fashion; he had been engaged only that year and was in the odd position of half-servant and half-guest.

It was impossible that a young man and a young woman, thrown together in glorious summer weather on a small island, in the same house, should not develop some interest in each other. Sitting down at the dinner table on the third night I found myself directly opposite Paul. I tried for a while to be cool and mysterious and treated him rather shabbily — aware always of Andrew at the top of the table — though he ate away enthusiastically, talked loudly and overbearingly to his boys, and seemed to take no notice of me at all. Then, one morning just into the second week, I was sitting in the dining-room, reading at the table, at about eleven in the morning, when Paul walked in through the open door.

'Oh, hi,' he said, surprised at my being in there. 'Not going out today, Miss Wyman?'

He made me feel like Whistler's mother with that 'Miss Wyman', seated in profile with my book, while the sun sparkled on the sea outside.

'Please — Starr,' I said.

'That's a wonderful name.'

'Thank you.'

'What are you reading?'

'Oh — it's only rubbish,' I said, embarrassed that I wasn't reading something more high-toned. 'Sabatini. I found it in the box room.'

'Ah.' He was silent for a moment. Then he said, 'Look I've got to go across to the mainland for the mail and newspapers. Do you want to come? If it's only rubbish, that is?'

He said that the boys had gone out to the yacht early and he'd kind of got the day off. So it wouldn't matter if I came with him. He was very sweet.

We walked round to the harbour and took the small dinghy with an outboard motor. Would I have lunch with him in the port?

The only perfect day I've spent in my life.

What did we do? Simply walked about. Had lunch. Visited a poky, dusty little museum. Sat on the long stone jetty of the port. Talked. Talked endlessly. He was twenty-three. He was going to be a painter. 'A commercial artist?' I said. No — a painter, he said fiercely. I poured out all my knowledge of books and art and said that it must seem really naïve to him. To which he said, with a serious and slightly puzzled face, that he was amazed to find somebody so well read and knowledgeable and serious-minded at such a . . . A what? A young age?

'Well, you're not very old, are you?'

'I'm seventeen,' I said in protest.

It was the first time I'd ever felt that young. I let him kiss me on the steps going down to the dinghy. I found we were holding hands when we walked back up from the harbour; I shook free gently as we came into view of the house.

That night at dinner, I was merry, talking animatedly across the table to Paul, joking with the children. Andrew looked down the table a couple of times. I avoided his eyes. When I did have to look that way, when Martha called something to me, I stared at him boldly. He smiled back.

I slept well that night, for the first time not taking any stuff. I was already half in love with Paul.

When I got up the next morning I looked for him at breakfast; he'd promised to show me the paintings he'd brought to the island. He didn't turn up. I asked the oldest boy where Paul was.

'I've sent Hamlin to the port for the mail,' Andrew answered casually. 'He was too late yesterday. Please don't dally with the boy, Starr. He's here to work.' He buried himself behind yesterday's *Boston Globe* again. Martha smiled, a little warning smile, and put her finger to her lips as if to say that I must say nothing back.

Andrew kept Paul busy all that day. He decided the children needed some schooling. Everything was getting too darn slack, he said. The boys, all but the two youngest — who were given to me to look after — were confined with Paul in the upstairs schoolroom most of the day. The women in the cottages had now got their husbands from the city, and they and their small children occupied the foreshore in front of the house most of the afternoon.

At four, Andrew allowed the children out for a swim, but they had to be under Paul's supervision. After a while I walked down the beach, scrambled over and sat at the edge of the rocks. Paul swam back to me and, looking up, said, 'I seem to have upset the old man. Sorry. Can I see you when we get back to Boston?'

I told him that I would be going back to school after the vacation; but if he'd like I'd give him the address and he could perhaps see me in the fall.

'If that's not too long?' I said.

But our conversation was broken into by Andrew bellowing from the house verandah, 'Hamlin. Hamlin — can you come up here a moment.'

'Oh, heavens,' Paul said. 'Have to go. Can you look after the boys?'

'They'll be all right,' I said.

And that was it.

God knows what Andrew told him. When he came back down to fetch the boys he passed me with only a quick sideways sheepish smile, running back with them up the beach, leaving me — literally — on the rocks.

At dinner his manner was constrained. Mine was puzzled and angry. Andrew was expansive, in a jolly mood. 'Thought we'd all go for a sail tomorrow,' he said. 'Game, Starr? You look a bit peaky. Put you right, eh? You've had hardly any air here. Can't send you back to Boston looking so pale.'

It wasn't until we got out to the yacht in the morning that I discovered Paul was not aboard. 'Left him to hold the fort. Telephone and whatever,' explained Andrew.

It did not take any great ingenuity on Andrew's part to

separate the two of us. Whatever he had said to Paul had had the desired effect. My sudden reversion to moody silence at the table must have only confirmed whatever 'neurotic girl', 'unfortunate incidents in the past', 'medication' story Andrew had given him.

He sent Paul back to New York a couple of days later.

The diary says nothing of all this. Simply, Stayed at North Haven about two weeks and four days. That was when Andrew and I left on our trip — the one to broaden Starr's mind — her 'once in a lifetime opportunity'. The diary gives hardly more than a list of names of towns and sights and hotels and all written in big childish handwriting. But the writing changes, becoming thicker and lazier — that's at night after the luminal I was now taking — for my sleep, you understand.

We put up at hotels mainly, stopping at most three nights in any one place. I was his 'niece'. I think he overplayed this, drawing the fact into each conversation with each desk clerk or manager. They didn't seem to mind what the hell I was. Usually he took adjoining rooms — I prayed for the odd times when we had to be placed a whole floor or more apart.

After dinner each evening in the hotel dining-room we would repair to whatever passed as a lounge and he would invariably meet someone he knew, or who knew someone he knew, and a lively and extraordinarily boring conversation would start up. This promised to go on for a long time — Andrew had the politician's gift for spinning things out. The convention was that I would sit in an armchair, straight-backed, look interested and intelligent and even throw in the odd remark or so of my own if asked. 'What do you say to that, Starr . . .?' or 'Well, I know my niece wouldn't see eye to eye with you on that . . .', but after a while I should yawn, and then again a few moments later, and Uncle Andrew would laugh and say, 'The little lady's tired I think.' At which, I would have to protest that I was not — but then excuse myself, saying, 'I think I will go to bed now, Uncle Andrew, if that's all right with you . . .'

And off I would go, knowing that the eyes of his new friends would like as not follow me, and that Andrew would watch them, and find pleasure in telling me later of the lust in their eyes and how they would try to hide it in front of the fond, but perhaps over-permissive uncle. If I'd been lucky and had a normal politician for a guardian he would have stayed up half the night drinking, or got into a poker school, or been lured away to the local whorehouse — but no, Andrew was an honourable man. Everyone agreed on that, incorruptible among the bag-men and gangsters who ran the states and cities; clean-tongued in the middle of the smokiest, oath-filled rooms full of tough politicians with no damn fools of women present; sober in the era of Prohibition. A man without vices. Some nights he would indeed stay up late, talking in the smoking-room, being introduced to the local dignitaries and fixers. When he got stuck on these occasions I could go to sleep sure in the knowledge that it was too late for him to visit my room. He was cautious over moving about the hotels after too late an hour. But if he got away in good time . . .

First would come the soft knock; hardly more than a brushing of his knuckles on the door. Then the knob would slowly turn, the thin line of dim light from the corridor widen to a narrow band, obscured by the dark bulk of his body. The whisper, 'Starr, are you asleep . . .?' At which I must stir, pretend to wake, sleepily, childishly murmuring, 'Who is it . . .?'

After half an hour — never very much more, sometimes less — he would slip away again. The door would open, his reclothed body slide through the dim light once more without a word, the door close with a quiet click.

HELEN

God — forgive my anger — when I look back I see that I have devoted my life to children who were ungrateful and men who were unworthy of me. Stanley, I see now, was exactly like all the others: feckless, scheming, obsessed with that *thing*, idle, naïve, untrustworthy — yet I believed in him. I wished to believe in him. America is its men after all, or it is nothing. Our barons of industry, our statesmen, our bishops, our heroes, our heroic dead — they are all men, aren't they? What are we supposed to do about them? They must have their way or the whole thing crumbles and falls.

So I believed in my Stanley. Life had been as unfair to him as it had to me. True, he cut a small, unheroic figure, but I was attracted to him, perhaps in default of any alternative; that is how most choices in life are made. He had said persistently that when he was free, when we were both free, then happiness would indeed be ours. Life, Liberty and the Pursuit of Happiness.

His wife passed.

Two days later, three days before her funeral, he appeared on my doorstep. 'I couldn't stay away,' he said. 'Don't say anything about right or wrong' — by now we had moved to the living room — 'I could not bear it. It was duty. My duty's done. What we say or do is our business now.'

On that day we first became lovers. On the sofa in the living-room. Tucker was at a friend's house; Starr I think must have been away too, or upstairs reading — she never stopped reading. Certainly she could have heard nothing. It was all over very quickly. I was hardly aware of what he had done, in any strictly physical sense — women feel much less than men imagine, but of course the disturbance in clothing, the panting and tugging, and the desire I had to accommodate him, to make him happy in the way that men like best and quickest, well that was the thing, wasn't it? And all at once we were again sitting up, he on the edge of the arm-chair, myself on the sofa, straightening down my skirts. He coughing. Adjusting his spectacles.

And that was the first time I had allowed myself to do *that* for — well, it must have been twelve, thirteen years. A little more than Tucker's age then, in fact. At least with a whole heart. I am not counting those few extra, hot summer nights with Wyman, even when we were out of sorts. It matters a great deal less to a woman, the actual act, but I had not realised quite how I had missed the warmth, the sense of belonging, which more than made up for the awkwardness, the general messiness.

When she came back from her holiday with Andrew I told Starr that I had put the divorce proceedings in hand and intended to marry Mr Faithfull as soon as decently possible. What did I expect? That she would throw her arms round my neck and say, 'Momma, I'm so glad for you. You deserve every bit of happiness' — the way they do in plays and movies? Or to curse me for deserting and driving away

132

her father? No. She simply sat on the sofa looking up at me and said quietly and bitterly, 'You too?' Then got up and walked out of the room.

That was when it started. She would not eat. Or go out of the house. She would go days without bathing, and then scrub herself endlessly in the tub and change her clothes three or four times in the day. This was her age, I told myself. And the New Age in which we lived. But these things persisted and grew worse when she went back to Rogers Hall. As I have said, I'd had complaints before about her, then one day I received a letter from the school principal, Miss Parsons. Would I go and see them? It really was quite important.

Miss Parsons was not immediately available — I was conducted through the school to an office where Miss Thompson, the assistant principal, awaited me. This made the matter seem less serious than I'd at first thought and I was a little annoyed at having to come all this way north. I sat down in the chair across the desk from Miss Thompson, and said, indeed, that I could not see why the problem, whatever it was, could not have been dealt with by letter as before. Perhaps I might have a cup of tea. I'd had a long and tiring train journey.

Of course.

When she had gone out and ordered tea, she came back and sat down again. She did not smile.

'Where is Starr?' I asked.

'In class.'

'She is not ill then?'

No, Starr was not ill. They had thought it best that she

did not attend this interview, or even know that I had been there.

The tea came in.

Miss Thompson started. What was my general impression of Starr? Was she happy with the school? With her work?

'Are you? That is the point surely.' I said.

'With her work — in general, yes. We are more interested at the moment in her emotional state of mind.'

Starr had always been a highly strung child, I explained. She was artistic, and that made her rather nervous at times. 'A little more than some girls of her age, perhaps,' I said. 'Her nature tends to lead her to make difficulties about things less sensitive persons would ride over, if that's what you mean.'

She did not wish to pry, but . . . Her questions were at first sly and only slightly probing. So, although Miss Thompson knew the sort of background Starr came from — 'It is quite obvious by her sponsors, Mayor Peters and Mrs Pargeter, that the child has money and a family of some substance behind her. But it is knowledge of the actual home background that we find helpful whenever there is difficulty. You live alone I believe. The War . . .?'

'My husband is alive and, as far as I know, well. In New York.' The schoolteacher knew what my circumstances were. I took delight in coldly confirming what she would not say. It is foolish to gain such small victories over those who may have some power over you. In the past I was not as careful as I am now.

'Oh — I thought,' said Miss Thompson, 'that because Starr seemed to have no father, that he had been lost to us in the great conflict.'

'This difficulty?' I said. 'You mentioned a difficulty — what precisely is that?'

It was plain from her increase in icy politeness that Miss Thompson knew she had not made a friend in me. She pulled out a piece of paper that had been peeping from under her blotter and held it out over the table.

'I would like you to read this and give me your opinion on it,' she said.

A small, blue sheet of writing paper. In the top right corner was printed the name of a hotel in Provincetown. Under that, in thick, crudely drawn black heavily curved strokes was a drawing of a crescent moon with a four-spiked star between its horns. Under the drawing a few lines were scrawled in, again, a thick heavy hand:

> The boat bobs useless and dirtied
> by the river's flow. The sea of this harbour
> is flat and dead, like all the black ponds,
> the night filled, starless holes

Below this the bottom of the page had been neatly torn off.

'You recognise the handwriting?'

'What is it supposed to mean?' I said.

'I have no idea. The style is modern — a form of *vers libre*, as they call it — that has become fashionable among the young. Presumably because it is easier than the traditional styles. The easy always appeals to the young.'

'I presume you haven't brought me here to discuss literature.'

'The writing? It is your daughter, Starr's? She has admitted it. Quite freely.'

'I don't understand why you are showing me this,' I said.

'Most girls write verse. I did so myself. Is this what you've called me in for?'

Miss Thompson's mouth at last allowed itself the tight little smile it had been withholding.

'Yes, indeed Mrs Wyman, they do — we all do — and mostly it is very bad. Not many of them write this, however — forgive me.'

She opened the desk drawer and took out a thin strip of paper. It was the torn-off piece from the one I had.

All that was written on it was this — and I shouldn't write it — but must:

FUCK YOU ANDY

I looked up from the paper. Miss Thompson was watching me in an interested, intense fashion almost as if excited by my reactions. And I was shocked. Much more than now when people say these dirty words all over and even put them into books, I hear. But then, to see them written out in the same handwriting that I had just been assured was Starr's . . . All I could do was to put the strip of paper down in front of me, and then turn it over to hide the message from both of us.

'You see now why I sent for you, Mrs Wyman,' she said.

At last I said, 'Where did you find this?

'In one of your daughter's notebooks. Every now and then, if we feel a girl is in some sort of difficulty we take the liberty of searching a girl's locker. I would remind you, Mrs Wyman, this is none of our doing,' she said sharply. 'Wherever your daughter has picked up such obscenities it is certainly not at Rogers Hall.'

'I hope you don't suggest that it is at her home that she has learned such expressions,' I snapped back.

'One would hope — and believe — not. It remains that such — well, I can really not find another word for it — such filth has reached your daughter from somewhere. This is not the first time, Mrs Wyman.'

I looked out of the window. Low white clouds proceeded at a stately silent pace across the blue sky at the end of the Rogers' grounds. Somewhere — always it is somewhere in a school — I could hear a piano being played distantly, jovially out of tune.

What had the girl gotten into? Not Andrew, dear God? What had Starr been up to with some awful boy? But not Andrew? The world was mad. Starr was mad.

That after all was the only sane, safe conclusion I could come to. That Starr must be suffering from some mental confusion. Some emotional upset so great as to cause her to accuse . . . But who had said anything about accusations? I immediately rejected any such thought. It was necessary to reject such thoughts.

Miss Thompson was twittering on about the moral tone of the school, unfortunate influences, how serious consideration must be given to the future. That I should seek some form of professional advice.

'What do you mean?'

'Well, this is not strictly speaking a medical matter, but the principal has suggested a doctor who has advised several of our families on emotional troubles. He is most discreet.'

'Does your school suffer so much from this sort of thing that you have to retain a medical man to deal with it?'

'Mrs Wyman . . .' She hesitated for a moment, gathering herself. 'Mrs Wyman — we get very little trouble with our girls here. Girls from this school range from families high in the Social Register, to deserving and intelligent girls from

137

more modest homes. One or two, as I say, do have problems from time to time — what I was trying to suggest is that more often the problems come from the family end rather than the girl herself.'

I opened my mouth to protest, but the dreadful woman went on.

'In all my time as a teacher of the young, here and elsewhere, Mrs Wyman, I must confess that I have never come across any such case as your daughter. No . . . let me finish. Starr is an intelligent girl, but on occasion can seem almost stupid. She is talented in several ways. She is a good artist — she will draw quite beautifully sometimes. Miss Webster, the art mistress, saw one drawing of hers, of a landscape I believe, a view of a harbour from a window, and told Starr that she wished very much to enter it for the show we have here every summer. Starr agreed. A few days later, when asked for the drawing, she said, 'Oh, you don't want that old thing. I tore it up.' Miss Webster was puzzled. Not so much upset as annoyed, as the sketch was such a fine one, she said, that the school could have taken pride in such a piece in its show. A minor thing, but indicative. The books Starr chooses to read. We do have forward and even free-thinking girls — these are tendencies impossible to separate from intelligent girls. But there are other indications . . . you wish me to go on?'

I made a sign, a turning down of the mouth, a slight lift of my left hand from my crossed knees, a tug at my skirt, all of which in female dress language means, Go on by all means, I don't believe a word of what you are saying but cannot think of a response and suspect some of what you say might be true . . .

'We allow our girls a degree of latitude. Young men may

take the seniors out at the weekends, as long as they are in foursomes, or more, and see that they are booked back in to the school, and indeed, safely settled in their rooms by ten o'clock in the evening in summer, and by eight in late fall and winter and spring. It is little realised — I must admit I am somewhat more radical in these matters than some of my colleagues — how much the conduct of women — young women in particular — is watched, how little they inhabit the world at large, what extraordinary constraints are put upon them. Men from an early age experience life in all its forms, travel, enter the world of work, live an almost wholly free life such as we can hardly imagine — but women, girls — and this is what we teach here, must learn that such freedoms are simply not available to them. They are to be, in Louisa M. Alcott's words, Little Women and Good Wives. We all know that since the War there have been extraordinary leaps and bounds in society and in what is considered permissible behaviour. We are not holding on to an untenable position in this school, Mrs Wyman, but we are holding a line. If that is difficult, so be it. It's just as well that the girls find our standards difficult at times — heaven knows, the world outside will be far, far harder on them if they do not heed our advice . . .'

'Miss Thompson,' I interrupted. 'I take this all into my thoughts. You have shown me an, an unfortunate . . . lapse . . . of my daughter's normal — you must agree? — good taste.'

Miss Thompson did not agree. There was not the slightest sign of conciliation in the muscles of her face, no relaxation into a smile of her pursed mouth.

I said, 'My daughter is, to me, a quite normal girl. It

seems to me that you — we — whoever — are blowing up a girlish prank into something, well, something absurd.'

'I see your point. I have to tell you that it is not quite like that.' Again her face was like stone. It seemed that the more I tried to reason with her, the firmer she became. She sat silently for a moment. Her face was pink and small — parents had been known to take her for one of the girls and ask the way to some responsible member of staff — but when she sat before me and the light came from the long high window and fell across her face, she looked to me not so much like one of the sixteen- or eighteen-year-old girls in this place, but like a child who had some wasting disease — small, pink, her skin beginning to pucker and wrinkle, not because of maturity, but through some version of childhood renewed with decreasing vigour each year.

And so I should have said, 'What on earth do you know about it? About any of it?' But of course I didn't, because I too was too well brought up ever to do such a thing, almost too well brought up even to think of it. So, once again, I said nothing at all. I heard a little more, a little less perhaps than I expected to hear.

'It is not simply a matter', said Miss Thompson, 'of this incident. There are others. As I say, our girls have some latitude. They are growing up. Starr when she came here aroused our concern precisely for the opposite reasons — she seemed to be a little behind in social matters and a little too advanced intellectually. The positions seem to have reversed themselves.'

She stopped. She held up a red leather-bound book. 'This is our disciplinary register,' she said. She put it down carefully on the table beside her. 'I won't read its entries to you. They are mostly minor infractions of our rules by any number of girls — failure to complete given scholastic tasks, lateness, rowdiness, excessive time in the bathrooms, infringement of lights-out times. Starr's are rather different, and more serious.'

Silent, my face demanded more.

'So the only person she has ever been out with from the school is, I believe, her uncle, Mr Peters. A most distinguished man . . .'

'He is a relative by marriage. He has only just ceased to be Mayor of Boston, as you know. As you say, a most distinguished man.'

'Starr has known him then since she was a child?'

'Yes. He has been very good to her.'

'This is the point, Mrs Wyman. I do not know how to approach it more gradually, more diplomatically — it is on the one or two occasions Starr has been out with Mr Peters recently that she has come back in a rather odd condition. She has appeared sometimes to have been drinking, though we find that to be quite unbelievable, and she has denied the fact vehemently. But she has plainly been intoxicated. It is difficult to connect the girl we see most times with the girl she becomes after these outings. Mr Peters is, on these occasions *in loco parentis* . . .'

'Mr Peters is no fool,' I interjected angrily.

'I never suggested he was a fool . . .' she said. 'But these latest incidents have grown worse. Starr tells me she spent almost the whole of the summer vacation with Mr Peters. Isn't that a little strange?'

I stood up and gathered my hat and gloves. 'I really cannot see any purpose in carrying on with this interview.'

Miss Thompson looked stonily up at me, but she said only, 'If that is your wish. You'll no doubt be in touch with us with your decision on Starr's future as soon as possible?'

'I will indeed,' I said.

Starr did not go back to Rogers Hall after the Christmas break. I didn't tell her of my visit or conversation. We could no longer afford the fees. 'What about Uncle Andrew?' said Tucker, who had been hoping to follow her sister to finishing school. 'We've received quite enough charity from Uncle Andrew,' I said.

But when Andrew visited us after Christmas and took us all to a show with Martha and their children, I could see nothing between him and Starr that was in any way different. Perhaps there was a certain coolness and snappiness in Starr's responses to him — but they were no more than you expect in the relations between people so close for so many years. Why, we were practically one family. The worst I supposed was that Andrew had made perhaps some clumsy, foolish middle-aged overture to her — or she imagined he had.

We owed him so much.

I was divorced from Mr Wyman in May of '24; a little later I announced my intention of marrying Stanley.

'I'm glad,' said my brother. 'A woman needs a man to provide for her, and you have been a long time on your own. He's back in business, I presume.'

'He has independent means,' I said. Stanley had told me of the insurance money from his wife's estate.

'I'm glad to hear it,' said my brother, smiling. 'He'll need them with three women to support.'

My women friends were less cynical. Martha said how good it would be for me. 'I'm so very glad. We're all dying to meet your mysterious Mister Faithfull.'

I think she was a little disappointed when she did meet him at our marriage ceremony. God knows what she expected — Warner Baxter, maybe? There are qualities greater than a handsome face. There are other disappointments too.

The wedding breakfast was held at an inn outside the city. Stanley had said that he would pay for the occasion, but my brother, again a touch too sardonically, told him to put away his wallet. That of course he, as head of the family until now, would settle it. Stanley said that was most white of him, old man, then pulled him over to one side to discuss some business idea or other he had, which, as I heard him say, 'Will more than recompense you for your kindness here.'

My brother, talking to me later, told me that he had declined to invest. 'Some cockamamie idea about making cosmetics from sour milk, sorry sister dear.'

So, after that, we went straight back to the new house I had taken in Grove Street, the two girls being packed off to one of the Aunts for a couple of days.

I was surprised to find Stanley an ardent, if rather precipitous lover. But, clean, pleasant, considerate of me in a rather pernickety way. No man can keep his dignity in a bedroom. Unlike a woman, who looks natural and feels at ease in nakedness, a man always appears slightly ridiculous and self-conscious.

'Stanley,' I said, 'May I ask you a favour?

'By all means, my dear.'

'Would you mind awfully, before you undress so completely, removing your spectacles? It does look so odd, somehow.'

'If it makes you happy, my sweet.'

Well, it did. He did. For a while. It was the return of the girls that produced some sense of strain. I had expected this and tried to prepare myself for it. With some trepidation I assembled them in the living room, persuading Stanley to go into the small rear garden and smoke a pipe while I talked to them. It would solve all sorts of problems, I said, if they would consent to take my husband's surname. I didn't want to force them to drop their natural father's name, I could understand why they might wish to keep it, but for simple legal reasons, and our bonds as a family, I would ask them to take the name Faithfull, perhaps keeping Wyman as their second name.

'OK,' Tucker shrugged, and asked if she could she go out, as her friend Emily had a new bicycle and had promised to let her ride on it.

'Starr?'

'Why not? It will be a change.'

A moment or two after Starr left the room, Stanley ambled in, his head cocked to one side, smiling a little nervously. 'Is everything all right?' he asked. I got the impression he had been listening outside the door.

'Perfectly,' I said.

'Do they like me?'

'I'm sure they will grow to love you. As they should,' I said.

'It's simply that I have reached the grand old age of forty-five without ever having had the blessing of children.'

'They can't always be described as that, I'm afraid, my dear.'

He smiled again, then turned and tiptoed to the door. He opened it quietly and looked out into the hallway. He closed the door softly to again. 'I didn't want anyone to overhear us. They aren't perhaps used to me being about the place and I do want to be as discreet as possible.'

'Starr's in her room. You needn't worry.'

'She spends a lot of time in her room.' He smiled at me in that pleasant way as if he knew that something in his remark might somehow jar on me, as if it was too intrusive for a newcomer to the house to say such a thing, but at the same time trying the limits of how far he could go in talking about the children. I made no comment and he went on, his voice light and cheerful. 'She surprises me,' he said, 'knowing how frenetic and pleasure-seeking the young are now, how very serious she is. Always reading. Quiet. It's good to see someone make so much good use of their own company.'

'She's always been a thoughtful girl, wrapped up in herself. Perhaps a little too much.'

'Has she a young man?'

'Young men bore her. That's what she says.'

'Ah, the cynicism of youth. No doubt time will take care of it. Now' — he put the pipe he had been fiddling with into his mouth and sucked on it speculatively — 'how about a ride out?'

If I had thought marriage would enhance my position in Boston I was right. In a way. A married couple receive more and more varied attentions than a lone woman. We began to be invited to dinner parties. But some invitations that I had expected were not forthcoming. My brother dropped a hint one day when I said I was surprised that one of our favourite uncles, one of my father's brothers, still had not invited us to dine at his house, when I had been a frequent visitor there before my wedding.

'Your Stanley is not perhaps the shining light you imagine in Boston society,' said my brother. 'There are people who hold some things against him. Let's say his dealings have not always been entirely on the square.'

No, no, he protested when I pressed him — he was not saying that Stanley was dishonest. One must be careful about using such words about anyone, let alone a member of the family. And then he said something that shocked me, and of which I had not had the slightest suspicion — that Stanley had last year been indicted for petty fraud — that his business was non-existent — and that he had only been saved from bankruptcy by his wife's fortuitous — my brother's unfortunate word — death and the insurance money that had been paid . . .

'He may rise again. There's talk of him starting a new company, he's looking for backers. I think he'll have to look farther afield than Boston. He's a little too well known here.'

Of course all this disturbed me. I had little enough money of my own. The relatives and friends who had helped me and the children out generously over the past ten years had assumed — and breathed no doubt a huge, collective sigh of relief — that by my remarriage I was finally off their hands. I did not bring the matter up with Stanley. He was unlikely to tell me before he was ready. Women have no head for business. I waited for him to tell me himself what his next venture was to be. I did begin to wonder quite what we were to live on for the rest of our lives.

Ours was an unconventional life from the first, though you grow habituated to any life and it is only outsiders looking in who remark upon its queerness. After Starr's death one of the reporters called us 'a very strange family indeed'.

But certainly for the first months we lacked for nothing, the girls were fed and clothed. On the last Wednesday of every month Stanley would give me a cheque for the rent. I presumed this was coming from the last of his insurance money and perhaps some investments. I had taken out a second mortgage on the Cape cottage to pay for new furniture and my share of the usual household expenses. Stanley was not idle; but where my first husband had hardly rested in the house, always at work, or looking for work, Stanley seemed able to conduct all his business from home. He wrote a great number of letters in connection with some lawsuit that had been dragging on for years. Patents for inventions he had made and which had been stolen from him by a partner. He received few replies. He made a great number of phone calls. No-one rang us. He went to New York for a few days to meet some people who, he said, were eager to invest in another company to manufacture cosmetics.

'From sour milk?' I said, rather sarcastically — we had just argued over some matter of an overdue account he had promised to pay.

He looked at me over his glasses. 'Lactic acid, actually. Who brought up the matter of sour milk?'

The investors took their time.

The children and Stanley? Tucker, now fourteen, regarded him as a new and not altogether interesting adjunct to the house, like a chair or a magazine. Starr's reactions were more complex. She was sometimes hectically gay, sometimes withdrawn and snappish. She had become beautiful, a little over medium height, slim, though she insisted she was overweight and dieted fiercely; you would have thought her an actress or some such. But with Stanley? She would, say, be arranging some flowers in the big cut-glass bowl on the parlour sideboard and turn her head suddenly as if to catch Stanley looking at her. And Stanley would be sitting in his chair, his damp pipe dead in his mouth, reading a book or the newspaper with no thought of watching Starr. Not in that way.

In those first few months she could be vicious. Coming up to me in the kitchen while I washed the dishes and muttering something like, 'Stanley is so dumb, how do you stand him?' or 'Why doesn't he buy himself a wig or something, combing his hair this way and that to hide how bald he is. It's pathetic.' Or the cry that came from both of my daughters, 'When's something going to happen? Why don't we ever do anything?'

Perhaps Stanley heard them, perhaps he didn't, but he came into the house after one of his jaunts to New York, and said, 'Well now, who fancies living in New Jersey?'

And Tucker rolled her eyes and said, 'No-one fancies living in New Jersey. Is it a joke?'

STARR

WHAT DID OUR new neighbours make of our pleasant little nest of gentlefolk? They must have seen the van pull up with our goods, and Mr Faithfull there to superintend, his family following by train from New York, and cab from the station at Orange, arriving in time to see one of the moving men walking up the front path with an armchair held over his head like a giant helmet, his mate following with the large dressing-table mirror, showing dislocated trees and chimneys, flashes of sunlit sky and a sudden glimpse of Stanley as if he was leaping into the air.

And they must have taken reasonably kindly to the first sight of non-leaping Stanley. For all the husbands more or less approximated to his type, small, rabbity men who looked like dentists. Their wives could not have taken exception to the furniture, just on this side of shabbiness. The right lack of ostentation, to meld in with the general slightly run-down tenor of the neighbourhood.

Once they'd allowed us to settle, the nearest of the males, instructed no doubt by the females, tied their neckties, put on their second-best suits, tightened their neckties, walked across to our little white wicket gate, unlatched it, came up the front path, and knocked on our front door . . .

As it was opened, they raised their hats, soft felt Homburgs all, dark brown and grey with sand-coloured or off-white bands, all dented with the same pinch of fingers at the front, announced their names, that they were neighbours and had just come to call — and were admitted.

Most often by Stanley, also dressed in a suit, but *sans* Homburg (in the house), pipe in right hand, book in the other, who would lead them off the hall into the parlour. To meet the gracious lady of the house; tall, thin, well-spoken Mrs Faithfull, and one, or, if terribly lucky, two of their lovely daughters.

Twenty minutes later, Mr Hoffman, or Mr Bradley, or Doctor Carey, or whatever names they had, would emerge from the front door, twisting round as they went down the two steps, giving a cheery goodbye, a Hope-You-All-Settle-In-Okay, and an avowal to bring their wives just as soon as possible to meet Mrs Faithfull, all this in the time they took to get to the gate, open it, go through, shut it again, waving a for-the-time-being farewell to the head of the household in the doorway, one hand on the door, the other raised in pipe-holding See-You-Again-Soon-We-Hope adieu.

And Mr Hoffley and Mr Bradman and Doctor Toothache, or whatever their names were, would hurry homeward under the low, heavy branches and broad shading leaves of the chestnut trees that lined that street, and turn into their own short front paths, and disappear through their own front doors. Inside not too dissimilar parlours — though probably not many of theirs I reckon had such prized relics of Presidential ancestors as the miniature of Pierce, or the glass paperweight that had come from the White House — they would describe to their families the new family at Number 528: The Faithfulls.

Nice enough, seem to be. The furniture good, though a little old. Don't know his business, bit cagey about that, but seems to have money. What is he? In business, he said. What line? Chemistry. Bit mysterious. Didn't seem to want to let on. Air of mystery wants to cultivate. And in reply to the questions to which their womenfolk really want answers . . .? Second marriage. Both. Two daughters. Hers. One about fifteen, bit forward, pretty enough, bit too sharp-tongued. Little fast perhaps, but what can you expect these days. Knife-box, eh? Yes — that sort. The other a few years older. Real beauty — Bea Harding will have to look out for her laurels with the boys round here now! What? What's she like? Medium height. Quieter, more demure than the younger. Oh yes, pretty, very. More than that. Well brought-up. Educated. Lots of books. Phonograph. Rather arty, perhaps. Not the husband — he seems a regular guy. Just the girls. And that's only to be expected.

They'll grow out of it, say the wives nodding their heads sagely. When they discover life . . .

And inside the Faithfull house?

The new house we moved to in West Orange was not so many miles from where I'd spent most of my childhood. We live in this open endless country and yet only twist and turn round and round in the same narrow dark passages, the same rooms, corridors, mirrors. Well, I guess that's how most people live their lives and it's somehow not good enough. Mother still wrote to her friends in Boston, but the replies she got back were shorter and almost off-hand. Things were not the same. To her Boston was a sort of dream. The truth was, and this she realised and it helped to sour her, the truth was that they had moved on in their lives and she had somehow stood still, and she realised also that she was not in the family's or old friends' thoughts as they were in hers. So when Aunt Editha died we heard of it weeks later as it had not occurred to any of them to ask Mother to the funeral. And perhaps it dawned on her after only a little while in West Orange that she had married a weak and ineffective man, that she had two grown daughters, one of whom, myself, was a trial and worry to her. She was forty odd years old, and that was that. What she'd got was all she'd get. That's why people like my mother change so drastically at that age. You suddenly cannot imagine them ever being young. What's worse, they can't imagine it themselves. They know, their bodies, their bones, every little nerve and vein knows that that's it, sister; you're on your own. They've wasted what chances they had. Bye. Bye.

It won't happen to me. I'll make sure of that.

So here I was, getting up to nearly twenty years old, spending my days watching my mother and stepfather row endlessly about money, my sister, adolescent, tough, sweet as a peach, waiting the long years for Mr America to take her to the altar, turning her hair into a brass mop with Golden Glint, saying, 'Do you know Jean Harlow's got five automobiles!' Whining, 'Momma, when can I go dancing on my own?' Without Momma. Without Starr.

And what does Starr do? She sits and watches them, and plays cards with them and goes for drives in the Palisades with them, and gets bored along with them and joins in their pathetic arguments about hair and dresses and hemlines and Stanley — whether he was in the room or not — and which movie show to go to. And waits, with fear and guilt and impatience for Andrew to ring.

Since I'd left Rogers Hall and this thing with Mother and Stanley had started, Andrew's opportunities had of course been limited. Oh good, you say. At last she is out of the clutches of that vile man. Well, yes. But it still went on, you see. I hadn't been released from him. I'd simply moved away a little.

Oh yes, Tucker and I were normal, fun-loving, red-blooded girls with our inalienable rights to be mauled round by boys and to be protected from vicious old mayors of big cities. We went to the dancing class in Orange; a big bare room above a café, with no carpets on the floorboards, cane chairs along the walls, red drapes to shut out the evening and the afternoon; I looked behind one once to see out into the night, and there was no window at all, just the blank, not very clean flock-papered wall. At the door was a small cloakroom and a little bar that served soft drinks only of course, Lemonade and Cola, and cakes and sandwiches that Mrs Bramah the owner of the place sent up from the café. At the top end was a small bandstand raised three or four inches only from the floor and here Ike Mooney and his Goodtimers played six afternoons and six nights a week; Jewish and Irish boys; a saxophone, a clarinet, a pianist — Ike Mooney himself — a violin — his brother — a boy wrapped in a tuba, a drummer with a big fancy kit with sunsets and palm trees painted on the drum faces. Hot dog! Well, it was New Jersey, not New York.

To this place Tucker was allowed to go — and I to accompany her. Sensible big sister Starr, much too mature and severe to let herself or her little sister get into any trouble with boys. And in this place we shuffled around with the cream of Orange, New Jersey youth. They were nice. I wasn't interested in any of them. Tucker fell for a different one each week, and each week was duly scornfully dismissive of last week's predecessor. The boys smelt of soap and hair-oil and youthful sweat. Their hands were dry if you were lucky. Once or twice the bolder ones, the ones who went out to the fire-escape and came back with whisky on their breath, would press against me and the unmistakable feeling against my leg would tell me they were getting hot. And that's when I would go cold on them. I got quite a reputation for being prudish, while little Tucker blushed and clung closer to them. Until she saw my stern eye on her, and my pointing at my watch, and she would come flouncing away from her latest conquest, saying, 'Oh, Starr, why do we have to go now? I wanna have some fun,' in that New Jersey whine that crept into her voice in this temple of romance and constrained phalluses.

Stanley would pick us up at ten o'clock latest in the second-hand Ford he had just bought and which we were ashamed to be seen in. All the way home Tucker would hum the tunes she had danced to and moan about me being stand-offish, and how I would never meet anyone being like that and would die an old maid with spiders in my hair. All this delivered in a whisper behind Stanley's thin back. And every time he would shout, over the chugging of the engine, 'Had a good time, girls? That's good.'

When we got home, if he and Mother had not been arguing and they had both had a little of the pre-war gin he kept in the loft, he would let Tucker put the victrola on and we would dance together, myself and Momma, Tucker and Stanley; old time stuff, Tales From the Vienna Woods,

Guy Lombardo. Then change partners and Stanley would waltz with me, holding me at arm's length as if I were a vase he was afraid to drop but didn't like to hold too tight.

So there was that.

And the movie house.

The rides out in the awful old motor.

Tea at the neighbours.

The neighbours for tea.

We had been there almost a year. One morning just after Christmas, for the first time in a week, the phone rang. My mother, standing nearest, snatched it up.

'Why Andrew! Why are you calling?' she said absurdly. But then she gabbled away at him, questioning — she was as dry as the rest of us for any sort of news from outside — about friends and Boston. What had he been doing? And her brother? And Colonel Drysdale? And Mrs Peabody? And the Saltonstalls? The three of us watched her, or at least Tucker and I did, Stanley sat in his armchair and read stolidly on, cocking an eye only now and again at all the excitement.

'Well I don't know,' she said. Then, 'Well, I don't know if she can.' Mother's voice had become somehow uncertain all at once. She put her hand over the mouthpiece. 'He wants to know if Starr can go to a show with him in New York.' Her face was confused. She looked across at me, then at Stanley. 'He was to have gone with Martha but she can't make it. He has only the one ticket and it's a most popular show. He says he knows it's your birthday in only a few days.'

'Oh, Starr. Always Starr,' said Tucker. She threw down her magazine and marched stiffly out of the room banging the door behind her.

'One moment, Andrew' Mother said into the phone.

'Well — do you want to?' she said to me. She sounded worried.

'Oh, I don't know . . .' I said.

So here I am, later that afternoon, on the train to New York. Outside the window the rows and rows of factories and yards and the miserable houses round them of New Jersey that I'm leaving behind. With the help of my mother I have been carefully dressed in a blue silk dress that comes to just below my knees, white silk stockings and brand new knickers and brassière, a pair of sensible walking shoes on my feet, my silver pumps in the purse Mother has lent me. And ten dollars. Though, as she said, I shouldn't need any money . . . 'I know how fond you are of Andrew, dear,' said Mother, brushing and setting my hair in the mirror upstairs. 'And he is our oldest friend. But remember, you're a young woman now. It's not like when you were a child. Things change. I'm sure he is a gentleman, of course. And he has been so kind to you in particular. But remember — it is only kindness.' Her eyes met mine in the mirror.

And her words called from the porch, as she clasped her arms round her body, shivering in the cold, and I got into the car to be driven to the station, 'Give Andrew our love.'

God, I hope not, I thought. But did I? I was sick with some feeling on the train. I was pleased with my appearance, and then felt that I was all prepared like a trussed chicken. A present.

There was snow on the ground and blearing the view as we got towards the city, through all the businesses and factories that were to go in three years in the Crash, that big Fall, that great Humpty-Dumpty that Stanley and Mother and all the adults blamed for their loss of dividends and interest payments and for increasing the already alarming number of radicals. Oh how Mother hated anyone who questioned the system that she accused of beggaring her. But then, in that year, the whole thing was alive still, the train going in among the tall factory walls through whose windows you could see doll-like people bending over machines, men talking into telephones in offices. Then plunging under the river for that shocking rattling clanging run through the tunnel, when the world disappears, inside is suddenly outside, the seats and heads and faces and yawns and cigarette smoke and a man brushing his too long blue-black thick hair, all reflected in the windows by the dim yellow bulbs which jerk up into whiteness only halfway through the tunnel, making all the faces go white and sick-looking. The Hudson Terminal. I was unlucky. I just met the last wave of commuters going back home after a day in the city. The men and women who go out tired in the morning and look haggard and intense and unsmiling, raincoats and overcoats flying behind them as they hurry down the steps and across the hall to the barriers, feeling in purses and pockets for their tickets; all of them fleeing, diving into the bowels of the earth, turning their backs on all that tremendous, wondrous glitter and trash, beauty and wildness that the city had to offer them. Turning all that down to hurry back to their Stanleys and Helens, their Tuckers and, God help them, their Starrs. Reading their papers about murders and airships, and heir-esses and movie stars, car crashes and burnings, lynchings and tomorrow's horses, cures for piles and advice for lonelyhearts (Give him another chance! No man is all bad. Can you be sure the fault is *all* on his side?). Turning the pages while they ride swaying and safe under the mud of the Hudson that flows away into the lovely ocean which this time of the evening will be silently and contemptuously absorbing the snow flurrying off the land. Or already, as soon almost as they are in their seats, squashed shoulder-to-shoulder with a stranger, dropping off into that half-sleep, their heads nodding forward, mouths opening, a tiny pocket of saliva beginning to well at the corner of the lips as the train rattles out into the open and they wake with a sudden premonitory jerk that somehow they've learned over hundreds of journeys because here is their station sidling up.

Then home by bus, or auto parked at the suburban station, to an evening of radio, bridge, finishing the paper, dinner, a go at a book, the head nodding to one side, the book falling from the fingers onto the carpet, the dog getting up, startled, turning round, settling himself at the fire again. Then lock-up, lights-out, bed. Sleep. No dreams, unless a little anxiety — boss appearing as unexpected and uncatered-for guest at important family function — panic. Situation not resolved. They wake tired and do the reverse journey in to the city. Is this what people make themselves for? They are pathetic. And I envy them.

I had to fight my way up through this crowd. I felt a fraud, swimming in what was for them the wrong direction, as if I had somehow deserted them and as if by my upright, proud, unhurried walk I reproached them for their scurrying flight away. I'd agreed, via Mother and her never-ending telephone conversation, to meet Andrew on Church Street above the Terminal, for fear of him losing me in the crowd. I hadn't seen or spoken to him for almost a year now. As I waited, feeling the cold, watching the traffic, the glowing interior of a restaurant across the street, having to look up between the terminal buildings to see the thin snow descending against the dark, my resolve began to fade. I wondered whether to go back down into that warm, noisy station and join all the other poor damn honest slobs on their way home. Then his hand gripped my arm.

He had changed. He looked older. He was older. And so was I. A year in a young person's life is a very long time, I guess. Stanley said sometimes how we must make use of our youth because when we were his age, why 'the years just fly past'. Well, to me the last had dragged on interminably. What I saw was an old man in his mid-fifties, large, but not as large as I used to know. His hat covered his baldness, nothing could hide the jowls that had formed and begun to hang each side of his face. He had always looked younger than his age I thought; like a lot of people with that sort of plump, bland, seemingly unchanging face, his had, over just a year and a day, collapsed irretrievably. I knew that whatever he wanted me to do, I was not going to be able to oblige.

'Hello Starr. Gosh, it's good to see you.'

'Andrew,' I said.

He took me by the arm and steered me to the curb, putting his hand up to signal a cab.

As we got in, he said, 'Sorry, I didn't think. Do you need anything? We can stop at a druggist on the way.'

He meant, Did I need any barbiturates? He had bought me allonal or veronal before, knowing how they helped.

'No, I'm okay,' I said.

He looked at me a little queerly, then smiled, settling back in the seat. 'I thought dinner first. At Gallagher's perhaps. You liked Gallagher's, I think. Wonderful steaks. You remember?'

'Fine.'

We headed on to Broadway, into that cold brilliant

inferno, Times Square ahead making the whole black sky retreat behind its blaze.

'Then a show. The Follies are good this year. Then we'll see. I've booked us into the Richmond.'

'I can't stay, Andrew,' I said in a level, determined way.

'My dear child, you can't possibly go back on a night like this. The trains may be snowed off or anything.'

'I can't stop,' I said again.

'We won't argue about it. Just here, driver.'

We ate. I was hungry. The normal things continue.

So, he talked in a pleasant, chatty, charming way over dinner. He asked about the family and when that was out of the way told me some stories about people in Boston we both knew, and the latest scandals in New York and what books I should read, which I never would because his taste was terribly old fashioned and I told him so and he laughed and looked at me and said seriously, 'But not for you, Starr. Not for you.'

We went off to the Follies. In the theatre there was warmth and darkness and light and companionship of a thousand or so strangers. I laughed at the comics and loved the new tunes we hadn't heard yet out in Jersey and would get for my phonograph tomorrow. *I want a little girl, to call my own* . . . sung sweetly by a young fairyish looking man to a girl on a swing going lazily up and down and showing her petticoat like that French painting. I don't know if Andrew liked that song. You don't connect these things until later, with the irony that colours and distorts your memory. He did like the troupe of girls in their white pyjama suits, almost transparent, as if they had been dipped in water. They clung so tight you could see the lines of their pink bottoms. I'm sure they wore nothing beneath but they kept moving and the lights were so clever, rose and blue, and the orchestra played something new called *Blue Room*, which was so pretty. The show lasted three hours and I wanted it to last for ever, that world of music and colour and illusion and good humour where everyone is either beautiful or funny and all of them immortal and unchanging.

As we emerged in the happy, bubbling crowd, I made out that I had a terrible headache.

'Do you want supper? To go dancing?' he asked solicitously.

I should go home, I told him. Would he get me a taxi to the Terminal?

'I'm not sending you home on a night like this,' he said. The snow was swirling down from the glowing sky, in thick fluffy flakes that melted when they hit the brilliant, wet street. 'I'll ring your mother,' he said decisively.

'This is ridiculous,' I said, but giving in. My feet were damp in the silver pumps I'd changed into in the powder room at the restaurant. Two girls passing by wore the new cloche hats that sort of fold softly on either side of your face.

'Get in the cab. I'll sort it out,' he said.

I stood in the lobby of the Astor, being noticed by the men who walked in, sometimes alone, sometimes with their wives, perhaps their wives, on their arms, dusting the snow from their coats. I tried not to meet their eyes, looking round every now and then to see Andrew squeezed in a booth, mouthing energetically into the telephone mouthpiece to Mrs Faithfull in West Orange, New Jersey.

'I've told Helen that you're booked in here, and that I'm at the Richmond,' he said when he came out of the booth.

'She insisted on that. You haven't said anything . . .? He stared accusingly at me.

I shook my head. 'Of course not,' I said.

'It's not quite eleven. What do you want to do?'

'Would you mind Andrew — my head is splitting. All I want to do is go to bed.'

He smiled, or rather, smirked. 'Reached the age for headaches already, Starr? Ah well . . . I'll see about rooms.'

He went to the desk. The clerk had been giving us those discreet looks every few minutes in between dealing with his other meagre duties. Middle-aged man, young woman. A five or ten dollar bill at least for him. Mr and Miss Peters, Boston. Father, daughter. Uncle, niece. Adjoining rooms. Would you like a connecting door? It's not necessary — said airily, signing the book with a flourish, as if it was a treaty, or a damn good contract at the least.

'I'm in 403, you're in 404. I'll take you up. You can settle in. Rest a while. Perhaps you'll feel better soon.'

We went up in the elevator, silent. The coloured boy gave us a huge ingratiating smile, white teeth and beautifully sculpted lips, as we stepped out. I wonder what they really think of us?

'Here we are.' He unlocked the door. I slipped in and held the door only half open. He stood in the corridor, paddling his yellow kid gloves in his hat. His capacity still for this boyish awkwardness and shyness astonished me. 'Andrew — I really must put my head down.'

'Of course. Of course. I've something to do. Perhaps I'll see you later.' Then he frowned at me, the lines on his head forming deep furrows, the hands, with hat in one, gloves in the other, falling impatiently to his sides. I closed the door. Engaged the lock quietly.

I undressed and got into bed naked. I had not brought any nightdress. That would have looked a little obvious, wouldn't it? I knew what the something was that Andrew had to do. He would go down again in the elevator, cross the lobby to the desk clerk — if he hadn't already fixed this — and ask him if he could procure a little something. A fifth? No, no a smaller bottle would do. Bourbon. He always had to have a drink beforehand. And knowing that I would not be at all amenable for at least an hour or so, he would ask the clerk to have the bottle wrapped discreetly and to drop it into room 404. Then Andrew would wander into the lounge and find someone from out of town, preferably New England, to chat to, perhaps someone he knew — he knew scads of people in politics of course. But not so much in New York. New York was for pleasure. Or he would sit in for a few hands of cards with any group there. Buffers mainly from out of town, who had no attendant nieces and didn't fancy a speakeasy.

I had no stuff on me, and my last Nembutal from the cache I'd kept had been taken the previous week. So I lay awake. For hours it seemed. But I had turned off the light, and drawn the thick drapes and at last, in the velvety dark, I got warm and sleepy. Perhaps I'd been asleep some time, or just drifted off; I woke up to a gentle knock on the door. I held my breath. After a moment the knock was repeated, as a double, still quiet but slightly more insistent entreaty. I curled like a foetus under the blankets. He did not knock again. The door was too thick, the corridor carpet too deep to hear his footsteps go away. It was a long time before I went to sleep again, conscious now of the presence in the next room and wondering what its thoughts were.

I got up a long time before dawn and sat at the window

waiting for the terribly slow January dawn. Not that you actually see a dawn in that open country sense here in the city. It is rather as if the stones and bricks of the walls begin to put on a little colour like an old whore in the morning and the wet tarmac of the street takes on a cold gleam and the high windows turn from lead to dull silver. The people in the street had never stopped passing; the dribs and drabs of solitary aimless figures. Where the hell do they come from, where are they heading, those girls hobbling on broken heels, the slow, wandering men their mouths filthied up with cheap booze, their heads cracking? Then the early workers who look weary already as they walk to the lowest jobs. The fashion store across the way is brilliantly lit, but empty, I can't read the price tags on the mannequins from here. The delicatessen across the way is open, the girls filling the windows with goods, a man turning a meat slicer like a hurdy-gurdy.

I watched till the street filled up and it was another almost normal day in New York. It was eight-thirty when he knocked on the door.

'I trust you slept well, Starr?' There was no hint of sarcasm, just the same, rather too studied solicitousness.

'Like a log, thanks.'

But we were cheerful towards each other, kindly uncle, dutiful niece, as we entered the huge dining-room. Warm, cutlery glinting, whiteness of whiteness the table-cloths, the waiters svelte, black-haired, looking as if they never needed to sleep. The place half full, with that murmuring subdued half-talk that people have in the morning. Two great round tables full of some businessmen's convention or other, starting to warm up with the jokes about each other's exploits last night, the tarts, the hangovers all washing away now they're together again.

Andrew guided me down the whole length of the dining-room to a table at the back. He liked to show me off.

Coffee and toast for the young lady. Ham and eggs, muffins, jam, cream; he ate like a one-man convention.

In between mouthfuls by him, sips of coffee by me, silence.

Then, when he was well into his breakfast, as if asking me to pass something, he said, 'So it's all over?'

'What?'

'Starr, don't play stupid. It is — it seems to me that it is — you wish it to be — all over between us?'

'What do you mean — between us? You talk as if . . .'

He frowned at me to be quiet.

The waiter poured more coffee into my cup; Andrew smiled at him as if he were a voter and then said we could look after ourselves just fine; the waiter bowed himself away.

'I'm simply saying how it looks very much to me,' he said, laying his knife down softly and reaching for the fork. 'You know that I love you Starr. I've always loved you.'

'Give me a cigarette.'

'You don't smoke. Neither of us smokes.'

Then I laughed at the ridiculousness, I was on the verge of being hysterical; a broad stupid grin crossed his face.

'That's better,' he said. 'Now what's really eating you? Something is. If you don't want me . . . don't want me sometimes, then tell me. I'll understand. You're a grown-up young lady now. Free, white, and nearly twenty, as they say.'

'I don't want to do anything again. Nothing like that. Not again.'

'Okay, okay,' he said soothingly. His brown eyes regarded

me with that kindly, worried look he did so well. 'You don't have to do anything you don't want to. You know that. It's always been like that.'

'For Christ's sake . . .'

He speared neatly his last square of egg and forked it into his mouth. He chewed slowly, swallowed, took a sip of coffee, put down the cup slowly and delicately on its saucer, and said, 'I don't want to lose you, Starr. We have meant a lot to each other over the years. I know I'm not a young man. If you want that part to end, so be it. I hope we can still be friends.'

I didn't look at him.

'Look, what do you want? Do you want money. New clothes? I can give you anything you want.'

'I just want — I don't know.' Then I did know. 'I want to get away. That's what I want. From my stupid family. From all this. From New York. I just want something else.'

He relaxed. He smiled.

I'd done it again, hadn't I? I'd left him with a hold on me, a line to me. Like that story, 'The Princess and the Goblin', where the girl has an infinitely fine, infinitely thin silver thread for ever attached to her, following her, however lost in a maze of caverns she becomes — though with her it was for her safety, with me it was to reel me back to his hands.

He reeled me in.

'I know, Starr. I do know. I'll think of something. I really will. I'm going to Washington for a few weeks next month, but I shan't forget. It'll be something special, I assure you. Now, before I do forget — I know that it's your birthday in a couple of days. I didn't know what to get, so please accept this.'

He took an envelope out of his pocket and held it out. I didn't lift my hands from the table. He placed it by the side of my plate.

'Now, do take it. It's meant in the best of spirits.'

I picked up the envelope.

'No, don't open it now,' he said.

'Thank you,' I said. 'I'd better go get my things. They'll be thinking I've done a bunk or something.'

'I'll get them to get you a cab to the Terminal.'

He didn't come with me. It wasn't necessary; he still had me, even by the thinnest of lines.

I opened the envelope on the train. It contained two hundred dollars in crisp new twenties.

Two weeks later I had a letter from him, a short note on a Boston Chamber of Commerce letterhead, 'What about this for a pick-me-up? I can book you 1st of July, Love and best wishes, Andrew.'

Attached was a brochure for the Cunard Line, a nine-week cruise of the Mediterranean on the *SS California*.

'With Andrew?' said my mother.

'No. On my own.'

'For nine weeks? On your own? Don't be absurd. And how could we possibly afford it?'

'You don't have to. Andrew says he will pay for the trip.'

'Bully for Andrew,' said Tucker. She hated me at that moment I guess as much as any sister ever hated.

'No. That is that. No,' said my mother.

'Now, Helen, Don't let's be over-hasty.' Stanley took the pipe from his mouth and spoke judiciously. 'If the thing is properly arranged and if Mr Peters is willing to pay. It could be a marvellous opportunity for her. Once in a lifetime. And if it would please Andrew. You're always saying how fond he is of Starr . . .'

'And how,' said Tucker.

HELEN

I HAD NOT wished to have to approach Andrew again. Especially with this trip for Starr. But at last I had to write him.

The reason, as usual, was a chronic lack of money — that had lately become an acute need. Stanley, the wily businessman, the merchant with a finger in many pies, the man of great expectations, the manipulator of investments, had revealed himself in little more than a year to be virtually penniless. He had been describing to me for some time, swearing me to secrecy, his plans to set up another manufacturing company with the help of some other businessmen in New York. And we had seemed to be living quite comfortably up until the spring. I had not had to apply to any of the family for help. I was glad of this. It was a great relief and good for my self-esteem that I had become an independent woman, married to this clever little man, no longer dependent on the goodwill of others. I was grateful also for my change in circumstances as I considered that any further requests might well fall now on slightly stonier ground.

So, swimming along quite nicely, I thought, until Starr came in, greatly upset one morning.

'I thought you said Ohlman's account had been paid,' I said to Stanley. He was in the small parlour that he used as his study. He looked up from his book.

'Why?'

'Why? Because Starr was turned away this morning.'

'Turned away, what do you mean?'

'They were most embarrassed about it, they practically apologised to her, but said Starr couldn't have the dress she'd ordered as our account hadn't been paid for over four months. The poor girl was humiliated.'

'Four months? That can hardly be correct, my dear. I have a system for keeping track of all our commitments.'

As indeed he had, a pile of folders in his bureau each neatly labelled with a creditor's name — from the lowest and most minor accounts of grocery and filling-station, right on up to the banks who held the mortgages on the West Orange house and the Cape cottage.

'I'll look into it.' He closed his book, got up, and went over to the bureau. 'They had a cheque promptly on their last bill. Some damn fool clerk at the bank has likely mixed things up.'

'Well, I wish you would look into it, Stanley. This kind of thing gets around, you know.'

'One thing's for certain,' he said, picking up his folders and beginning to go through them, 'they've lost trade by their stupidity. I don't want any of you going there again.'

That mollified me somewhat.

Until I went into O'Brien's, the general store, a few days later. Their bills, like all the others, were sent directly to Stanley, as he had said that he wished to be head of the household. Anyhow, I had spent twenty minutes in O'Brien's, pulling things off the shelves, and getting the girl to fetch down tins and packets from behind the counter, to slice ham and grind coffee for me, until I had three large paper sacks on the counter, and she stood waiting for me to pay. I thanked her for her help. It was a lovely spring day outside. I was feeling particularly well in myself; Stanley had been extra affectionate earlier in the morning.

'Would you just charge it to my account, my dear,' I said, when everything was bagged.

'Yes, certainly, madam. The name?'

When I said, 'Faithfull,' the smile sort of withered on her mouth. She gave a quick small grimace that might have been attempting to recover the smile. 'Please, if you wouldn't mind waiting a moment, madam,' she rattled out, and disappeared behind the curtain that led into the O'Briens' living quarters. Another woman shopper placed her filled basket on the counter and smiled at me with stupid, half-pitying curiosity. I smiled bleakly back at her, said, 'What a lovely day it is,' in my best Bostonian manner and turned away, pretending to look at some leaflet or other on the counter, extolling the virtues of a laxative drink.

Mr O'Brien came through the curtained doorway, followed by the girl — she hurried up the counter to serve the other woman, avoiding my eyes. Mr O'Brien was charming, and embarrassed; he had a long strip of paper in his hand. If I wouldn't mind — his voice was lowered — if I wouldn't mind, it was simply a matter of the account — they tried to be accommodating — no doubt it had slipped my busy mind — but it was almost two hundred dollars now . . . if I could see my way clear to settling?

I couldn't see anything clearly, my mind was filled with a

hot rage and shame. The other woman shopper turned away with her goods and gave me another hideously sympathetic smile.

Of course, the bill would be settled, I said grandly. I couldn't understand it. My husband . . . Now if Mr O'Brien would place these new items on the bill I would see that a cheque was delivered that very day. Mr O'Brien pondered for a moment, his look wandering speculatively over my purchases, his hand reaching out to hand me the account on the long strip of paper, then he said slowly, 'I don't think I can do that Mrs Faithfull . . .'

The humiliating compromise we reached was that I was to be allowed to pay for the goods on the counter by cash — luckily I had just enough on me — and that the account would be settled in the next seven days. Oh, we parted sweetly enough, with Good Morning, Mrs Faithfull, and Good Morning, Mr O'Brien, and smiles, and the little mousy girl smiling insufferably too, and I drove home to Stanley with utter black rage in my heart.

Ah, but I loosed into Stanley. How could he do this to me? I screamed. What the hell was wrong? He started muttering about some mistake. I demanded to see the accounts.

They were not available. They were in his office in New York.

'Don't be ridiculous. What office in New York?'

The syndicate and he had taken an office in New York to conduct their business, he said . . .

He was floundering, drowning. I pressed him under.

'I will pay these bills,' I said, with a new firmness. 'God knows where the money is to come from. I shall have to raise some more on the cottage.'

'You will not. I have matters in hand,' he said, making a

sudden rally. Nothing emasculates a man more effectively than questioning his ability to provide. Stanley's primitive blood, however thinned by years of civilisation, rose slightly in him. 'Really, Helen, you are being unreasonable. All businesses experience their ins and outs, their ebbs and flows. If your faith in me is going to desert you at the first small difficulty . . .'

'Difficulty! To find oneself humiliated in front of trades-people and their assistants.'

'This is New Jersey, my dear. Not Beacon Hill. I dare say everyone round here gets into difficulties at some time or other.'

'Most of them have a job.'

He reddened. 'These bills will be taken care of — I assure you. Now please excuse me.' He jammed on his hat and almost bumped Starr out of the way as she came through the door.

'What's the matter with him?' she asked. 'Are you two fighting again?'

We had to continue living. I had shaken Stanley. The bills were cleared by him immediately. It took the last of his insurance money I think and I felt a little guilty. I told him I was taking out a second mortgage on the Cape Cod house to tide us over until his business plans materialised. No, no, he protested, he could not let me do that. But when he finally relented and allowed me to borrow money, he was at once more relaxed, his eyes shining behind his glasses. 'How about a drive out? A meal?' he suggested.

'We aren't millionaires,' I said tartly.

'Not yet. Not yet. But we will be one day, old thing.'

So we were happy again. Somewhat. Instead of criticising him I realised it might be better, and safer, to take an interest in his affairs.

The next time, I sympathised when he began to complain of the slowness of his partners in reaching a decision to float his revolutionary new drug or cosmetic, or whatever it was by then — something again to do with the chemical treatment of milk by-products. He spent hours at his desk when the girls were out, with books on chemistry propped in front of him, or perched on his lap, making notes, scribbling away at formulas. He believed he was working and I was willing to suspend my disbelief, watching his narrow back hunched against the desk light.

I couldn't help wondering exactly how foolish a thing I had done by remarrying. But you make your bed and lie down in it with someone. I did not admire Stanley, I did not even particularly like him sometimes. But I did, I do, strangely, love him sometimes. It is an odd belief of men that women are totally consumed by devotion to them. What is that thing of Byron's — something about women's love being the whole of their life, but men's being only a part? Not so. Most marriages are practices in a manageable sort of chafing together. We are weak creatures and we cling to each other. The business of middle age is the orderly handling of the decay of passion and its gradual replacement by routine, conformity, comfort, and an increasing level of interest on one's investments. 'That is what people are willing to kill for,' said Stanley, and I agreed — we could cheerfully have shot every hobo and labour agitator and Socialist in the country. They did not understand the way we lived, really lived. Stanley announced one night after the radio news of some other big demonstration or strike that if this sort of thing was allowed to go on, all would be over for this country. The Reds would rule everything.

And we had frightened each other by the violence of our

arguments about money. He affected, in a most infuriatingly insouciant way, not to have any worries on that account. One man with a good idea was worth another with a million bucks, he said. I agreed, but suggested it might be better if he went up to New York and saw what his partners were actually doing. 'You never seem to speak to them on the telephone,' I said. 'There's no correspondence. There's no money. What sort of a business is that?' He seemed strangely reluctant to go. 'You can't hurry this sort of thing,' he said. But I forced him to get in touch with Frishberg. Frishberg was out every time he rang. I insisted; he must go to New York to find out what was happening and to try and get a quick decision on the new company from the other prospective investors.

He went — and came back silent, grey-faced, angry, his lips set in thin lines. They had welshed on him. Their promises, drawn up in contracts, had proved to be worthless. They were unwilling to invest. Frishberg had closed his office and disappeared with the thousand dollars that Stanley had given him to invest. 'I have the documents. I have their signatures,' he kept saying, his hands scrabbling through the papers on his desk. He would sue them for breach of contract. 'We have more lawsuits than *Bleak House*,' I said.

I don't know how much of his story I believed — or how much of it he believed. But he got down to work immediately again, drafting letters to a firm of lawyers in New York, giving page after page of details of the negotiations, of promises given and retracted, of expenses incurred — all of which he got me to type up on the machine he had brought with him at our marriage. That, and his fifty or so books, and a picture of his mother and father, were about all he did bring, come to think of the matter. Anyway, this gave me something to do too, and gave us both the illusion of being busy bees involved in a family concern. Certain of his success in his up-coming law-suit, Stanley took out a second mortgage on the West Orange house. I only found this out by looking through his bureau and discovering the papers. It did not shock me as much as I thought. It meant that he had money in the bank of his own, giving him some measure of independence and the ability to pay bills — we had changed all our stores of course. It seemed a lot of money. I didn't tell him that I knew. We now had no less than four mortgages, with repayments due each month and no income coming in.

If the worst came to the worst, there was always Boston. That's what I supposed.

I shut my eyes. Until the summer of '26. Here was my daughter about to go on the trip of a lifetime and we could hardly buy groceries. I did not begrudge her Andrew's kindness at all — he could not know what a situation we were in after all. The late bills had started to come in again; the polite, then less polite, then decidedly unpolite letters from the shops. The only recourse I had then to raise cash immediately was to apply to my family. I spread the requests. A little from each so that they would not assume we were in too dreadful trouble. The letters went to my brother, to Aunt Julia, to Andrew. My brother wrote back, enclosing a cheque for twenty dollars and cheerfully advising in his letter that Stanley might consider getting himself some gainful employment. Aunt Julia did not reply. Andrew sent back a rather cagey letter typed, I presume, by a secretary on his official letterhead. He hoped Starr was well and looking forward to her voyage. He would be in New York in June and would try to see her off. Perhaps we could meet then and discuss whatever problems I had.

STARR

MOTHER CAME ROUND to the idea of the trip in the end.

I couldn't wait for the spring to pass. For the first time in my life I had something good to look forward to.

Two nights before I was due to go, the phone rang. Stanley answered, with that preposterous 'The Faithfull house' that made us sound like an inn. Then, 'Oh, Mr Peters. Stanley. Yes. How are you? The girls are always talking about you. Yes. All good.' He hee-hawed down the phone. 'Yes, she is. Let me just say, Andrew, if I may, how pleased we are that you have given Starr this wonderful opportunity. Yes, educational. Sure. Wish I could get educated that way. Haw . . . haw . . . Yes, here she is.'

Andrew wanted me to come to New York that afternoon. He was passing through; he wouldn't get another chance to see me. He wanted to buy me a few little things to make my trip more pleasurable. See another show. Terrific one at the Palace. Get me back in good time for the night train. Run me back if I liked . . .

My mother, just coming into the room now; What is it? her voice harsh and suspicious.

Me; quick explanation of Andrew. Invitation.

Mother, impatiently, asks for the phone. She wants to speak to him anyway. She cradles it away, facing the wall, her long back hunched slightly, her shoulders high as if trying to shield the phone from us. She talks very low. Letter. Thank you. We must meet. Tomorrow? I'll see you at the Biltmore then. Well, I do want something arranged. Starr — I suppose so. If she wants to. Yes. Fine. Where? All right, I'll tell her. Bye, Andrew.

'He says he'll meet you in the lobby of the Astor at four this afternoon,' she said, her mouth giving that impatient little twist it had started to do lately.

I went to the city happy. White silk stockings, white chiffon dress, white cloche hat, my long white belted mackintosh because there was a little rain about when I left. In two days I would be away from New Jersey, New York, Mother, Stanley, Tucker, Andrew — the whole menagerie.

Meantime I could even enjoy meeting Andrew.

'I'm taking you to Fifth Avenue,' he said. He seemed tense and bubbly at the same time, like a boy out for a treat. I almost liked him then. Well, I did have some feeling for him. I wished he hadn't done those things to me. If I didn't look at him too much I could almost imagine that he was my kind uncle and that we were out on a spree.

'Why Fifth Avenue?'

'I want to buy you everything you want for your trip. You must have clothes, new luggage — well, you know better than me what you need.'

'No,' I said, rebelling all at once. There was an innocence to that day which was rare enough, and I wanted to keep it intact. 'I mean it, Andrew. I have had too much from you already. I don't want to be looked after. To be provided for. You musn't buy me anything else. I mean it. I'll stop the cab and get out unless you promise.'

'No clothes? No leather luggage with your initials on?' He laughed. 'Okay.' I thought I'd spoiled his plans, but he just laughed at my cross expression. He leaned forward and said through the half-open partition, 'Marcus and Son,' to the driver. 'There's something I have to pick up,' he said, and smiled at me and laid his hand over mine, and smiled again when I withdrew my hand and pretended to look for something in my purse.

We got out in front of the shop. The window wasn't full of glittering junk like the cheap places in Jersey City and Newark; here diamond necklaces hung around ebony necks that had no heads and no bodies except discreetly rising half-busts, a small select group of these giving the impression of a conversation at a very exclusive party between a few women so rich that they had no need of coarse bodies or empty heads; diamond rings and impossibly slender gold watches on hands that reached up out of black velvet cubes like packets of night. It was all very discreet, and discreetly forbidding; no-one would ever step in here for a five-dollar ring for his girl. The truly rich like things done in this understated, sombre way, they deplore deeply the vulgarity that attaches in the ordinary mind to huge sums of money. In fact, the rich don't possess money in that sense at all; they have riches the way the rest of us have blood. Andrew held the door open for me, his eyes bright, that big smile again.

As we walked between the crystal cabinets filled with such fiery and deeply glowing treasure that you could hardly call them anything so coarse as shop counters, he said, in a whisper in this cathedral of wealth, 'It's good to do good by stealth, but even better when someone knows,' and took my arm, his hand cupping my elbow.

The man who sat behind the table at the end of the room rose to greet us at exactly the right moment; neither too eager, nor too tardy. He was tall, distinguished, his hair wavy, beautifully greyed at the sides; he looked more like an ambassador than a shop assistant. Well, a South American ambassador maybe, but very cute.

'Mr Peters, so nice to see you. Madam.' In a split second his eyes politely devoured, evaluated, and delicately spat me out.

'Mr Marshall — you have my package?'

'But of course.' He slid open a side drawer of the ambassadorially sized desk and took out a small, square, flat, leather-covered box. He leaned forward slightly over the desk, clicking the catch on the box. As he did so, Andrew reached out, almost snatching it from him. 'No, no,' he said, 'I'll see it later. Um?'

Mr Marshall straightened and gave a little self-effacing nod of the head. 'As you like, Mr Peters. It's just that we like to know that our patrons are satisfied.'

'Quite so,' said Andrew, slipping the box into his pocket. 'But I can hardly imagine Marcus and Son ever giving cause for complaint.' He laughed in a gruff, matey fashion.

'That's good of you to say, Mr Peters.'

'Shall you charge it?'

'Whatever you wish, Mr Peters.'

We walked away back up the shop, I turned to see Mr Marshall making a discreet entry in a ledger with a silver fountain pen. He should have had a quill.

I was all ready to refuse an expensive gift from Andrew

— which what I was sure was in the box. But he didn't offer it. 'What about tea — at the Astor?'

It was now about half-past five. When we got to the hotel he settled me in the tearoom then said that he had to go up to his room to change. He had a plain business suit on and didn't want to go in that to the theatre. 'I don't want to go full fig, you understand,' he said, laughing. 'Just something a bit darker and more New York, eh?' I was glad he didn't ask me up to his room; I didn't want to get into that offer or refusal nonsense so early in the evening. In fact I was hoping it wouldn't come up at all; he was acting so nice and friendly, with no hint of anything else.

We had tea. There was no mention of the visit to the jeweller's and I let it slip, with some reluctance, out of my mind. Then we took a cab — not to the Palace, but to somewhere really downtown, in the not so good part of Chelsea. The show was boisterous, rude, a burlesque theatre. I had never been to one before. I said so to Andrew. 'You'll enjoy it,' he said. And I did.

The MC was a thick-set man in a blazer with great broad red and white stripes and a straw hat to match, which he kept sweeping off to introduce the acts. He told the most lurid jokes. There was a dog on a bicycle. The girls were bigger and plainer than the ones you get in the regular shows, with thick thighs and their breasts bouncing up and down out of time to the music. But it was funny and fun and the band was good and had a hot trumpet man as good as some I've heard on record since. And when we spilled out of there, Andrew said, 'Don't tell your mother, though, that we went there.' He was in such a good mood. I felt beholden to him for the good time. It had started to rain really hard while we were in the theatre and we hurried into a cab. We were past the Terminal before I realised and said to Andrew, 'I really must catch the train back soon.' 'Not in this weather, Starr.'

'Not again, Andrew,' I said. 'What the hell will Mother say?'

'I'll tell her there's a storm. I'll put you up at the Biltmore. For God's sake, Starr, relax. Your mother is coming up to town in the morning. You're sailing in forty-eight hours. Do you really want to go back to them?'

No, I didn't really. I didn't want to be here either, but I'd handled it the last time. I was a big girl now. So back to the Astor.

He could phone from his room. I didn't think to ask why he didn't use the public booths. I followed him docilely into the elevator. Same boy, same wonderful smile. There was an inevitability in all this, as if I was beginning to act a part Andrew had designed.

In the room, a room of great, surpassing boredom, like all hotel rooms, utterly unlike the dream palaces in the movies, he rang Mother. 'No,' he lied, 'she's not here. I dropped her at the Biltmore. If you're coming in the morning we'll meet you in the lobby there. No, I'm at the Astor. I'll come over to wish Starr bon voyage. No, she's perfectly all right. See you in the morning.'

He turned away from the wall phone. 'I've got a little surprise for you, Starr. Which it very nearly wasn't thanks to that man in Marcus's.' He went to the closet and reached into the pocket of his grey suit hanging there. He came over to me. I moved almost unconsciously a step away from the large double bed.

The box of course. He undid the catch and passed it over,

opened, to me. I took out a bracelet, silver, inset with tiny diamonds in a single line around.

'It's got an inscription. On the inside.' His voice was sort of husky.

To Starr, with fondest love, ever AJP

I put it back in the box and closed the lid. I held the box out to him.

'Aren't you even going to put it on?'

'I can't accept this . . .'

I held it out to him. I even enjoyed that. He had, after all, made me the way I was. I felt the petty sexual power of a mistress.

'You were right, Andrew,' I said airily. 'It is all over. I'm grateful for the trip and all. But nothing else. It must end. Don't you see? I can't take any more from you.'

This time though he did not beg. He seemed to swell up in front of me, his eyes bulged, his cheeks flushed, his head cocked back and forward again.

'You can't accept? You can't accept?' His voice went high. He dug his fists into his coat pockets and then he spoke in a hard, hoarse voice. 'What the hell else do you think you've been doing for the past ten years? That's all you have been doing. You and your family. I loved you, you stupid little bitch. Money. Clothes. Education. Where do you think it all came from? What the hell was it all for?'

He came forward. His hands jerked out of his suit and he pushed me back so that I staggered and sat down hard on the bed.

'Well, it's about time you gave something back.'

I still held out the box.

'I never asked you for these things, Andrew. I never asked you to touch me. And now I think I want to go home. You

183

can have your cruise. And your damn bracelet. If you gave me things, what were they for?' I began to cry.

'You haven't got a home. Your home is with me. You're not going anywhere.' He leaned over me and took my hair in one hand and with the other hand gripped my shoulder, pulling and twisting. 'You turned me down at Christmas. I haven't forgotten that. Do you think I'm a fool? I'm a man of position, of standing, and you are mine and you have always been mine, and now you're going to bloody well deliver what is mine.'

Then he is lying on me, flattening me to the bed, my hands strong, and weak, trying to push him off. His hand is between my thighs and pulling at my underclothes, his other arm is pinning me across my chest.

I don't want to do that, Andrew, I'm screaming and crying. Not that. I told you — not that. Never that. We agreed. But, to my muffled sobs, that is what he does, panting, a sudden flaring pain inside me, his huffing and puffing, his weight, then — it couldn't have taken more than a minute — he groans, and pulls away from me.

'You owed me. You owed me,' he said, staggering back, trying to compose himself, his grotesque, pathetic thing already shrinking away, his face looking down at me with an expression of utter horror.

I sat up, covered myself up, not looking at him.

'Get me some stuff,' I said mechanically. 'You want to make a night of it. What does it matter?'

HELEN

WHEN I GOT to the hotel, Andrew was sitting in the lobby, watching the entrance. He got to this feet as soon as I came in and waited for me to cross the long floor to him. He looked rather tired and out of sorts.

'Helen, good to see you.'

'Where's Starr?' I asked, looking round.

'She's gone,' he said. 'Do you want coffee?'

'Gone. Gone where?'

'Home. She left early. She wanted to get home. Said she had things to get ready for her trip.'

'She might have waited for me. For her own mother. Really, the child's most annoying,' I said.

'She's hardly a child any more, Helen. She's quite the young lady.'

'To speak frankly, and while we are grateful, Heaven knows, I sometimes wish you had never thought of this trip, Andrew. You've quite turned the girl's head.'

'I thought she needed something like that. I was worried about her. She doesn't seem well.'

'She's not sick.'

185

'Disturbed. Emotional. You know Starr.' He smiled, quickly, insincerely — it was like Mr O'Brien's smile in refusing me credit. 'Now, what was this business you wanted to talk over?'

The interview in the hotel lobby was less than satisfactory. Andrew was off-hand in his manner, and kept glancing at his watch. Ploughing on, I laid the facts before him as best I could, half-jokingly . . . a recurrence of the old troubles . . . until my husband's business was running smoothly . . . the two properties as security . . .

'Helen. Put this down in writing to me,' he said, cutting me short. 'I really must be in Washington this afternoon. If you'll excuse me . . .'

Well, my whole day was ruined. I had no heart — and no money — to face the stores. I had about five dollars in my purse I remember. I felt their puniness, insulted by the immense shouting wealth about me as I stepped out of the hotel. I had expected to go shopping with Starr. Did I think she would have money? I don't know. Perhaps I hoped so. Her uncle was very kind after all.

How kind I discovered when I returned home.

I got back about four. The house was quiet when I let myself in. Usually the phonograph or radio was playing if Tucker was home. Not a sound. As I hung my coat on the hall stand, Stanley came from the parlour. I didn't turn round, patting my hair back into place in the mirror. Reflected in the mirror, his face looked oddly unfamiliar, as if he was a visitor I couldn't quite place.

'Starr's back,' he said.

'I should hope so,' I said. 'She's quite spoiled my day, hurrying off like that. I wanted . . .'

'No.' He held his finger to his lips. 'Don't speak so loud. Come in here.'

I was not so much in a mood for humouring him, after two journeys on a hot day, but I followed him. 'Get me a soda or something,' I said. 'I swear Andrew was downright off-hand . . .'

'In a moment,' said Stanley. 'Something has happened.'

Looking back, it is all a little like a stage play. We enter the room. I ask again for a drink. He faces me, hands thrust into his jacket pockets, thumbs jutting out. I brace myself for a revelation. I speak:

'Oh God, not money again?'

'No — Starr. Something has happened to her. She came back early this morning. Just after you left. She was very upset about something. She won't tell me. She wouldn't speak to me. She's upstairs.'

'What do you mean — something happened to her? What do you mean?'

'To do with Andrew. Something to do with Andrew.'

I mounted the stairs towards our future. Did I know what it was? We always know what our future is, we just pretend we don't. We meet, make love, marry, have children, go to a house, arrange its furniture, read books, listen to the radio, eat out, watch our friends drift away, make new ones, know, suddenly, that our children are growing, have grown, that they despise us; and at the same time ourselves spy, as if through a turned-about telescope, on those who once over-shadowed our whole lives, and see them dwindle and become yellow and shrunken like Aunt Editha and be buried with or without us there — they could scarcely be con-cerned, but it only seems decent for the sake of the rest of us — and others are meanwhile born and we go to their

187

christenings and hear their innocent bawlings echo and drift in the same big high churches of our marriages, our deaths — and we mount the stairs to hear from our child her report of our world.

'One thing we must not do is to be hasty.'

Stanley had pulled his armchair close in so that we sat with our knees almost touching. I had got him to light a fire though it was summer. I felt cold. Tucker had come in, rolled her eyes, said, 'How ludicrous,' and gone over to a friend's house. Starr was upstairs; Stanley had prepared a sleeping draught for her.

I was silent. In my hand a tumbler of gin and warm water. I believed Starr and did not wish to believe her. All of it was of a piece. Our happy times at Martha's. The sight of Starr smiling and waving from the boat that Andrew rowed off the shore at North Haven. Starr tearing across the lawn at the Chestnut Hill house. Playing tennis, gravely, intently, with a boy I never saw again on the back lawn there. Starr loading her bags into the back of Andrew's roadster; her turning away of her cheek when I tried to kiss her goodbye. The month's holiday she had spent with him. The outings from Rogers Hall. The gifts. The clothes, the riding lessons, the cards on her birthday, the postcards written by her when she was away; the same occasional messages we all send, perhaps salted with a little of her bitter humour, but I'd got used to that. *This place is so dull. I think I shall go mad. Andrew is looking over my shoulder! Wonderful, wonderful, wonderful place — he tells me to tell you. O-kay!*

The riding accident. The bitter drink she swallowed. The book he read to her. 'I can't remember — I can't — a dirty book. Then he made me . . .'

I couldn't repeat it. A gradual leading in, as she described, from the reading, to fondling, caressing . . . The ether, brandy sometimes, then to feel him, to have him touch her . . . But, no, she had never let him do that. Never. There was always a piece of her he couldn't have. Until last night.

Her sobbing. Her body curled on the bed in that white lovely dress, creased and soiled along the hem . . .

'And — I don't want you to take this wrongly, Helen,' said Stanley, 'but can we be sure? This is a serious thing we're talking of here.'

'What do you mean — sure of what?'

'Starr is a very sensitive girl. An artistic girl — she has an imagination, that is what I mean.'

'You think she imagined this?'

'I don't know. I don't know what went on. But it is possible. We must be very careful. If she is correct . . .'

'If?'

But the devil is there to put doubts in your mind. The matter was not as simple as I had thought. Stanley was not stupid in that respect.

'Your discussions with Andrew this morning . . . You must put them down in writing, quite coolly with no hint . . .'

'No hint — how can you say that!'

'. . . no hint that you have any knowledge of Starr's accusations, and not say anything to imply that these debts are for the family to settle, but just that you wish to acquaint him with the facts — as he requested.'

So the next morning, still much against my will, the letter was written — a queer little letter in Stanley's words, and typed and signed by me, setting out the debts I had mentioned to Andrew at the Biltmore.

'I don't see the purpose of this,' I wailed to Stanley. 'How can I ask this man for money?'

'Trust me.' He read the letter carefully and began to fold it.

'And what about this trip of hers? She can't possibly go now.'

'I can and I will.' Starr stood in the doorway, holding on to the door handle. She was pale but appeared perfectly composed. 'I presume you've told him?' she said, not looking at Stanley.

'Starr . . . You should still be in bed. I told you not to get up.' I had to say something; I was suddenly terrified at what she may have heard of our conversation.

'I left a book in here,' she said. She had changed into a woollen skirt and a pullover; she looked like a schoolgirl once more. '*Jurgen* — I want to take it with me tomorrow.'

Stanley fussed ostentatiously among the books on the table, and in the little pile on the floor beside his armchair. 'No, I don't think I have . . .'

'It's all right — I've got it,' she said curtly, taking the book out of the case. 'It said in the brochure that they have a library on board the ship but they probably won't have this.'

'Starr — we want to talk to you. This trip — you can't possibly go off all on your own after this.'

'After what?' She stared at me, she seemed to be at an immeasurable distance from the room we were in.

'I think a change is just what Starr needs,' said Stanley quickly. I hadn't expected him to speak, but he went on, 'I don't know the ins and outs of your problems, Starr. I'm not going to be so presumptuous as to enquire what took place between yourself and your good mother. If you want to go ahead with this trip, so be it.'

'Well,' said Starr. 'I will go. And you can stay here and

argue about money with Mother. Because that's all that will happen if I stick around here. I must — I must get away. After all, the trip's been paid for, hasn't it?'

We went over and over it again and again. The letter to Andrew lay in its envelope all day on the sideboard. Was taken out, re-read, rewritten. Sealed once more. But not yet mailed.

'If it were untrue . . .?'

'She would have to be mad to say such things.'

'Yes, she would, wouldn't she. We must go carefully in this thing, Helen.'

My first impulse on hearing Starr's confession had been to contact Andrew immediately. But he had gone to Washington. Martha? Stanley had talked me out of any precipitate action. 'We must see to Starr's best interest,' he said. For the first time in months my estimation of my husband rose. I leaned on him for support in this awful time. He was a comfort. He could see these things with a clear head. Fond though he was of Starr and Tucker — and he never ceased to tell me he was — his view was essentially that of an outsider. It was easier too to let someone else take up the strain.

So, the following morning he announced that he would accompany Starr on the train to New York, arrange a cab from the Terminal, see her settled on board the ship.

'When I come back — that's when we can get to grips with Mr Peters,' he said quietly to me. There was a spring in his step as he went down to the car ahead of Starr. She got in without looking back. I went down to the gate and saw the car turn at the bottom of the street and disappear towards Orange. As I turned away too, a mother's tears in my eyes — who can dismiss them cynically? — I looked up and saw Tucker staring down at me from her bedroom window. She mouthed something at me but I couldn't understand her. She shrugged her shoulders petulantly. I went into the house and looked for a stamp to put on the letter to Andrew.

Yes, I agreed at last with Stanley, the best thing we could have done was to let Starr have her trip. I'd telephoned the Cunard Line to check if there was any system of looking after lone passengers. How old is your daughter, madam? said the Englishman's voice. When I told him twenty, he sounded surprised. Oh, he thought I'd meant a child. The company did not actually approve of lone women travellers — for obvious reasons — but he would make sure that she was placed at a table with some suitable ladies — he stressed that word — and would ask the officers to look out for her. I'd be pleased if he would — she is convalescing from an illness, I said. He sounded most reassuring and not entirely unbelieving.

Well, she was gone now anyway.

A level, businesslike reply to our letter came from Andrew. Our immediate debts were to be settled by an agreement he had come to with the family. He was very pleased to be able to help . . .

Tucker was able to have new clothes and some other treats to help mollify her chagrin at Starr's holiday. I hadn't told her anything about Starr and Andrew. I had simply said that we must look after Starr; that she had had a most unfortunate experience. Tucker said, 'Oh that pathetic stuff with Andrew, I suppose.' I was astonished. 'What do you mean?' 'You must be blind,' she said. 'He's done nothing to you?' I said, shocked. 'Of course not,' she said in the most blasé way.

When I reported this conversation to Stanley, he stroked his chin and looked very serious. 'That, in a way, confirms Starr's story, I suppose,' he said.

'You're taking it very calmly, I must say,' I said. 'I know that they're not your natural children, but . . .'

That was not it at all, Stanley explained. It was obvious that justice must be had for Starr. And equally obvious that this holiday cruise was to be regarded as only the first step in her full recuperation and rehabilitation. He looked very pleased with that phrase.

'Reparations must be made . . .'

'But if what Starr says is true, surely we must do something about it,' I interrupted. 'I don't know what. What he has done — the law is involved, surely — it would be monstrous if he went unpunished.'

'Of course, there is that aspect of it. These things are horrid enough. But do consider, Helen. It would mean the police, the courts. Disgrace for Andrew — and what for Starr? He is a lawyer, he would have the best of lawyers. They might be able to twist Starr's words — believe me, I know how these things are done. Put her in the wrong. Perhaps make out she was lying. Or that she had somehow entrapped an older man. Remember, he is most respected, Helen. A public figure.'

'But something must be done!' I bleated.

'Oh, he must pay. No doubt of that. He must pay. What we must do,' he said, his eyes gleaming excitedly through his spectacles, 'what we must do is to draw up a careful plan to deal with all this. We must be careful, Helen. For Starr's sake . . .'

One letter the whole nine weeks she was away. From Naples,

where her cruise had put in. The letter got back to us only a few days earlier than Starr herself. The views were magnificent, the churches dirty, she had fallen in love with all of the officers; there was dancing, and all the liquor you could wish — 'which isn't much, Mother, I do assure you,' in her sloping thick hand, which brought into my head that drawling voice she put on to show boredom. The sun, the unbelievably blue sky and utterly unbelievable sea, the utter lack of New York, New Jersey — she never wished to come back — 'nothing personal Tucker . . .' The letter was an odd blend of willed cheeriness and snide sarcasm.

Then she was back herself, looking wonderful, tanned and relaxed and radiant in our small parlour, as if she was a glamorous visitor, charming, hiding almost totally success-fully her slight impatience at our provincial ways.

She had brought small presents back. A black lace shawl for me; inevitably a curly-shaped pipe from Italy for Stanley; a bottle of perfume for Tucker — who looked puzzled for a moment, then quite touched, and leaned over and kissed Starr on the cheek.

'And what do you know, Tucker,' Starr said urgently, 'I'm in love. With the most divine man. He was our Cruise Doctor.'

'Tell me, tell me.'

And it was quite ravishing to my heart to see them happy together for this while at least, and as if nothing at all unpleasant had ever happened to any of us.

Stanley mixed us all Martinis — even Tucker had a small one — and put a Whiteman record on the phonograph and we were all so happy for an hour, with Tucker and Starr dancing together and Stanley changing the record over, then over again, smiling across at me and tilting his glass, conservatively filled, in toast.

How fast our neighbours must have thought us — this was only mid-afternoon — and then somehow the spring suddenly ran out of our merry-making; I guess Starr was tired after her journey, or the tune wore us down. Stanley locked the bottle back in the bureau. Tucker slumped in a chair. Starr said, 'I must go across to Lind's before they shut,' and looked at me meaningfully so that I thought she was talking about her monthly, you know. 'Will you run me over there, Dad?' That was the first time she had ever called him that. He blossomed like a Christmas rose. 'Certainly, certainleee . . .' he sang out.

They came back after quarter of an hour and Starr said she had to go and unpack upstairs. No thanks, she didn't need any help. Tucker sat in the parlour looking through the books Starr had brought back and the postcards of the places she had been to. Stanley turned his new pipe in his hands. He lit a match and turned the pipe over it, scorching its mouth. 'Have to baptise a pipe,' he said. 'Burn the varnish off.' After three matches, an ouch when he scorched himself, he at last filled the pipe from the tobacco jar and lit it, leaned back, and drew in the first smoke and puffed it out a moment later, removing the pipe from his mouth and regarding it contemplatively. 'Good pipe,' he said. Then he drew on it again, blew slowly out again, repeated the process, turned the newspaper over in his lap, and said at last, 'Starr's quiet upstairs. She must be tired. Would you mind, Helen, seeing if she's all right?'

I mounted the stairs. Her door was shut. I knocked softly, thinking she might have dropped off to sleep. 'Starr?' I said quietly. 'Starr?' Hoping I wouldn't have an answer; opening the door insinuatingly, like a burglar, afraid to disturb her, hoping at last she was resting, feeling with the gin and the music and the happiness that all that *other* business had been a bad dream and could now be forgotten, I looked into the room. The thin curtains were drawn. The room was full of a warm, lemony light from the sunlight outside.

Starr sat on the bed. Her case was open beside her, but she had unpacked hardly any things. Neither had she changed out of her travelling clothes. Her hands lay clasped loosely on the taut lap of her dress because her legs were spread oddly wide. She stared at me with a fixed, but somehow unfocused look.

'Starr?' I said, coming into the room.

'Hello Momma.' Her voice was childish.

'Starr,' I said, '— you haven't . . . ?' I knew now why she had gone to Lind's pharmacy.

'It takes me away,' she said slowly. 'Like the boat. It takes me miles away. I don't ever want to come back.'

The Debt

STARR

So, by telling did I free myself? No. Now I was trapped in the machinery of lawyers, of doctors, of pity and disgust. What had been secret was known and it Had-To-Be-Put-Right, in Stanley's phrase to Mother.

Arrangements had been made for me. 'All this time — I never knew,' mooed mournful Mother. 'He will not be allowed to escape his responsibilities,' vowed valiant Stanley. 'Let them twist him for all he's got,' whispered wicked Tucker.

The secret must be told and retold and tested and proved, and a settlement must be made, then the secret will become another sort of secret, known, but not to be spoken of ever again, because that is part of the settlement. Mother went to Boston and told the secret to a relative of Martha. This lady just happened to be the wife of a lawyer friend of Andrew. The lawyer summoned Mother back to Boston, read her the riot act about slander, but didn't budge her. The Andrew camp wrote asking how she could say such terrible things, although no-one would specify what the things were. Mother wrote back — or rather Stanley did, I heard his voice droning on, dictating these hateful letters, while I hid my head under the pillows in my bedroom above.

'Helen' — Stanley paused for thought, went on slowly — 'has friends of her own in Boston and if she should communicate her knowledge of Andrew to them . . .'

Then I must go and tell my story. Not once but three times I tell it to stern, middle-aged men who sit behind their desks and watch me and make careful little notes on yellow paper while I tell them of nights in hotels, of afternoons in the study at Chestnut Hill — I see them now, those grave-voiced lawyers whose books and minds contain knowledge of all the depravities and atrocities of man and they must listen to this poor, commonplace tale told against one of their own. Of course they don't say whether they believe me or not. They retire into conference with each other; they reply in guarded terms to the lengthy letters that Stanley loves to write, pinned to the reports he has received from the private investigator he has hired to track back over the old hotel registers. It has given my stepfather a whole new occupation. He has borrowed money to fight my case. He keeps careful accounts, so as to be able to charge them to Andrew when this thing is finally settled. Mother is quiet, nervous, slightly hysterical. She sits in the lawyers' offices pale and shrill. At home she nags Stanley. Can he not speed things up? When is there going to be an end to it all? Her friends in Boston are not pleased to see her now, she can sense it. How long before their doors close for good?

I know she blames me, for ruining Boston for her. But she won't say a word in reproach. I am a valuable, if damaged property. I have been hurt, and, as in an accident, I must be compensated. They talk in an exaggeratedly quiet, calming way to me. At first. The only real animation between Mother and Stanley comes when they talk over the progress of the battle with Andrew's lawyers. How bluster and threats of counter actions have turned into guarded denial and willingness to discuss the matter more fully. Stanley travels to Boston with fresh detective evidence. He sends copies of Dr Garretson's confidential memoranda to him, giving chapter and verse of my trauma.

I must go to see Dr Garretson up in New York. First because he will attempt to put the genie back in the bottle — a lot of bottles now — and make me a normal healthy girl again, and secondly that he may provide more ammunition in the form of confessions and enormities committed against me for Stanley to lob over to Boston. The appointments are twice a week. They begin three months after I come back from my trip. He is expensive, you see, and the lawyers have only just got round to talking about money, but Stanley has high hopes. I am allowed to go to New York on my own. I am the family silver, after all, and must be allowed considerable freedom — everyone's hopes are riding on me. So I am a queen, a holy termagant, what I say goes. Tucker and Mother and Stanley wait upon me. I don't do a hand's turn in the house. I am allowed drink and Stanley himself fetches me veronal from the pharmacy. In my search for normalcy I am allowed to visit a friend I'd met at an art class I'd taken last year in New York. And he is a friend — Edwin. An artist. I visit him in his studio after I have been to see Dr Garretson to put my mind right. Edwin, with great sweetness, kisses, embraces, comforts me. Mother encourages me. Dr Garretson has told her that I must seek some normal form of sexual relation. Dr Garretson is a very advanced alienist. Mother meets Edwin; Tucker too. I am in love with this man. They are partly in love with him too, I am sure. I say to Mother why doesn't she have an affair with Edwin, it might improve the monotony of her life. I enjoy making them jealous. And poor Stanley goes nearly out of his mind when we all talk admiringly of tall, dark, handsome, strong, artistic Edwin and by aspersion draw the contrast with short, weak, balding, most inartistic Stanley. When I come back from my Freudian conferences with Dr Garretson, who convinces me that I am in love with my father, and with my stepfather and with Andrew, that I hate myself and my mother and sister, and who doesn't believe a word I say, but gives me the most wonderful prescriptions, when I come home from him and if I haven't seen Edwin I come home so low and on the verge of hysteria and pick arguments with Mother and Tucker and I start to scream at them and we sometimes fight each other and punch and kick at each other and being poor weak women do little real damage. When these arguments rage, Stanley shuts himself in the other room and, when we have finished, I open the door on him and he is sitting in the chair, pretending to read a book, his hands trembling. And so we all live in Hell.

Not a pretty picture is it? What picture did I have of myself? None. Whenever I looked in the mirror I was surprised to see myself and wondered who the girl was who looked out and what the hell was she doing in either that reversed world, or in this one where she lifted the comb slowly and pulled it through her beautiful hair, above her beautiful face, down towards her fine slim body. I was relieved of my secret and found I had nothing else. I would fall — I fall — into the deepest moods, when I seemed to be looking over a black void; when the prospect of life became unutterably horrible; the thoughts of growing old, older, fat, sick, ugly all became insupportable. The world was a cold, pitiless place and the only ways out of it were by means of my drugs and, if I could not get them, by drink. I still then thought that love was possible. That someone, perhaps Edwin, someone else, unknown, unknowable, would love me. But what the hell did the word mean? Sex was risible, bearable and even enjoyable sometimes if I had taken my stuff — otherwise it was a comic, inexplicable pursuit of men. Love was what was in the books and the poems and the songs. All those spoke of tenderness and beauty and moonlight — and not of tufted, pale-skinned, large, ungainly mammals clawing and twisting about each other to the most pitiable accompaniment of sighs and squeals and commonplace words.

And so I made love with Edwin. By arrangement almost. I'd asked if I could spend the night at his studio instead of having to go back to West Orange after art class. At last he gave in. And was this normal? I suppose so. I was wondrously excited by all the preliminaries, and at almost the last moment — I had gotten expert at this with Andrew — slipped to his bathroom and took two grains of veronal to go through with it. The next day I was terribly dizzy and dazed. I took some more dope.

I saw him a few more times; he was always a friend, and sometimes I enjoyed the other thing, and sometimes I didn't. We went to his studio, and I made him take me to a hotel because it felt different. Then it ended. I broke down in Dr Garretson's and told him and he seemed pleased and made notes on his pad and said I had a long way to go but that I was beginning to make headway towards a normal way of life. I told Mother and she cried a little and then said I was very brave and gave me a lot of stuff about babies and how not to have them. I would murder one, I believe. I have utterly no feelings for children. Garretson said that it was because I saw them as rivals. I wondered sometimes if he was mad. As a reward for my normal immorality I was told by Stanley that he had nearly reached a settlement with the lawyers. One more trip to see the lawyers, in New York this time — to tell my story simply and truthfully. We went up early one morning in June '27. I was in a simple black dress, no make-up, my hair styled. This was the last time I met the lawyers. Once more the dreadful recitation. Papers spread in front of them, to which they referred every now and then, clucking quietly to each other. Then Mother and Tucker were called in to give their accounts. I met them when they came out, we waited for Stanley. He came down from the room rubbing his hands. It was all settled he said. I was believed. A few details and a settlement would be made. 'Do you mind,' I said, cutting him off. 'I am in an awful state. I want to be on my own.'

Sympathy, coddling, worried expressions from Stanley and Mother, a cold stare from Tucker. In fact, I had already arranged to meet Edwin. We had lunch, went to a movie theatre, to a pharmacy, then I made him take me to another hotel. 'I'll pay,' I said grandly. 'I'm a rich girl now.'

Each time after Edwin I felt tremendous excitement and happiness. A few hours later these feelings would be succeeded by the most appalling darkness and misery; a terrible fear of the world. Outside the sunniest sky would be black, the ridges of the houses like beaks, the windows blank stupid eyes. If I went for a walk the trees seemed to lour over me, the warm summer air lay across my mouth like a horrible feathery mass, suffocating, the eyes of the people as they passed me were huge and staring as if they saw something terrible. These — what shall I call them — these crises of horror, of a total lack of joy and confidence in the world, always came as a reaction to happiness; the worst and blackest came after Stanley had given me the news that I was to be rewarded with another cruise — this time to England, and a guided trip there to Scotland. Tremendous excitement — the assembly of clothes again. Mother said, 'It is probably for the best anyway, apart from a wonderful holiday, you will be away from all these awful arrangements Stanley has to make.' And yet — the day before the trip another reaction. Terrible depression. And a last-minute hitch. Stanley was waiting for the release form from Andrew's lawyers for the money he had negotiated. It arrived in the post an hour before I was due to leave. Wonderful, Starr. Twenty-five thousand dollars. And more for expenses.

Miss Gilbert, my escort to Montreal, waited outside in the taxi to take us to the station. I departed, saying, yes, yes, wonderful, wonderful, yes, yes, thank you, thank you, smiling, sick at heart, thirsting for freedom, for simple absence from this place, these people. Away, Starr, for God's sake, away.

From this tiny airless room in New York, I look back on the sea. It was on the *Aurania* where I met Bill Carr. Most romantic. Introduction by means of a stomach pump. Ship-board romance with handsome ship's doctor. Oh Christ. That journey — I wanted it so much — and then contrived to bitch it up from the start.

Once we got to Montreal I managed to give la Gilbert the slip and went into a drugstore and bought some Dial to quieten me down — I was so up, so excited at being away, and yet frightened at the same time. Then I got on the boat and, it being British waters, the drink was flowing before we left. I met a boy I knew from somewhere I'd been with Edwin in New York. Pretty soon I was drunk. The boat sailed out; next thing I know I am crying, feeling horrible, the doctor — Bill — having finished pumping out my stomach, after first removing from on top of it the boy who had been making love to me when we were found.

The start of a perfect friendship. Yet, I recovered. I was as good as gold the rest of the trip, smiling palely at Bill on deck, requesting an interview with him, apologising. Saying that I was not normally like that, that I was under treatment for my nerves. And he so kind and always finding time to talk and so totally uninterested in me as a sexual being. That's what attracted me to him. I guess he understood. He must have been used to young women draping their infatuations about him; all of which he managed to elude gracefully and politely. I've seen him on three voyages. But last week was the end, wasn't it, when I tried to stay on board on the *Franconia* — the last of the drunk scenes. I won't bother him any more.

How could I? How can I go on now? There is no money. No more trips — even if there were I can't simply travel the rest of my life, growing fatter and older and single and a little more expert in concealing my drink, and hang round, chattering less and less brilliantly, in the saloons of the liners until I become, fairly rapidly, a joke. A ship's officers get a lot of attention from women, from the young romantics to the blowzy widows who spend their legacies on cruises — their legacies from the husbands who used up their half-million hours of life running America and then dropped dead, purple-faced and pop-eyed, on the day of their retirement.

And when I started, the cruises were booming. I could lose myself in that crowd that flooded the cheap tourist class; the teachers and students on vacation, the 'artists' and, sometimes, the artists, and the tourists from the West going to 'do' Europe. And if the old money and the eminent names went first class, it made little difference; with the right clothes and the right voice you could soon get an invitation to the first-class saloon. Anyway, the War had ended all that nonsense; the first class would join in the same dances, the same Treasure Hunts. Being older than most of us in the tourist cabins, they didn't maybe go quite so wild. The drinking started as soon as we were twelve miles out — just as well because most of the young guys had emptied their hip-flasks before we even left port. It was fun, for God's sake — licensed, enclosed, travelling fun. I loved the sea that surrounded us without limit, day after day, the stars that I never saw at home blazing at night above our brave little lights, our music, the flirtations, sex if you wanted it, the promises to see each other again, the exchange of addresses, the look me up when you get fixed in London, or Paris; the see you back home in Trenton, Brooklyn, Chicago, Pittsburgh. This democracy was at its craziest on the smaller one-class ships; though I travelled also on a couple of the great ships, where the saloons were like the staterooms of hotels, though swaying ever so slightly as if they shivered. Here there was wealth and power from Europe and America; only on these great floating parodies of their own homes would you see the movie stars and boxers and the kings and queens and princes and princesses who had lost their countries but could be monarchs here in the middle of the ocean for a little while longer. God, I could have stayed on the boats for ever.

Some people did stay for ever, as legendary and seldom seen as ghosts. There was one extremely old lady of great wealth who had enough to book herself endlessly on back-to-back cruises, once supposedly being on the *Mauretania* for three whole years, keeping her cabin while the ship emptied, was cleaned, refuelled, made ready, filled again with passengers, and sailed again, going from London to Le Havre, to Boston, and New York, to Kingston, and Port of Spain, and the Bermudas; circling the ports of the Mediterranean — and not once was she seen to emerge on deck to look at the sea, or at the ports in which the boat settled, let alone actually going down the gangplank into any of these places. No, the ship was her world; assisted by one or other gold-braided, infinitely solicitous steward, along the corridors and into the library, or entering the dining-room, accompanied by the most junior and unfortunate officer, to sit alone, tiny, spectral, and silent, at her own small table.

Because that was all she needed — the ship. The cocoon, the steel, inviolable womb of the ship. And that was all I wanted. I never saw that woman, but by God I envied her refusal to leave her dream. Because that is what a voyage is — a licensed dream. The filthy city dropping away at last into mist or below the horizon, the prospect before you of a place where no-one will know you. And, in between, this interregnum of silliness, drink, happy expectancy, the calmness, other-worldliness of the gods and the servants of the gods who run this little universe.

I had a good run of it. Five trips in four years. The West Indies. England twice. The second time there marred a little by Tucker and Mother coming along. But they stayed in some cheap little hotel and I swanned it on my own. I didn't want to think that I'd brought New Jersey with me. Men asking me to marry them, to live with them, to go to Paris, to Budapest. Gifts, little gifts.

'Are you going to give me a little present . . .?' Afterwards.

But they did not often come back a second time. I was not a very good whore. And, remember, this was part of my therapy.

It would be good for me, said Mother, to meet men of class and good breeding. If they should offer me gifts or accommodation I should not alienate them by a curt refusal. There were ways of doing these things acceptably and with good grace. A bracelet. A ring.

'Are you going to me a little present . . .?'

After we moved to New York, and when the money finally ran out, I went to a party uptown. The others were chorus girls mostly, or girls trying to be actresses, the type you meet in the Village. The party was on one whole floor of a Manhattan hotel, a dinner party for businessmen and political types, men with silver hair and good suits and wives and children out in Westchester. And by each girl's plate was a cheque for fifty dollars. Unsigned. The party got rowdier and rowdier and each girl paired off with one of the men and went away to a bedroom. To get her cheque signed. I got mine signed, sure. I found it in my purse the next morning, all screwed up, but signed. I don't think I can have done much for the man — but some of them want surprisingly little. At other times there was a weekend on a boat, or a good dinner in a good restaurant. Rarely anything as sordid as actual money. I wouldn't earn a lot in the trade, I think. I did not give so much satisfaction as I might have done;

Uncle Andrew's teachings had left me ill equipped I fear for the world of adult and reciprocal pleasure.

Yet I still fell in love. Whatever that means. With untouchable Bill. With officers and stewards and cruise directors on the boats. With Edwin. I fell in love with large, good looking, powerful men, older than me — Hi, Andrew — or with young, aesthetic, slightly weak types — Hi, Paul. But above all, and over all, I fell in love with the sea. Not with the rackety, boozy, slightly hysterical gaiety of the cruises, but with the great, dark swell, and tug and race and stillness of the ocean, the darkness and deepness that I could sometimes make in myself with barbiturates or booze.

HELEN

OF COURSE THE money that Stanley negotiated for Starr could not last for ever. And it was for Starr; to pay for her doctors and her trips abroad — which seemed to be the only thing that released her from the dreadful depressions she suffered. Sometimes I thought it would have been better for her if she had never told us of the whole wretched, sordid business. Better for us too, if I may be selfish. Certainly no-one emerged from the knowledge with any advantage. Sleeping dogs are better left to lie I think sometimes. She was no happier for our knowing. I lost some of my oldest friends. On the rare occasions I went to Boston it was I who sat right back in the taxi-cab going from the station to the lawyers so that I might not by chance see or, more painfully, be seen by any of my old acquaintances. New Jersey was hardly any exchange for New England. In the end we had to settle for New York.

For none of Stanley's business endeavours prospered. Indeed it was as if he had exhausted himself in bringing off the great coup of arranging the settlement from Andrew; that he intended that we should live off it for evermore; or at least until, like Mr Micawber, something 'turned up'. Far from lasting for ever, it was inevitable that the money lasted a far shorter time than we had envisaged in that first heady rush. Debts were paid, Starr and Tucker fitted out, a new car bought, the house redecorated; we rose in our neighbours' estimation because we had seemed to be lagging behind them in the boom; and we still had money when the Crash came. Stanley's lack of employment became less of a jealously regarded luxury and more the common lot of many of our neighbours. Or so I thought. Stanley told me that he had not suffered too badly in the '29 Crash.

I was a fool to believe him.

Things had gone quite well for two years despite difficulties with Starr, who it seemed would never settle, who drank too much and still needed those drugs I hated so. Life was dull in West Orange, but I prided myself that we were not as dull as some! The Faithfulls did have a certain style after all. New York was practically next door, but far enough away to control Starr and ration her visits. She went on two cruises that year and I must admit that it was a great relief and relaxation when she was away, though it may be wicked of me to say so. Every time she came back madly in love with some man she had met on the ship, or in London. And then the inevitable reaction when life closed around her again and the glamour quickly faded. To the local young men she was beautiful, aloof, scornful. When not influenced by her drugs or drink she was such a kind, intelligent, talented girl — she could draw beautifully, and she should have been a writer according to the letters from her friend Dr Carr, which I read while going through her correspondence when she was out one afternoon; sitting on her bed, the afternoon light coming through the slats of the blind, carefully refolding each letter along its original creases, and keeping them in the same order and putting them back in exactly the same place beneath her sweaters in the dressing-table drawer.

You may think this devious of me, but Dr Garretson said that it was essential to keep a watchful eye on her for at least a couple of years. I didn't see anything to worry about in her letters to Dr Carr — he seemed an eminently sensible man, fending off her protestations of love with good humour and sensible advice.

Some sensible advice is what Stanley could have done with. The old difficulties began again; the unsettled bills, the charge accounts suddenly closed. There was not a great deal left in the kitty, he said. But he had great hopes of the legal action against his defaulting partners — now dragging on into its third year; and he continued to search for investors for his inventions. The newest was a face cream. He produced some in the wash-house. It was yellowy-white and smelt peculiar. Neither the girls, nor I, would put it on our face. A great jar of the stuff remained outside the back door until it began to turn green and grow a mould. Such incidents would have afforded amusement to a family who did not depend on such ridiculous contrivances for a living.

Here and there, he found gullible fools to buy some share of his non-existent wash-house company, but sooner or later, in that time of Depression, seeing no results for their money — Tucker suggested they be sent a share of the green mouldy stuff — two or three of them, all local people, almost simultaneously demanded their money back. Bad news travelled fast along those quiet tree-lined streets. Now Stanley not only had our array of mortgages on the two properties, but also fresh — or rather, stale — tradesmen's debts coming out of his ears — so that we had to shop farther and farther afield and mostly for ready money because credit was not so forthcoming after the Crash. And Starr continued to demand her clothes, her trips. Something had to be done.

The usual. We fled again; leaving the house, and our furniture. We could not hire a moving van — even if we hadn't been immediately set upon by creditors, the nosey neighbours would have noted the hire van's name, and the driver would have our new address and we could be traced. This was Stanley's reasoning. He read many detective novels and seemed to organise his life to their rigid and deceiving rules. So we spent the whole of a Sunday packing all our clothes into suitcases and loading the car at the rear of the house at night. It was so full that Stanley drove in on his own to New York, and the three of us took the train, as if we were off on a shopping trip.

That's the last we saw of West Orange.

In New York, Stanley put us up at an apartment and went off and booked himself into some cheap hotel. This he said, in his stupid, mysterious way, would make it much more difficult for anyone to trace him immediately. If we were contacted we were to say that he had deserted us and left us in near destitution. Which he damn near had.

I told him that he had to pull us out of this. I was not willing to live in some poky little apartment — God knows I'd started my first married life like this and in nearly thirty years I had got no further and what the hell was he going to do about it? And Tucker whining that she had no clothes and no money to go anywhere. And once in New York, Starr became quite uncontrollable. She went out nights and stayed out till all hours, coming home sometimes so intoxicated that Tucker and I would have to douse her with water and lock her inside her room. Then other times she would quieten down, be sweet and thoughtful, stay in her room and never move. She began to talk excitedly about her summer trip. I didn't see how we could afford it. Christmas was a dismal affair and we entered 1930 bickering and despondent.

Then things began to look up somewhat. We had derived some income from letting the house in West Orange. But instead of putting that aside to pay towards the mortgages, we used it for our living money and in the end I had to come to an agreement with the banks, the property was put up for sale, we would make enough to pay off at least the West Orange mortgages and have some left over. Not enough to buy another house but a few thousand dollars.

Then an old friend of Stanley — I was astonished that he had such a thing — offered him a job selling pneumatic mattresses. It was commission only — a mere stop-gap, Stanley assured me, until he could at last form a new company of his own. We had been fools to stay so long in New Jersey, he said. This was the city of opportunity. If a man could not make a success of business here, well, he couldn't anywhere. And through this same friend, Stanley learned of the apartment at St Luke's Place.

We had scarcely been there more than a few weeks when Starr came home in good temper. She had run into a friend she had met on the *Baltic* the previous year. Constance something or other. They had been the greatest of buddies. It was rare for Starr to have such a close girl friend. She was going out with her to a party down on one of the liners. 'Now you won't drink too much,' I said, smiling. She seemed perfectly normal that day.

'Well — no,' she said. 'But I must have the one to keep

Constance company. She does like a little drink now and then.' And she laughed and I thought she'd be perfectly all right. To be on the safe side, to keep her away from Prohibition rot-gut, as Stanley called it, he even mixed her a flask of Martinis.

'That — and no more, between you,' I said. And she smiled and said yes quite gaily. Then she went and got changed. And sat in the front living-room looking down into the square and waited for this Constance girl to arrive. And waited. And waited. I went to the room after an hour or so of cleaning in the bathroom and kitchen and was surprised to see her still there; she seemed perfectly all right. 'I guess she's already gone to the ship,' she said. 'I'll go down there.' 'I'll tell her you've gone on then, if she comes?' 'Yes,' said Starr, 'If she comes . . .' After she'd gone, I saw the flask on the table. I picked it up meaning to run after her, but it was empty. She had drunk the Martinis while waiting.

Her friend didn't arrive. Starr didn't come back.

The afternoon went into evening; then night. Starr often came in late, but one of us always stayed up to see if she was, well, all right. Sometimes she had had too much to drink, or took too many of the pills the doctor prescribed. That night she didn't come home at all. Stanley grew very agitated and rang the police and the hospitals. That was when we found her in Bellevue. She'd gone to some hotel and got beaten up by a man when she was drunk.

'I will not stop in this goddamn city,' she screamed when we got home. 'It will kill me.'

'Well now, Stanley,' I said. 'I think this city will kill us all this summer. The doctor says that we must get Starr away. In her condition I can't possibly let her go on her own. I have the money from the house sale and it's about time Tucker and I had a holiday. Starr needs to get away.'

And I told him that we were off to London for a month while Starr sorted herself out and remade the friendships she had in London. Our hope I think was that one at least of her friendships might become more serious and stable. While we were gone he could get the furniture out of store and generally get the place straight. I was a little hard down on his idleness at that moment. But he just smiled his thin, accommodating smile and said, 'Of course, my dear. Of course.' We hadn't got the money for the house yet; but I borrowed some from the bank against it. I was determined to get away.

In the event we stayed too long in London. The money I had got, Starr insisted, was hers. That Stanley and I had milked her settlement fund so that there was nothing left. If we were coming to London with her, we were certainly not going to spoil her chances. And with all this I went along. Bitterly. But I went along. Starr knew a lot of fine people over there. This was a chance too for Tucker perhaps to meet a man and make a good match. Things were not done as they had been in my day. I knew my daughters met men, that Starr went with them. All I could tell her was not to cheapen herself. To insist on a present or some sign of goodwill from the man concerned. I still hoped she would settle with one sooner or later. God knows she knew enough of them.

So, when we got to London, she insisted on living separately from us. She put us up in a quite inferior apartment and would not even tell us where she was living. Once a week she would visit us, always beautifully dressed and appearing in the pink, as they say over there. She had her allowance direct from the bank in London, transferred from New York. Poor Tucker and I saw hardly any of this; how we lived I do not know. Occasionally one of her friends, Mr Haybrook, would call and take Tucker out, sometimes both of us. When he saw the poor way we were living he was most surprised and loaned me some money — much against my will. We stayed for the whole summer and fall — Starr would not go back and we couldn't book passage without her. She seemed to enjoy us being dependent on her charity. Did she not want me to know what she was doing? I could guess from Mr Haybrook's guarded comments: 'Oh, you know Starr, Mrs Faithfull, she's having a good time, I believe. Theatre — things like that.'

I knew she was involved with several men; how far these matters went I really can't say. She was always a little wild and flighty in her emotions, but she was mixing with the very best of gentlemen. I hoped, sincerely hoped, she would make a good match over there and, as I say, I realised that things were not done now in the regular way of the days of my youth. If she accepted gifts from them it was out of her innate good manners and a rightful disinclination to offend. But to my disappointment she settled with none of them; disparaging to me the last one, while singing extravagant praises of the qualities of the new one. When I asked if she had any money she could give to us, she only smiled rather nastily and said, 'Why, Mama, you know I only have what I earn.'

Only Mr Haybrook was her constant friend and when she deserted him he paid court to Tucker. When Starr got to know of that she quickly took him back for herself. But at last Starr too ran out of her rich friends, or ran a little too fast for them, or froze them off. She'd done this before, a year or so back, staying on and on until all she had were the clothes she stood up in and she'd had to beg a trip back from Dr Carr; he let her sail and guaranteed her ticket himself.

Now there was no Dr Carr. He was at sea. We were all at sea, come to that.

Starr was thrown out of one hotel after a rowdy party in her room. She flitted from another hotel. Then she moved back in with us. The sisters argued bitterly. The trinkets were pawned. That money went too.

At last we couldn't hold out much longer. Starr didn't want me to, but I asked Mr Haybrook to send a telegraph home to Stanley, saying that I was desperately sick and would he wire money to pay the hospital bills, signing it with Tucker's name. We had some money from the house sale left, but I knew the only way I could get Stanley to disgorge any of it was to make my case seem desperate.

In November we at last sailed for home.

So that was how we went on. The West Orange house money went soon enough. I was still paying the mortgages on the Cape Cod house, and now the summer letting money was our sole regular income. It was nowhere near enough. The complex debts that Stanley had built up, each one serving to pay back some of another, now began to devour each other. Creditors were calling us from all directions. Stanley's lawsuit had finally foundered, leaving him in further debt. The demand for pneumatic mattresses was not as great as he had expected. The world was not ready for green, mouldy face cream. Just then, as if the gods took pity on our wantonness, I received a whole 4,000 dollars insurance settlement for an old motor accident. It all began again. Starr wanted to use some for another trip to London. I had to tell her that our debts were too pressing to allow another adventure. She must come to terms with our life, our circumstances now. Perhaps when Stanley's commercial activities picked up again . . . She looked at me with such horrible contempt. 'You certainly know how to pick them, Mother. For all of us.'

What she meant by that, I do not know.

The insurance money tided us over the early part of '31. But it was quite evident to me that we could not go on indefinitely, borrowing to spend, not earning a penny, except what the girls brought in from their gentlemen friends — and they could not accept more than small presents, for the sake of their reputations, could they?

It was not evident to Stanley, who — living in a dreamworld of fortunes to be made, commercial empires to be conquered, seeing himself as the great American capitalist — trudged, more like Charlie Chaplin, from store to store trying for small orders for his wretched mattresses. As in all these cases, it is the woman who has to spur on the man, to wake him from his illusions. I had exhausted the family's goodwill, I told him. I had no intention of surrendering our one last asset, the cottage. Or of allowing him to sell any more of our valuables — small though they were by now. It was up to him, I said, to pull us out of this mess.

'Well,' said Stanley thoughtfully. 'Only money can make money.'

We needed another lump sum, he said. One big enough to settle our debts and so that he could finance his own projects. This time round he would know how to use it properly. Now was the time, in a Depression, for a man with capital to secure a niche in the market and hold out for the upturn which was bound to come. There was only one place we could turn to for long-term help of that kind, said Stanley — a once-for-all, final windfall . . .

'Where?' I asked.

'The gentleman in Boston,' he replied.

STARR

I CAN'T HEAR anything in the house now. This room is as hot and silent as the centre of a pyramid. There's no New York. No America. Just inside.

This room. This house. No-one will believe me when I describe them. People say that St Luke's Place is one of the prettiest places in the city. It's a little different inside. Like most things. We have the upper floor; below are people we don't speak to, and below them the landlord. As I am a prisoner again today, I can tell you that my room fits very well. When I'm inclined to think that way, it looks just like the stage-set for some third-rate Broadway comedy. No window. The two longer walls have a door; one back to Stanley and Mother's bedroom; the other to the front living-room. The third door, stage right, leads on to the landing passageway.

Inside? One lamp with a parchment shade showing the Russian Ballet. Two book cases, one each side of the dressing table. A grand name for the chest of drawers with a mirror hung above. Jars and tubes and sprays for the body and face beautiful. The usual junk. A wardrobe packed as tight with clothes as a taxi-dance.

Tucker has the front bedroom. I couldn't stand the yelling of the kids in the park below. When the windows are up in summer you can hear their chants and catcalls, and the sirens from off the harbour, and those great, calling hoots of the big ships as they set out from the piers. Which was wonderful — but not the children.

We — the family, Mother, my stepfather, my sister — have lived here for a year now. And in a dream. Like all dreams, when you wake from them the only things you remember are the few, ragged, lit pieces at the edge and whatever the whole dark dream was has vanished and you cannot recapture it by any waking means. So you make up and falsify the dream to tell it to others, and in time you come to wonder yourself what is true and real.

At times I've almost loved this room. When I was well and sober and not using anything and could lie face down on the bed and read and read, about people who never existed or if they did were safely dead, and be — not a child again, not exactly that — but no age. You see? That was paradise. To be back. Before. That's the definition of paradise, I suppose. To be always before. So, I'd lie and read, say, Keats, and the beauty of the lines would pierce me — not as a pain, but a sort of pleasing, a pleasant ache. That sort of furry, sexy feeling you get as a child when you are coming down with a cold.

I remember the night in good old Bill Carr's cabin on the *Aurania*, when we talked half into the night. I was a little drunk, or more than a little, and I started to say that poem, 'Bright star, would I were steadfast as thou art . . .' I suppose to draw attention to myself — to draw his attention to me.

Halfway through I forgot the rest. He smiled and said he'd never heard that before. I wanted to say that it was for him, but went all bright — bright Starr — again, wanting another drink, making myself ridiculous. I cursed myself later, because I wanted him to see me at my best. But that never comes. I have come to the melancholy conclusion that there is no best.

And I suppose last week on the *Franconia* was the last time I will ever see him. I had to get drunk too then. Afterwards I went down to his cabin and waited and waited and he came along the corridor at last and said that he couldn't see me now. That he was busy. And I swore at him. And swore he would never see me again. I went up to one of the cabins where there was a party going on. And while I was there I swore I would, could, not get off and go back to that damned house, to that damned family. All week I'd been telling everybody grandly that I was going to London — oh, yes, sailing on Friday.

So I drank and drank and when the party broke up, with people starting to go ashore, the ship getting ready to sail, I went and locked myself in one of the toilets. I reckoned by the time I came out we'd be well out to sea — and I'd get to London one way or another. But I guess I'd had too much. After an hour or so and the boat still didn't get under way I fell asleep. When I woke up and emerged — it was a farce. I made my great entrance to the sight of New York behind us, but not very far. They damn well soon spotted me. Called up a harbour tug and put me off. It was like being taken back to prison, pulling away from the ship.

Oh, and all the people looking over the rail. Oh, what a most sad sight, they all must have said. This young woman, this girl, being taken down in a sling onto the tugboat, not because she is sick, but drunk, and shouting obscenities and goodbyes — they're the same thing sometimes. They put me ashore at the pilot station and let me go when I'd sobered up a little and promised to go straight home.

And did Bill see my hideous exit?

What a pathetic dream I had for a while — that I could marry someone like him. There is no one point at which our lives touch, except the sliding, false one of the sea. He pities me, and has no comprehension of despair.

Because for him, you see, life is a gallant enterprise; a whole world mapped out for him when he was young; school, and small triumphs and defeats the way boys have; and then his training; his girls, voyages, career, and talking so calmly to stupid and uncomprehending people, telling them they will get better even if they won't, and they believing him, because he is the doctor they have come to see and they expect him to say something. He writes me such sane, sensible letters. That is their fault. I don't mean to disparage them. They are wonderful. They are full of the ordinary; the thoughts of a strong, normal mind. He sees the world as a rational, understandable place. His honourable ancestors lie in their graves, and his charming children await him in some unused womb. He gets up each morning in hope. He works. Whatever sicknesses he treats, he alleviates with kindness and skill. His sun rises in the east and sets in the west. His clock ticks purposefully on. He is of use to the world. He is even patient with my false bravado and fake intellectualism and bad poetry; not quite so with my lying about under the influence of some lousy, delightful drug or drink, my speakeasies and hotel parties, my waking in strange beds with some man I've never seen before and never want to see again and sometimes don't. I bet he hasn't been drunk for twenty years. If he does take a drink it is to relax, to be happier — not to be less unhappy. He doesn't want what he can't have — doesn't even know its name. And he doesn't hate what he gets. And what I say is, the world is not like that.

He told me over and over that I led too hectic, too frantic a life. That he didn't know what drove me. That I should settle down. He wrote me that I should think about the future, about marriage to someone my own, young age. Ruling himself out that way. But I suppose he will marry someone younger than himself, won't he?

Whoever she is, she will be pretty. Not beautiful, as I am. No vanity: it's simply that I've been called that, 'beautiful', so many times that I no longer know what it means, or what men see when they utter those words softly, caressingly, 'Oh, you are so beautiful, Starr . . .' They are all fools.

So, Dr Carr, your wife will be pretty, but not outrageously so; she will not drink cocktails in the morning or soak herself in veronal; she will be a virgin and produce several wonderful children.

You will live until you're ninety-nine and see nothing at all wrong in life that can't be fixed by a balanced diet or a good stiff walk. You will have money, but not be rich. Feed and clothe your family and provide them with that horrible amber Pears soap you had in your cabin, clean linen, and good educations. And they will grow up just the same as you: bright, clear-eyed, clear-headed. The world will be for them as it is for you — a sane, well-ordered place with awkward spots and lurches in its history and unfortunate and disadvantaged people who can and must be helped. I don't mean to sound sarcastic. I am envious. Envious that you will never see the truth of the world. That it is vile and disorderly and selfish, devious and violent. And irreversible.

So what for me now? I must get away — and see no way to. If I could even work my passage, somehow . . . Though that is naïve and fantastic. What can I do? I can't stay. I can't go. I even wrote my friends in London that I was definitely coming on the *Franconia* last Friday. They'll be expecting me any time now. Perhaps floating into the bar at the World's End or the Six Bells. 'Buy me a drink, Rupert . . .' And all the stares and welcomes and smiles and handshakes and Where are you staying? And, There's a party at Frieda's, or Why don't you come and stay the night? No strings, unless you want them . . . Kindness, kindness, love. But I know too that that wouldn't last long. In my absence the lives of my London friends would alter and shift; over the next few years they would change partners, marry, move away; other, fresh faces would appear in the Chelsea pubs — you can't know how I long after them — and soon I would be the only constant, revisiting them every year, like a comet. An ageing comet — because the thing about the milieu of places like that, the bohemian, shifting crowd I loved, is that they replace themselves, rebreeding every four or five years, and those who stay must have a damn good reason, they must be famous, or rich, or be in some way tolerated for their eccentricities — for those read, 'money to spend on drink'. If they are only pretty, or momentarily exotic, attractive for their strangeness, well, that will soon pall; the face will lose its youth, strangers who become familiar quickly bore; and there are always others arriving to provide novelty and new experience. I would be yesterday's news.

There are other places. There's Paris. I met a lovely girl

who has an apartment there. Down in that club in the Village — 'where freaky people go' as the song says — and the more freaky, the better human beings they seem to be. At least they don't count costs and love poetry and music above all things, and each other; the boys go with the boys, and the girls with the girls, and sometimes they share each other around — but who the hell cares? My dear Starr, she said, any time you're in Paris just look me up. Stay as long as you like. Or that English girl, Georgina, who I knew at the Six Bells, who has her family in Calcutta, with her father a colonel or general or some damn big thing in the British Army there. Do come, Starr. You'll be a sensation over there. I do envy you, she said the last time I saw her in London — you're a free spirit. Nothing seems to tie you down.

But if the free spirit turned up on their doorsteps? Oh, I would be welcome as the wealthy, beautiful, fashionably dressed young American, suitable as their friend, the consort of their brothers, eyed up by their mothers as an eligible partner for their sons. And when I got drunk — that would be amusing. Took drugs? A little fast and dangerous. Flirted? Acceptable. Slept with one or two men who were not too discreet? Extended my stay by another, and another, week. The few outfits I had beginning to be worn a little too regularly. No new clothes on shopping trips. No dinners stood, or drinks bought. Hanging back when the cabs were paid. Then the questions would start to be asked. How long, exactly, is she staying, my dear? Who, exactly, are her family? Where, exactly, do they live? What, exactly, do they live on?
Exactly.

Perhaps it's just as well the *Franconia* did happen that way. But perhaps not. I'd rather starve in London than go through with much more of this. If I don't go tonight or tomorrow it will be too late. I will be back in all that horrible dark country of Andrew and lawyers and depositions.

Where else though? Leave my family? Take a room, no matter how poor and run-down the area? Get a job? A job as what? There are no jobs about for anyone, let alone a spoilt little tramp. I have earned a bit in the past modelling for Edwin's friends — but they have no money for that now. And it was amusing to take off your clothes and pose and maybe sleep with them — but to go back now and beg them for a few dollars? They've had me once after all.

The last straw was when Mother told me that Stanley had again approached Andrew's lawyer. Now we are claimants on Andrew's charity once more. The money we had from him to, what was Stanley's phrase? — 'to rehabilitate Starr emotionally and morally'. Well, as in so many old fairy stories, the coming of money changes us, but perhaps not in the ways intended.

I even feel sorry in a way for Andrew — they say he has aged awfully. And there is another thing that does not seem right to feel, sometimes I felt a sort of affection for him. Does that astonish you? Not when he was doing those sexual acts, but at other times I would find myself thinking almost fondly of him. For he did treat me with some kindness after all, at first. There was no brutality or forcing in his behaviour, at my slightest resistance he would stop — that was what the ether and pills were for of course, so I would not resist, would not want to while under their influence. There was never any question of what the lawyers called 'full sexual intercourse'. It was always on the level of childish play — if a six-foot-tall, portly man in his late forties can be classed as a child. The need for him to possess me fully grew only as

I grew. As I became less childish, so I became also in some strange way the stronger partner. It was I who had power over him. Or so I thought. He showed me how limited that power was. That was when he had me, and lost me for ever. When the silly, mucky little dream came to an end.

It couldn't have gone on anyway, could it? After Mother married Stanley, Andrew must have known the game would be soon at an end. Soon I left my last school, we moved from Boston, a new father was installed at home; there were no further chances for him. And it was of course stupid, greedy Stanley who blew the whole thing apart, who led me to the doctors, the ships, the money — to this life where, at the age of twenty-five, I have utterly no rest, no hope, no contentment, no future . . .

So, I've resolved to get away one way or the other whatever the outcome of Stanley's visit to Boston. If he gets more money or he gets none — what difference will it make? In any case, we can hardly keep going to the well every five years or so, can we? — getting older and fatter and revolving round each other in this awful compact of silence and gossip and poisonous argument. Is the responsibility for the rehabilitation of Starr to be handed on to Andrew's sons when he dies, on and on, so I become an ageing, pitiable family curse?

I wrote to Bill earlier this week that I intended to do away with myself; a neat, characteristically tart letter I thought — but writing such things does help to put off the actual execution. The dream of doing it — of killing oneself. I've gotten pretty close to it by accident. I work out a scenario: I'll go into New York and have one last good meal, on my own. I will pick a glorious day. Later, as the sun goes down, I'll go to Penn Station and catch the train out to Long

Beach. Someone told me once — the way people you never met before and can't remember apart from a few words — that Long Beach is the last place in America, that from the beaches there you get the last best view of the ships going out. It will be fine to go there and watch the *Carmania* or the *Olympic* or the *Ile* going out, with all their brave lights and engines and music and the people chattering excitedly, and looking back at America gliding away and everything trembling slightly when they hit the swell of the ocean. I shall watch them and smoke a cigarette. Then when it gets utterly dark and the sea is empty and the stars are cold, I'll take enough veronal and simply walk slowly and dreamily down the beach and into the sea, and swim and swim until I'm too far out and too sleepy to care . . .

I don't know — romantic enough? How the hell would I really go about it? It is not easy to live; it may be easier to die.

The only remotely good thing about the *Franconia* disaster last Friday was the man I met in the party. His name was Jack. He was having to hurry away; but before he went — before I got horribly drunk — he asked if he might see me again. I said yes and wrote my address and asked him to wire or write me. Stupid Stanley hasn't paid the bill and we have no phone at the moment. Jack seemed to like me.

I've been going round this week, saying my goodbyes once again. And sort of apologising to some people for the way I've behaved sometimes. And trying to hustle enough money for at least a one-way fare to Europe. After the *Franconia* thing, I rested up all weekend, waiting for a note to come from Jack — hoping he'd not heard about what happened on the boat. I don't know what I expect from him. Perhaps nothing. Perhaps it will all fizzle out again; I don't think I could bear that.

There was no note or cable Monday. I read in the shipping news that the *Mauretania* was in. I rang down to the pier and managed to speak to one of the officers I knew, Don Shaw. We went out for a drink or two and he took me to lunch. I sort of asked him if there were any passages left to England, but didn't dare ask him to smuggle me on board or anything. We arranged to meet again. It was stupid. Did I expect him to hide me in that tiny little cabin of his?

There was no message from Jack on Tuesday either. I went out and wandered about and found myself in Edwin's neighbourhood. He is my friend now not my lover. I don't want any of that from friends; it spoils everything. So I sat and chatted for a while and had a drink and told him how foolish I was to drink, and about the *Franconia*, making light of it, making a funny story out of it; another amusing misadventure. But it came out as pathetic and foolish. I had been going to ask him for money, but then couldn't bring myself to it. He asked me what my plans were, and I told him that I had my ticket rebooked for this Friday to sail for London — I said this brightly and cheerfully. Then I went back home. There was nowhere else to go.

I at last got a note from Jack on Wednesday morning. This was the morning Stanley was leaving for Boston on his errand of — what shall we call it — inducement? Or just plain blackmail? I said to Mother that I wanted nothing more to do with it, and whisked out. I phoned the number Jack's note gave and met him on the corner of Sixth and Carmine. But he was with the same friend he'd been with on the ship and I got the distinct impression he was pimping for him in some way — it must have got around, mustn't it?

We went to a speakeasy in the lunch hour and had not lunch but cocktails. The conversation was light and funny and I buzzed along on the surface, jolly old Starr, witty and outrageous and beautiful and tipsy. I chatted to a girl I knew from the club and saw the other character, Tom something or other, tug at Jack's sleeve and mutter something in his ear. Jack came over to me, smiling. 'Forget it,' I said. 'Take me home.' Next time I met him would be without his creepy friends or not at all. 'Sure, Starr, sure.'

That was when he said he couldn't see me the next day, he was out of town. But Friday, when the *Ile* went out — we sure would go to the sailing party. Where would we meet? I'd ring him on the Friday evening and probably meet on the pier.

Thursday, I went out again. The round of artists — to see if there might be some work. Drinks at the club, at a hotel party — waste, waste, waste — nothing to be done till tomorrow night and then probably nothing much but disappointment, degradation of one sort or another, another few steps down to a dark, dark cellar . . .

All this week has been a tangle of contradictions, as if my whole life was summed up in six days; all the childish, adult, selfish, selfless, mature, immature, drunk, sober, faithful, multiply unfaithful, singularly attached, affectionate, harsh, cynical, criminally innocent qualities; the good daughter, wicked sister, tormentor, soother, virgin, whore characters who make up this problem that is set by God knows who for God knows what reason for me to solve; all of them stagger and fly and whistle and walk and sit in front of the mirror and pose to strangers and lovers and friends and people who hate me and the whole savage bitter skyline of New York bends over me whispering, 'You're better off out of it, Starr. You don't want it. We don't want you.' And Stanley, that funniest of funny little men, our very own Harold Lloyd, who goes walking on tightropes and pirouetting on the tops of lawyers' flagpoles, telling his tale, my tale, again and again, dragging out the old documents from that folder he keeps in the bureau, the brown manila cardboard concertina marked AJP in large blue crayon letters — and comes back today on the steamer and walks in empty-handed and says that it's all over . . . Or do I hope he has brought the money for my passage? Positively the last money.

Stanley came back about nine on Friday morning.

He summoned us all into the drawing room. Mother sat on the sofa, with Tucker perched on the arm, and her hand on Momma's shoulder. I stood behind them. Stanley stood in the centre of the room, by the chess table. He took off his eyeglasses, polished them, put them on again, and said, 'This affects Starr more than anyone.'

'It always does,' said Tucker.

Stanley went on: he had seen Rowley, the lawyer, and another man. There was to be no more money from Boston. Their client was obdurate.

'I told you there'd be nothing. I didn't want you to go,' I said. I was feeling sick.

'The lawyers say', said my stepfather, 'that we have overstepped the bounds set down. That what was — well — what was hidden is common knowledge. The things that you say took place . . . that did take place . . . Well, they're known all over Boston.'

He is leaning against the chest of drawers now. We are in a business meeting. He is relaxing. This is what he likes to do. He is in a meeting and getting his point across. His confidence is increasing. He has a book called *A Hundred Ways to Increase Your Sales* in his bookcase. This is why we are broke.

'I know it is difficult for you, Starr.' His voice dropped an octave. 'But we have had a good life together. We can continue to have. But you must be reasonable. I think, if we remain cool and calm, that Uncle Andrew may come round . . .'

I just stood there, at the edge of the sofa, twitching at the hem of my dress. I said, 'Well, that's all right then, isn't it? We'll just leave it at that, and say Andrew has had his money's worth.'

'Oh Christ, not that again,' said Tucker and got up and stalked out of the room. A minute later we heard her bedroom door slammed to.

Stanley didn't blink or take his hands out of his pockets. After a moment, he said, 'It was a condition. For our life — your life — that nothing was to be said. Andrew — I didn't see him — Andrew's lawyer says that someone has been talking. That the whole thing has become insupportable.'

'Insupportable? Insupportable?' I said. I began to laugh and perhaps I was getting a bit hysterical by then. 'You don't know the half.'

'I'm only telling you the position as it is,' said Stanley.

'I don't want to hear any more. I've got an appointment.'

'At this time?' said Mother.

'I told you — I'm invited to a party tonight. On the *Ile*. I want to get my hair fixed.'

She went to say something else, but Stanley intervened.

'Do you need any money. For your hair, Starr?' he said in that horrible soft voice he used when trying to be extra pleasant.

'A couple of dollars.'

'What time will you be back?' Mother asked.

'Midday. This afternoon. I'll go out again tonight.'

She looked at Stanley; Stanley smiled. 'That's fine. Run along, Starr,' he said. They wanted to discuss Boston without me.

I picked up my purse and hat. 'See you later,' I said. When I got out on the landing, Tucker's bedroom door was shut.

Come down about noon to the ship, Don had said. Things would be quieter then. So I mooned about. Bought a coffee, a paper. I never did make the hairdressers.

We went to his cabin. As soon as we got in he went to his locker and took out a bottle of Scotch. 'You want some of this?' he asked. Sort of a rough type. Direct. 'Help you relax.'

So over a drink I poured out my troubles to him — well, a version of them at least. I simply must get away, I told him I'd go mad if I had to stay another day in New York. He sat down beside me on the bunk and poured out another drink. 'Know what you mean — has the same effect on me, kid,' he said.

Would he help?

Sure, if he could.

I let him kiss me. Then, when he went to top up my glass, I said no. Not to spoil it by getting drunk. I asked him to excuse me a moment. I went out and along to the evil-smelling crew's john along the corridor and took four allonal. You know I love that stuff. You float. You die. When I came back in I began to strip off and got into his little bed. I don't know what he did. I never cared. I even forgot why I was doing it. It wasn't much good. After a little while, he stopped. Then someone banged on his door and called his name. 'I have to go,' he said. 'Get dressed — let yourself out.'

'You will help?' I said drowsily.

'Sure. Sure.'

Next thing I know, he's shaking my shoulder and saying, 'Come on, Starr, it's two o'clock for Christ's sake.'

I mumbled something. I was still a bit groggy. But he was angry and said, 'If I'd have known you were going to go like that . . . I couldn't wake you.'

'Sorry,' I said. 'Sorry.'

We went through the ship to the crew door in the side. I must have been swaying and looking a bit tight, because some of the crew were about and grinning and calling, 'Hey Starr — how are you today?' And I was waving and shouting back to them. Don had a hold on my arm, pulling me roughly as if I were a whore towards the gangplank. 'For Christ's sake,' he said again. 'Can't you behave?'

I felt marvellous. You know? When he'd said two, I thought he meant two in the morning, but here we were, bright afternoon, the gulls calling overhead and all the high white buildings come down to meet me like kings. 'I feel like a princess,' I said. 'I'll get you a cab,' he said, and walked me across the front, whistled up a cab, and got in beside me. 'Where do you live?' he said.

'Twelve St Luke's Place,' I told the driver.

So I got home.

I leaned, swaying slightly, into the cab, holding on to the door. 'You will try and help? I'll see you later today? Tonight?'

'Stay home,' he said. 'Just stay home.'

Mother was waiting for me in the living-room. Stanley hung back behind her at the bookcase, cleaning away again at his glasses with a handkerchief. She started in on me — and he polished away, trying not to look at me, squinting down at the carpet.

'Where, young lady, do you think you have been?' she says. 'I saw you come from that cab. What on earth people will think . . .'

'Excuse me.'

I swept away into my room. But if I thought that ended it — well, she pursued me in a moment later like the wrath of God.

'It can't go on, Starr,' she shouted. 'What will happen to you? Your father thinks . . .'

'He's not my father,' I said. 'You should know that.'

Stanley appeared behind her, his glasses dangling from his hand. At last he decided to put them on. 'Helen,' he said, 'there really is no point in shouting. Let me speak. Starr will listen to me.'

Mother steps out of the room with one last glare at me, swinging the door shut. I'm left with Stanley, still holding the handkerchief, like a flag of truce.

'Now, Starr, listen,' he says. 'I know you're upset. But as I was trying to tell you this morning — your uncle, your uncle's lawyer in Boston . . .'

'I don't want to hear about it any more — uncles, lawyers — the whole damn thing . . .' I sat down heavily on the bed.

He smiled down at me. He put the handkerchief back in his pocket, adjusted what he has for shoulders in his suit jacket, and went on.

'We have always given you everything you wanted. Your schools. Trips. Wonderful holidays. You've had more than any of us. More than your mother. Or your sister. Why, we've hardly been out of this place for a year.'

I can switch off his voice so it seems to come from a long way off, like a fly buzzing between blind and window in another room.

'You must understand, Starr — there is no trip. There is to be no trip. There is no money any more. Uncle Andrew . . . Peters . . . Mister Peters has said . . . his lawyer has said — that we have breached our agreement. I know this is not pleasant for you, Starr . . .'

'Where's Tucker?' I cut in on him.

'Your sister has gone away. For the weekend,' he said. 'Some friends.'

'She hasn't got any friends,' I said. 'Has she gone to Boston? To make the peace? In whatever way you all think best? Anyway, I'm going out again,' I said.

This gets to be even more play-like. What happens is, the door to the landing is flung open. Enter tall, gaunt-eyed Mama, her long black dress hanging so it seems to stand, quivering, all on its own. Stanley, stepfather, steps farther back. Almost disappearing into the wallpaper.

For he always defers to her. After all, they are lovers. God, the thought. I've heard them making love. Most discreetly, like a pair of mice. The merest hint of bed creaking. A few quiet words exchanged. A water glass set down. Coughs and sighs. Goodnight. Turn over.

I said, in my coolest, best Boston voice, 'I have a gentleman to meet and that is what I'm going to do.'

Mother shut the door and stood in front of it. 'That is all over,' she said. 'You can't do that any more.'

'I shall do as I please,' I said.

'Starr . . .' Stanley's voice was so soft and imploring, it ebbed away as he spoke.

I gathered up my purse and coat from the bed. I could get out by way of the door to their bedroom.

Stanley stood still and blinked.

'I wonder if anyone else lives like us,' I said. 'Anyone on earth.'

As steady and firmly as I could, with what I imagined as a determined grace that would impress them into silence and inaction, I made my way through the doorway into their bedroom. I was going. Going my own sweet way through this big room with its almost blue-skied window and the windows of our neighbours looking in, and I felt free as a bird. Mother shouted behind me, 'No, Stanley — she mustn't do that. She mustn't.' The sash window raised high so that half the city could hear her.

And all at once she was behind me, grabbing at my purse with one hand and at my coat with the other, crying, 'No. No,' over and over again, and I was kicking out at her and twisting and struggling to get free, and Stanley was there, assisting, but all the time trying not to touch me and saying in that same soft, horrible voice, 'Starr, Starr, do what your mother says. You must do what your mother says. Be sensible, Starr, can't you see . . .' Then I was raging and my mother had her arms round me, shouting, 'Lock the doors, Stanley. Lock all the doors. She is not to go.'

Mama and I were left struggling together, panting, staring at each other with such hate, our faces so close that she breathed, her breath over-sweet, into my mouth.

Then I was freed by her. Because dear Stanley had locked the only other door out. He stood, hoisting his glasses up on his nose, straightening his necktie. Which is what he always does after one of these spats.

They stood and stared at me. The whole thing struck me as too ridiculous for words. I would have laughed, but I caught a sight of my puffy, inflamed face in their long mirror and I looked away again quickly.

'Give me some stuff,' I said. 'Just a little.'

Oh, the look of triumphant contempt on Mother's face; the relief spreading under Stanley's thin, pink skin.

We went back into my room. Mother went out into the passage and along to the living-room. She can never stand me doing this thing. If she doesn't see it, it doesn't happen.

Stanley came back with a tumbler of water and the small brown bottle and left them on the table in my room, not looking at me. It was as if I was not in the room at all, and that he was laying these things out for someone else, a stranger he was expecting. I lay on the bed with my back to him. I heard him cough into his hand — to say that it was ready but really it was nothing to do with him. The stranger would come and drink the drink; go away; leave a sort of peace for them all.

He went away. I heard the lock click. After a while I got up and mixed the stuff in the water and drank it. I lay down, waiting for it to take effect. I heard Stanley say something sharp and loud, then his voice was lowered, and I heard my mother's insistent nagging whispers begin.

I must have slept three, four hours. The stuff has worn off. I still feel a bit muzzy but I'll freshen up. I'll try one of the other ships. I'll go down to the *Carmania*. Not the *Mauretania* — I couldn't stand to see Don again. I've blown my chance with him anyway. I'll ask if Charlie Roberts is on board. I've seen him this week. He said come along any time. He may give me some veronal in case I need it later. I'll stay sober and not embarrass him. We can sit and talk and I know he won't try anything. I can stay with him until it's time to meet Jack.

It's all really down to Jack. He agreed to pick me up at ten tonight, if I can get out again, and if we can find a party on the *Ile* or another ship we'll go. If we're too late for the *Ile* I'll get him to drive over to Long Beach. I've not told him that I may try and hide away on one of the boats. He's my back-stop if all else fails. Of course I'll not tell him about Don today. A trampish act. One thing does give me heart, and that is to look round this dreadful — literally — room and know that I may never have to see it again. Whatever happened, that would be a mercy of its own.

It's half-past six now.

Will Stanley let me out? They're very quiet. I'll get dressed. Take my coat; it's warm now, but it will get cold in the night. I don't intend to come back here whatever happens. It's all over whatever happens. It would be too much of a defeat to come back.

The Settlement

SHE KNOCKS ON the door. After a moment or two she hears Stanley's footsteps in the passage. The key turns in the lock.

'Why — you're all dressed up, Starr. Are you okay?'

'Perfectly.' She appears calm and collected now. Despite the warmth of the evening, made closer in the windowless room, she has on a black coat over her blue and white dress.

'Where's Mother?'

'She's gone over to Mrs Foster. For tea.'

'I'm going out for a little while.'

'Well . . .'

'I'll be perfectly all right, Stanley. I can look after myself.'

'Well . . .' he says again, and then smiles. 'Of course you can. Never said you couldn't. Do you need any money?'

'Three or four dollars. That's all. I'm going to see a friend.'

'When will you be back?'

'I'm not sure.'

'Not late, Starr. Not late. Your mother . . .'

'No, I won't. By midnight. Like Cinderella.'

And for the first time for many months she smiles at him.

'Well, toodle-oo, Daddy,' she says. 'I suppose you are my Daddy now.' And as she passes him in the doorway she kisses him fleetingly on the cheek, and he watches her go down the stairs and disappear from view along the landing, then hears her steps on the next flight down into the hallway. Then, distantly, the front door opens, and closes.

On the beach the group of people has grown and shrunk, been reinforced and then diminished; up in the dunes people from the nearest avenues are looking down at them. The beachcomber who found the body stands a few yards off, now peripheral to the professional enquiry going on over there. Questioned, his answers noted down in an off-hand way, then ignored, he feels his initial importance draining away. First the uniformed patrolman had come; then the ambulance; the detectives in their suits; the doctor who came and went; the photographer whose flashbulbs were brilliant and insignificant in the bright day. Cars on the road, their drivers seeing the official cars, still slowing to see what the fuss is. Some drive on after a minute or so. Some get out.

Who is it?

A girl.

A girl? A beautiful young woman.

Is she dead?

Drowned.

How?

She has been washed ashore. She has come off one of the ships. She has dived off one of the ships. From a drunken party. Or fallen. She has been murdered down there on the beach. She has committed suicide. She has been assaulted. She has staggered down from one of the speakeasies with a man, perhaps two, and been held under the water until she drowned. Someone had heard shouting from the beach the night before. A woman says that she had seen a liner stalled on the ocean far out on Saturday night and perhaps they'd stopped and were looking for someone. And a fisherman contradicts her scornfully saying that there was no way that that body had been in the water for more than a few hours. Could be a day — perhaps two — says another. The sea is a strange thing. Some can come out fresh and some like dead bait. Perhaps she has never been in the water at all, but killed elsewhere and dumped here. And all this idle and hushed talk goes on and is added to and subtracted from by comments by the patrolman, the ambulancemen, the other beach-combers, the neighbours, the motorists who have stopped and go reluctantly back to their cars after a while, having business to conduct or appointments to keep.

At last all the official work is done. The body is lifted on to a stretcher, a blanket drawn over it, and it is taken up the beach to the waiting ambulance. The detectives get back into their cars and pull onto the road and away. The thin line of people in the dunes stand a little longer, looking down, talking among themselves, then drift apart, becoming fewer, until those left, feeling at last rather foolish and isolated in morbidity, and as if they have overstayed their welcome, turn away too from the beach.

That same evening, small knots of people, later only one or two, gather to look down at the site of the reported discovery in the idle and slightly awe-stricken and not entirely rational way people do; drawn by the recent presence of a death, a body, in peacetime that least seen, most common and terribly fascinating thing; the legitimacy of their curiosity confirmed

247

in some odd way by its absence now, and by the emotional resonance given to this piece of beach, by the chill in the darkening air, the screams of the few gulls, and by the slimmest evidence of any happening, even that confusion of footprints and trails up and down the beach from the one shallowly hollowed spot, already beginning to be washed away by the lapping incursions and trawlings back, and again rolling forward tide.

AFTERWORD

This novel is based on the true case of the finding of Starr Faithfull's body on Long Beach, New York in June 1931. Speculation as to what happened between her disappearance on the night of Friday 5 June 1931, and the finding of her body early on the morning of the following Monday, the suspicion of murder and subsequent scandalous revelations about the dead young woman filled the New York and, to a lesser extent, London newspapers, for weeks on end.

There are two factual books about the Starr Faithfull case: Fred J. Cook's *The Girl on the Lonely Beach* (Red Seal Books, London, 1956) and Jonathan Goodman's *The Passing of Starr Faithfull* (Piatkus, London, 1990). Cook's lays out in detail the family background, mainly from transcripts of court actions and the drawing together of newspaper reports and his own interviews. Goodman has had access to the original police files and statements and what was left of Starr's own diary and has used them to fill in many gaps in the Faithfulls' family history. He marshals an impressive body of other evidence to suggest an ingenious solution to the mystery of the actual death, and I have hinted at alternatives, but the mystery element in itself was not my own chief interest.

For, whether Starr's death in 1931 was homicide or suicide is irrelevant in a way; her true destruction was begun long before, in the early summer of 1917, at the hands of her abuser. So although the two books on the case, and contemporary newspaper reports, provide detailed records, what they could not include was the narrative of Starr and her relationship with Peters. The affairs of the Faithfull family were magnified by the huge publicity given to the sensational aspects in 1931; but like all human beings the Faithfulls and others are interesting and unique in themselves — this is the true mystery that obsesses all writers of fiction, and a sort of truth beyond the documentary is what they must try to provide.

I am indebted to the two books cited above, and to the many reports of the case and related matters in American and British newspapers and magazines, together with a number of secondary books on the social and political history of Boston and New York; what I have invented or distorted or where I have differed in my interpretation of facts is my own responsibility and should not be laid at the doors of any of the previous reporters or researchers. My thanks to staff at the British Library and its Newspaper Collection at Colindale, and in particular to those at Birmingham Public Libraries for assistance in tracking down books and other material in their own collection and elsewhere.

Also my gratitude to the Society of Authors for their financial help during the writing of this book, but most of all thanks to the endless and unlimited support of my wife, Gill. I'm still trying to write the book she deserves.